T0090563

LIFE ACCORDING TO FRED:

One Man's Search for the Sensuous

Ernie Stech

Order this book online at www.trafford.com
or email orders@trafford.com

Most Trafford titles are also available at major online book retailers.

© Copyright 2010 Ernie Stech
All rights reserved. No part of this publication may be reproduced, stored in a retrieval
system, or transmitted, in any form or by any means, electronic, mechanical, photocopying,
recording, or otherwise, without the written prior permission of the author.

Printed in the United States of America.

ISBN: 978-1-4269-4120-7 (sc)
ISBN: 978-1-4269-4121-4 (e)

*Our mission is to efficiently provide the world's finest, most comprehensive book publishing
service, enabling every author to experience success. To find out how to publish your book,
your way, and have it available worldwide, visit us online at www.trafford.com*

Disclaimer

All the characters in this novel are entirely fictitious. They are not based on any human beings I have
known. The soul quest and visit to the monastery at Snowmass, Colorado are based on the author's
experience but do not represent actual events. All the places including the forests and mountains around
Flagstaff, Arizona; Walnut Canyon National Monument; Moab, Utah and the surrounding canyon
country; Canyonlands National Park; and Buena Vista, Colorado are real. The name of the small lake,
Stanley Lake in the novel, has been changed to avoid having people troop into and around the real lake
in Michigan, but it is a real lake on which the author at one time had a cottage.

Please note that no camping is allowed in Mill Creek Canyon outside of Moab, Utah. The trail into the
canyon is accessible.

Trafford rev. 8/06/2010

 www.trafford.com

North America & international
toll-free: 1 888 232 4444 (USA & Canada)
phone: 250 383 6864 ♦ fax: 812 355 4082

Dedication

*For my teammate, hiking partner, friend, wife, and soul mate, Yvonne,
who has had to put up with me at the keyboard for hours on end.*

Words from
the Narrator

This is the story of adventures, physical and spiritual, starting eleven years ago. I have reconstructed the story out of memory and a journal I kept.

You will meet Fred on the first page of the story. I spent parts of three years with Fred or his cohorts. In that time, I had conversations with Fred, sometimes about his beliefs and wisdom, sometimes about the words and actions of others..

Fred had the ability to summarize in a sentence the essence of any experience or lesson. I wrote those sentences down and have dubbed them "Sayings of Fred." They are collected on the next few pages. Each of them is buried somewhere in the text that follows. Most of the sayings don't make sense until you read the text. There is a kernel of wisdom in each. I thought it would be interesting and, for me, fun to compile them into a single list for anyone who wanted to review the lessons.

SAYINGS OF FRED

Somewhere between rationality and randomness is where we live.

Most people are in a tunnel to oblivion, not a tunnel of love.

Don't own anything anyone would steal. Don't own anything you would miss if it were stolen.

Be ready for random opportunities, and go looking for new experiences and acquaintances.

Pee clear at least once a day.

The more you try to control anything, the more you are controlled by it.

Life is a constant struggle to balance all the rules and regulations of society against the dictates of your soul.

Check your bowel movements to get an assessment of your soul.

Create a life by dreaming and then finding ways to get around whatever blocks the dream from happening.

The here-and-now is the place where your soul meets reality and your personal story line meets the possibilities of tomorrow.

Your soul talks to you in the pauses in life, and that's why you need to create pauses.

The real demons and devils are inside of you.

Never get sunburned on your genitals.

Without a lot of pain, a person is hollow.

It's easier to live a life without choices.

Everyone has a soul place where they really belong.
The problem is in finding it.

You have to go through hell to get to heaven.

Learn to dance your ideas.

Approach every human being with awe and reverence.

Find someone and dance your feelings for one another.

Look for the spiritual way of making love.

If you have a need, satisfy it. Just don't make
someone else responsible for your satisfaction.

The spirits do not appear on command.

Sensuous doesn't mean sexual.

It would be a pretty dull world if every bit of knowledge
had to be useful.

Be careful when you roll over after making love.

The harder you try, the harder it is to get hard.

It's not how often you make love but how well.

Very few people are in transit in life.

You learn more by getting wet
than by reading an instruction manual.

Honor your connections.

Learn from everyone you meet.
It's not the size of the task but the soul you put into it.

Enjoy the process because most of the time the product
isn't worth shit.

The world is made up of very small sounds.

You will understand a lot about human behavior if you
realize that most people are striving to become immortal
or else doing everything they can to ignore the inevitability of
dying.

If your only goal is to catch fish,
you will spend most of your life disappointed.

The more you are able to adapt,
the less you need to control.

Intuition is just listening to subtle signals.

Smart people have to
ask dumb questions in order to learn.

Some of the most interesting people in the world
live on the margins of society.

If God didn't have a sense of humor,
how could we?

Look for the small wonders of the world where you live.

Learning is just an attitude toward experience.

Maybe underwear really isn't necessary.

Very few people are in transit in life.

Talk about all your mundane and bad experiences;
remain silent about the precious ones.

Sometimes you're better off with your assumptions
than with real knowledge of what someone else thinks.

You become more and more like who and what surrounds you,
and you can choose who and what surrounds you.

Organizations always outgrow their missions
because the organization becomes the mission.

There's no need for One Book, because you can learn
from all books, all places, all people.

Pass on what you have learned, not what you have been taught.

Your possessions own you as much as you own them.

BEGINNING

1

Little did I know that my life would change, that I would go through several transformations, because I had to take a piss and stopped at the Hittle Landing rest area on the Colorado River between Cisco and Moab, Utah. Fred, who I didn't yet know, was sitting in an old folding chaise lounge with a mixed breed - mostly black with white paws and tail - dog at his side.

And so I owe my current life, a life of fulfillment if not success, to my bladder.

Leaving Grand Junction, Colorado an hour and some minutes before, the morning coffee stimulated a greater and greater need to pee as I drove the winding two lane road deeper and deeper into the red rock canyon cut by the Colorado River. As I approached Hittle Landing, I saw from a quarter mile away the cement block outhouses. The need to relieve myself was overwhelming.

The unisex latrines were a reddish stucco, painted to match the red rock canyon walls, and I pulled my Wrangler up directly in front of the first one. Racing inside, I managed to hold back the pent up fluid until I unzipped my jeans. Great relief spread across my groin and lower abdomen as the urine streamed out.

Coming out of the toilet, I saw the old man reclined in the chaise lounge, the dog at his side. He sat up as I came out and looked over at me. I ignored him.

The river flowed gently and silently in a wide bend here. I walked down a concrete ramp to the water's edge, a launching site for rafts, canoes, and kayaks. I had heard that the Colorado flowed easily from here to Moab. No major rapids or white water, particularly this late in September.

A few minutes spent at the streamside and I walked back toward the Jeep. The old man motioned to me. He wanted me over. I hesitated. I am basically shy and reclusive, and I was enjoying this solo journey into the west, into the desert and canyon country after crossing Colorado's mountains.

He motioned more vigorously. "Come on over," he called in a raspy voice. The dog looked at me and blinked. As the Old Man made that announcement, he held a small stick in his left hand and drew two lines of equal length in the sand: one vertical, the other horizontal, intersecting in their centers.

I looked down at the crude cross, bewildered.

'That's the secret to life," said the old man.

It just looked like a cross in the sand to me.

"Are you curious?"

"Well, I guess. But I need to get on the road again."

"Where you goin'?"

"West. I want to see Arches and Canyonlands," the two national parks in the area, "and then I'm going down through Monument Valley to the Grand Canyon."

"Vacation?"

"Not really." He was friendly but too inquisitive. I wanted to leave.

"Sit down a minute." He motioned to the ground across from the dog.

Seemed as if I had to. Even though I didn't want to.

"My name is Fred," said the old man. "I've been expecting you."

How could he? Until four days ago, I didn't know I was going to be here. I left Chicago on Saturday. I'd been driving, looking at scenery, thinking, and on occasion going blank until this moment.

"Well I wasn't expecting to meet you," I said.

"I know."

"So what are you here for? Why are you expecting me?"

"Because you need me."

"I do?"

"Yep. Now tell me *why* you are heading west if you're not on a vacation."

"Because I need to. I need to go somewhere but I'm not really sure where."

"So something happened in your life?"

"A couple of things." Here I was starting to tell this old man about something I hadn't told anyone back in Chicago.

"And they are?" He squinted at me, friendly, with a gentle smile on his narrow lips and small mouth.

"Well, my Dad died seven years ago, and then my Mother died last year about this time. Last month we settled the estate. I've got enough money to take off for a few years. No need to work to make money. Last spring, when I saw how much money I was going to inherit, I started to feel really uneasy about my job. I knew I wasn't doing what I really wanted to do. Somehow or another I drifted into a marketing, publicity, the public relations world. There were a few interesting things to write. Most of the time, particularly recently, I was not too motivated. In fact, I was bored.

So I resigned two weeks ago. Just walked out on a Friday. Told the boss I wouldn't be back. No notice. Just left. Packed up my personal stuff in a box and left. Never looked back."

"So you're free to travel. And you're heading west."

"Right."

"What about a wife or female friend?"

"I was married for six years. We divorced. The marriage was a mistake. We both knew it. We split amicably, as they say. She is still a friend. I have a girl friend back in Chicago. She couldn't understand what I was doing in quitting and all that. She expects me back in a month or so."

"Will you be?"

"I don't know." A pause, a silence. "No, I guess not."

"So you're here in Utah looking for something. Your story tells me that you're not running away from anything. You're looking. And I'm going to be your guide, off and on."

"Guide? Maybe I don't need a guide."

"Everyone needs a guide once in a while. I'm not going to direct you or push you. I'll just be here -- or there -- for you at times. Now look at these two lines. This is the secret to life. Okay, maybe not *the secret* but one of the secrets."

He pointed to the cross.

2

"See this vertical line? It represents a continuum from inside of you, your soul, the lower part of the line, to the world outside of you, the "real" world, the upper part of that line. The dead middle of the line is where 'you' meet the world. It is what we call 'here.'"

He looked at me. I shrugged my shoulders thinking: So what?

"The horizontal line is time. The left side is the past. The right side is the future. And the dead center is 'now.' So the center of the cross is the 'here and now.'"

"I don't see how this explains anything. Or helps me," I said after a few seconds.

"You will. You will. We actually live in the here-and-now. That's where we should live. But we spend a lot of our time and effort on the past and the future. We spend a lot of our time on what's 'out there.' But here's the strange thing. We don't spend very much time on what's 'in here.'"

"So?"

"That's what we need to learn. And we need to learn how to take our history, our future, the world out there, and what is inside of us to the here-and-now which is where life is. But more of that later. Let's go to my place."

"Wait. Wait. Go to your place? I don't even know you."

"Hey it's a free night's lodging. And I live in Moab, just a few miles from here. Why not? I'm not going to attack you. I'm not going to trick you into joining a cult. I'm just offering a night at my place."

I was reluctant. Yet there was an aura about the old man. He certainly wasn't dangerous. His dog jumped into the cab, looked over the scene, and turned to look back at me with a questioning look. So I followed Fred and the dog to Moab.

3

Fred's trailer home, located on the Mill Creek Road, was parked under a couple of scraggly but adequately leafed trees with one larger tree centered in front. I pulled my Jeep in behind his pickup camper into his small plot of land with flying dust settling behind us on the road. There were some anemic bushes and scattered clumps of brown long grasses around the trailer. The rest was dirt. Tan, brown, and red sandy dirt.

He motioned me to the door that was unlocked, and we walked in. Furnishings and decor were Spartan. In fact, Fred had nothing on the walls of the trailer except one piece of paper thumbtacked to a small bulletin board. There were several bookshelves jammed with mostly soft cover books. I would look those over later.

"You get the front bedroom, through there..." he pointed to the right and a slightly ajar door. "No bed linens. Sleep in your sleeping bag. That's what I do." And he turned and walked to the rear of the trailer past the small kitchen, what appeared to be the toilet door, and into another bedroom. "I'll be out in about half an hour." With that Fred closed the door.

I was alone in this trailer home of an old man in a town I had never been to before. What had got me to follow him and agree to stay here tonight? Nothing rational, that's for sure. There was an aura about Fred. I trusted him. It was intuitive.

He was different. Simply the way he'd introduced himself. I was curious, my curiosity aroused by his very direct way and by the two crossed lines, the past to the future, the outside to the inside, and the hear-and-now at the intersection. What was that all about?

I went out to my Wrangler, unlocked and opened the tail gate, and pulled my sleeping bag from the floor. I rarely packed the bag in its stuff sack. That only caused a more or less permanent crushing of the fibers, and it was the loft in the bag, the ability of the fibers to stand upright, that made it warm on a cold night. Draping the bag over my left arm, I pulled my athletic bag with my right hand and walked back into the trailer. Within five minutes, I had the bag arranged on the bed. I unzipped an end pocket to the athletic bag and pulled out my shaving kit. Now what? I looked through the slats of the venetian blinds on the front window at the red rock cliffs ahead and to the left. Farther away, to the right and the west, lay another line of cliffs. Moab nestled between them.

4

After half an hour or so, Fred emerged from the back bedroom. I didn't know what he had done. He was dressed exactly as when he went in: faded, worn jeans, a black T-shirt under a tattered denim shirt. In fact, later, I never did know what happened when Fred disappeared for short periods. All I could guess is that he took "power naps" or maybe spent a brief time meditating. He never said. I never asked.

"Hungry?"

"A little," I responded.

Fred lit a gas burner on the small stove in the trailer and proceeded to make a stir fry, all vegetable, which he served over re-heated rice scooped out of a plastic cottage cheese container extracted from the small refrigerator. It tasted good.

5

Describing a human being is fairly easy. We can detail height and body build, picture the face - eyes, nose, mouth, general proportions of the face - whether the ears stick out or are plastered against the skull. Hair and eye color help. Put words together about texture and color of the skin.

But how do we describe the mind and soul of a person? I got insight into Fred looking over the books I found on the shelves in his trailer home and in his camper. Later, I read or skimmed some of them. I made a list of the books in my journal:

Mysticism, Evelyn Underhill
Toward a Psychology of Being, Abraham Maslow
Pilgrim at Tinker Creek, Annie Dillard
The Way of the Sufi, Idries Shah
The Tibetan Book of Living and Dying, Sogyal Rimpoche
On Walden Pond, Thoreau
The Alchemist, The Pilgrimage, and *By the River Piedra I Sat Down and Wept*, Coelho
The Old Man and the Sea, Ernest Hemingway
The Heart Aroused, David Whyte
East of Eden, John Steinbeck
Transformation, Robert A. Johnson
Soul Making, Alan Jones
Science and Sanity, Aflred Korzybski
Man's Search for Meaning, Victor Frankl
Mount Analogue, René Daumal
Franny and Zooey, J. D. Salinger
The Birth and Death of Meaning and *The Denial of Death*, Ernest Becker
Zorba the Greek, Nikos Kazantzakis
The Outermost House, Henry Beston
The Tracker, Tom Brown
Wilderness Essays and *Mountaineering Essays*, John Muir
Modern Man in Search of a Soul and *Man and His Symbols,* Jung
The Prophet, Kahlil Gibran
The Book of the Vision Quest, Foster and Little
The Glass Bead Game, Peter Camenzind, and *Siddhartha,* Herman Hesse
Love in the Time of Cholera and *One Hundred Years of Solitude,* Gabriel Garcia Marquez
The Hero with a Thousand Faces, Campbell
A Path with Heart, Jack Kornfield
Contemplative Prayer, Springs of Contemplation, and *New Seeds of Contemplation*, Thomas Merton
The Hero Within, Carol Pearson
Poems, Rumi

and a partial collection of the works of Carlos Castaneda.

At the end of our journey together, three years later, that eclectic collection made sense.

A piece of paper, five and half inches wide and eight and a half tall, was posted on the wall next to the door to Fred's trailer. The following had been neatly lettered by hand:

True joy is:

To have no objective and yet to achieve many lofty goals.
To live among people but not need them; to live among
them and love them.
To have the stars above, the mountains to the east, and
the desert on the west.

That seemed to sum up Fred after I got to know him better.

6

Fred was, in fact, short, five feet five with a wiry build. His skin was well wrinkled from exposure to the sun and advanced age. He was, in that out of date expression, sprightly. He moved quickly but not jerkily. His eyes sparkled and were twenty years younger than the rest of him. They reflected his mind. No, they showed, displayed his mind.

Of all his features, Fred's hands were the most fascinating and revealing. They were delicate and expressive at times and were functional and strong at others. It was as if they changed depending on the needs of the moment. When he talked, Fred provided small gestures that were always appropriate and helped to illustrate his point, even when we discussed the most abstract topics.

The overall impression of Fred was one of energy, a latent energy, waiting to come out, but always in a controlled and deliberate way.

FIRST YEAR

Section I

Moab

1

So I spent the night in my sleeping bag on a bed in the front room of Fred's trailer. I didn't sleep well. The surroundings were strange. Originally I thought I was going to get a motel room, watch TV, and doze off. Instead, Fred left me alone in his trailer. He drove off somewhere and came back much later. I sat, for a while, under the tree in his yard. Fred's black and white dog wrapped himself around himself and looked up at me with those questioning black dog eyes. Then I sat for a while in the front bedroom. The dog stayed outside. Eventually Fred returned, nodded to me, and ambled to his bedroom in the back of the trailer. That was it.

In the morning, Fred walked to the door and out. I sat up and looked around, knowing of course where I was but not why. Fred came back in.

He cooked something on the small propane stove and offered it to me along with brown sugar. It tasted funny. I looked up. "Quinoa," he said. Later I found out that quinoa is a grain, native to South America, introduced to the U.S., and popular among some people of the Southwest. It tasted funny. One problem is that it tasted, that is, it had a strong taste. Not the blandness of oatmeal or some other cooked breakfast cereals. Even brown sugar couldn't mask the flavor. I ate it anyway.

Then Fred motioned me outside, and we perched on the old folding aluminum chairs under the tree in his yard. "So you're traveling the

Southwest." His dog flopped onto his side between us, yawned, and closed his eyes. Fred pointed: "His name's Barker… because he never does." I nodded to Barker who paid no attention.

"Yes. We went over my situation yesterday." I was irritated, partly from lack of good sleep.

"And I interrupted your trip yesterday. I knew you were coming. Well, hell, I knew someone was coming. And when you stopped to piss, I knew you were the one."

"You make me sound like some kind savior. 'Someone was coming.' I was just taking time off from my work back in Chicago."

"I know. I know. But you see something brought you out here. Not to Maine. Not to Florida. Not to Texas. But out west. To Colorado, Utah, and Arizona. There's a reason for that."

"Not that I know of."

"Of course not." Fred looked over at me. "Most of what we do is stuff we know about. We just do it. But see I think it's because of something inside of us. You know, like a soul."

"Wait a minute. I don't want to get into a religious discussion with you. If you're trying to get me into some kind of church or cult, you have the wrong guy!"

"No. Hell no. Soul has nothing to do with church. In fact, you can lose your soul in most churches."

There was a long silence. I didn't know what to say.

Fred continued. "Look here's an opportunity to learn about life. You've got a college degree. But they don't teach you about life in the university. Oh some few professors may give a little bit here and there. Most of 'em are too busy building up their professional resumes and advancing their careers to worry about life. They have disciplines, areas of study. That's where they focus their thinking and their lives."

"So where do people learn about life?" I was a little curious and less angry.

"Not at a university. Not in a classroom. You learn about life with people out in the world. Different kinds of people. Old people. Young people. Women. Men. Gay people. Dying people. That's where the lessons are."

"So what does that have to do with me being here in Moab?"

"A lot. You didn't get here by accident. No one ever gets anywhere totally by accident. They also don't get there by reason. You know, rationally. Somewhere between rationality and randomness is where we live."

I had to think about that. Later I realized that was one of my first lessons about life.

Barker opened his eyes, looked at me as if to confirm that I had gotten the lesson.

**Sayings of Fred
Somewhere between rationality and randomness is
where we live.**

"So let's look at your life."

"Gee, I would like to, but I think I should be shoving off to go see Arches and Canyonlands."

"My god, boy, they will be there tomorrow, the day after, and decades and centuries from now. Quit rushing along!"

I sat back. Okay, so I didn't need to go right at this moment.

"So what about my life?" I wasn't going to go easily into this conversation.

"For some reason you needed to get away from your job and away from Chicago. You could have stayed. You could have gone on doing what you were doing."

"Well sure. But I had a chance to get away for a while. I think I'll probably go back sometime later this year and dive back in."

"I don't think so." Fred looked down at the ground and stirred the dust with his sandaled left foot. He looked up at me.

"Why?"

"Because something is pulling you to a new place."

"You mean like Phoenix or L.A.?"

"No. A new place in life."

"And what does that mean?"

"I don't know. You see we can never know about the future. There are people who study the future. Call themselves futurists. But you can't study what hasn't happened yet. Studying is for things that have happened. In the past."

"So what about the future?"

"We create the future."

That made me think. I had to stop and really think. Fred let me do that.

He went on. "You see, you are at a point where you can create your own future. You have gone away. You have put away a lot of your own past. Now you can create who you will be, where you will be, what you will be."

I still didn't have a response.

"You're very lucky. Most people are trapped in a straight line path. They are controlled by habits and rituals. They don't have any choices, at least not many. They're all hemmed in by what is expected of them. What they expect of themselves. That means the voices inside. And what their friends and lovers and co-workers and bosses expect of them. All of that creates a tunnel, and they are carried through that tunnel."

"To what?" I could see the tunnel. I could feel the tunnel I had been in.

"To oblivion!" That stunned me. Yes, he was right. You just marched or swam on to nothing. There was nothing at the other end.

Sayings of Fred
Most people are in a tunnel to oblivion, not a tunnel of love.

"So now what?"

"You've opted to get out of the tunnel. Now you can create a future self. All of your friends and co-workers and bosses are back there in Chicago. Your parents are dead. And you sit here with an old man who can introduce you to some other people, people who will have no expectations of you. And old man who can introduce you to some experiences that will let you explore possibilities. Ain't that hotshit?" The dog cocked his head sideways and looked up at Fred as if surprised by the swearing.

Fred surprised me then and he would again and again. He combined some kind of crazy wisdom with earthiness and profanity. That, I would find out later, is another lesson in life. Wisdom and profanity go together.

"So why don't you drive over to Arches and check it out?"

I nodded.

"If you want to, come back this afternoon. You will have a place to sleep as long as you want." With that, Fred got up and shuffled off to the trailer.

I got my stuff together, threw it in the back of my Jeep, and drove off to Arches National Park. Barker got up and watched me leave.

2

Naturally I came back to Fred's place that afternoon. I was hooked. I wanted to find out how to create my new life. In that I would be disappointed because Fred had no formula. But did he have an incredible set of adventures for me!

3

When I returned to Fred's trailer, he wasn't there. And neither was Barker. So I sat in one of the plastic-strap chairs and waited. Impatiently.

An hour later, Fred's camper truck rumbled up the road and into the yard. He slid out with dog following right behind. "Man, you could have gone inside!"

"I didn't even think to try," I answered. "Is the place unlocked?"

"Hell yes."

"Aren't you worried about someone stealing your stuff?"

Fred laughed. "Are you kidding? There's nothing in there worth stealing. That's Fred's security method. Don't own anything anyone else would want."

Sayings of Fred
Don't own anything anyone would steal. Don't own anything you would miss if it were stolen.

Instead of going inside, Fred sat down next to me. "How was Arches?"

"Fantastic," I gushed. "That's one of the most incredible places I've ever seen. Those gigantic blocks of red sandstone. Just unbelievable."

"Well, you just experienced the past. All that stuff in Arches is millions of years old. It is nothing but the past! There's no 'now' in Arches National Park. Oh yeah, there are the visitors, but they're nothing. That place is pure past."

With that, Fred bent over, picked up a stick and drew a line in the dirt. "Look," he pointed to the line. "Here's the past…" pointing to the left end of the line "…and here's the future" pointing to the right. "Right in the middle is 'now.'"

"The park was in the past. But now the experience of the park is in your past. While you were there, it was 'now' for you. Sitting here, it is in your past."

"So?" All this seemed pretty obvious to me.

"Let me go on. With every act you create a future. If you repeat acts, then your future doesn't change. But if you try on a new kind of act, then your future may change.

"Most of our acts come out of our past. They come out of our personal history. And they come out of our people's past. Something we call the culture. You can't act in ways that are different from your past and your people's past. You're stuck in that."

"You really believe that?" I frowned.

"Sure. But there is one thing. If you meet someone new or experience something new, then that person or experience becomes part of your personal past. And allows you to create a different kind of future. Different from what you would have if you just kept acting in the same way."

"So today I opened up a possible new future for myself?"

"Could be." Fred was silent. He looked up at the tree leaves wobbling in the soft afternoon breeze. More silence, and I was getting uneasy.

"How does this work, then?"

He looked directly at me. "You can meet new people randomly. If you give them a chance. Same for experiences. You can have them randomly. Or you can be guided by someone. A person can suggest a new experience. Or introduce you to a new person. And you can do it by yourself if you decided to do that. Not many people are willing to take the risk to go out looking for new experiences or finding new people to meet. But it can be done. Some folks do it."

Sayings of Fred
Be ready for random opportunities, and go looking
for new experiences and acquaintances.

I didn't know it at the time, but Fred would be my guide. And he would introduce me to some incredibly unique people, among them Venus, and take me out for life changing experiences. But right now it was all words.

4

"Today," Fred started out, "we need to talk about urine."

So we moved from a conversation about life and making a future to a discussion of urine.

"What?" I was having trouble following him. I expected more talk about looking for guides and having new experiences.

"Yeah, urine. Piss. The stuff we do every day. Very important in learning about life."

"How? What does urine have to do with life?"

"Health. Body. All that stuff."

We were walking from Fred's place along a rutted dirt road up toward Mill Creek Canyon. Just as we started, a convoy of four vehicles, three passenger cars and a van bounced up the road and passed us, flailing dust into the air. Fred walked ten yards off of the road and waited for the dust to settle.

"Yep. Piss. Very important. You have to learn to assess your own body, your own health. And urine is one way to do it."

"It is?"

"Oh yeah. Here's the secret: you need to piss clear at least once a day."

He walked on ahead. So we moved from the highly abstract and intellectual, at least for me, to the completely organic.

"You see," Fred continued, "if you piss clear at least once a day, it is a good indication that you are flushing out a lot of toxins."

I was silent.

"Here's the deal. If you read anything about hiking in deserts or dry climates, they will recommend that you drink a lot of water. The test for seeing if you drink enough is the color of your piss. If it is dark yellow, your liver and kidneys are working overtime to get rid of bad stuff in the body. If it is yellow, there is some stuff being worked out. But if you pee clear, like weak lemonade, there are no toxins, no bad stuff coming through."

"This is for real?"

"Absolutely. One thing you're gonna have to learn is that your body is sending you messages all the time. One message is in your piss. Look at it. And smell it!"

"Smell it? You mean lean over the bowl and smell it?"

"No, you don't have to do that. If you are passing a lot of bad stuff through your kidneys, your urine will smell. Hell, you've smelled it before. You just haven't taken notice of it."

"That's a relief," I nodded and then smiled at my inadvertent pun.

"That's pretty good!" Fred chuckled. "But it's a bigger relief if you see clear piss once a day. At least."

"And how do you get to that?"

"By drinking lots of water. Actually, you can drink lots of sodas – even beer – and get the same effect. They are diuretics. That will move liquid through you in a hurry. The problem is they will also make you dehydrated. So water is the cure. Yellow piss is the symptom!"

Sayings of Fred
Pee clear at least once a day.

5

Fred handed me four sheets of paper and said. "Here, read this whenever you get a chance. And then let's talk about it. So I read:

The Dragon That Would Not Be Slain
A Fable

Sir Kendred, renowned knight, pursued the demons of the Kingdom with zeal, He was pure of heart and never spoke an unkind word to any man, woman, or child. This purity allowed Kendred to face every situation with equanimity and certainty. Ever since being knighted, Sir Kendred sought out and conquered the most vile creatures of the kingdom having even saved a young woman from the jaws of one of the ugliest monsters of the South District of the Kingdom.

Thus it fell to Sir Kendred, in his thirtieth year, to go out in search of the largest and most dangerous dragon in all the King's lands. This required traveling many days to a forest in the extreme West near the border and the sea. Kendred moved deliberately through villages and towns, across open plains, following the path to the Dark Forest.

On the edge of the Forest he paused, in the bright morning sunshine, to look into the gloom, able to see only a few yards beyond the outer fringe. Urging his mount onward, Kendred leaned forward in the saddle as they penetrated the outer ring of trees. The forest was thick with old trees – and new – making progress difficult. Often the horse had to move sideways as much as forward to avoid thick growths of saplings. It took several hours before the knight first heard the grunts and then roaring of the beast, the beast which now sensed the approach of a human being into the very heart of the forest.

The enormous sound grew louder until Sir Kendred and his mount stood at the edge of a clearing. A clearing, yes, but dark with roiling clouds overhead and a mist creeping along the ground. Where the morning outside the forest had been bright, here there was nothing but dark greens and purples and even grays and blacks. In the center of the clearing stood the dragon, staring at the knight.

A bellow from the depths of the monster's gut shook the forest and set the armor on the knight to rattling. Yet Kendred experienced no fear. He was here to slay this beast and then return to his King for another mission and one beyond that. This was just another adventure in the life of a brave, no, the bravest knight of his time.

Looking over the position of the beast very carefully. Kendred decided to attack the right flank, avoiding the large jaws. So he kneed the horse into a gallop and raced alongside the huge belly swiping at the flesh with his sword. The blade ripped into the flesh to a depth of a foot or more but then, before his very eyes, the wound disappeared as quickly as it had been slashed. There was no scar, no evidence of injury. No blood or other juices oozed from the place where the sword had penetrated.

Kendred and mount circled and made another attempt with the same effect. Again and again, he ripped at the dragon's hide, inflicting long slices into the flesh, only to have it mend immediately. The beast simply looked on with disdain. Its warted ugly face betrayed nothing.

In desperation, Kendred rode directly across the snout of the brute and took two great swipes at it. With exactly the same result. The dragon was impervious to exterior injury. Retreating, Kendred thought quickly for he feared retaliation from this formidable foe. Without hesitation, he charged full force at the chest just as the dragon raised its head, and Kendred's sword plunged into the chest wall and sank up to the hilt, a full three feet. Then a most amazing process occurred. The sword was sucked into the chest of the dragon, and the knight had to let go lest he be pulled into the body of the beast as well.

Sir Kendred, white knight, honorable warrior, conqueror of all manner and means of evil creatures, sat in his saddle looking at the blank face of this dragon and felt a great melancholy overtake him. This dragon could not be slain. There was no fear in Kendred's heart now because the beast looked down at him with pity and shook its immense head slowly from side to side, emitting a rumbling but unaggressive growl.

The knight pulled the reins to the right, and the steed turned. They plodded back into the forest leaving the dragon in its lair. A heaviness pulled at the heart and chest of the knight. Had he known how to cry, he would have sobbed and wailed, but the training of a knight prevented any such display.

For three days and three nights, pausing only to let his horse graze and get water and for himself to sleep a few hours, Sir Kendred traveled back to the castle and his King. At noon on the third day, Kendred's horse clacked across the drawbridge and into the walled castle. Inside, he dismounted with the help of a squire and removed his visored helmet. Holding it in his right hand, Kendred asked for a audience with the King that was granted immediately.

The knight walked into the dining room where the King was having lunch. Slowly, sadly Kendred walked forward, bowed, and knelt and addressed the King. "I have failed to kill the Dragon of the Dark Forest, Sire." Then he told the King his story. At the end, Kendred placed his helmet on the table and said, "I can no longer be a knight, My Lord."

The King nodded and looked at the sad knight. "You have been brave and true. You have not failed, dear knight, but have indeed learned a great lesson. From this time on, you will be known as Kendred the Wise." With that, the former knight rose and walked to his quarters where he doffed the armor.

Clothed in the rough attire of the peasants, carrying a staff and a simple sack, Kendred the Wise, even though a young man by many standards, walked the land telling all who would listen of his encounter with the Dragon that Would Not Be Slain. They listened and some told Kendred stories which he learned and repeated. For many years, Kendred the Wise wandered the land from north to south, east to west, telling, learning, and repeating stories.

The old king died and his son took over the kingdom. Then the son, too, passed on, and his son in turn became Lord over the Land. In that reign, Kendred, who now numbered close to a hundred years, lay down one autumn day in a patch of sun near the path to the town of Sumnet. He placed his old worn bag under his head and closed his eyes. Thus he lay for an entire day when one of a group of passersby, knowing who this was, came over to him thinking perhaps he had died. The old man opened one eye just a bit and smiled briefly. Assured, the townsman walked on.

The next day, Kendred the Wise continued to lay in his place near a few trees on the high plateau close to Sumnet. Townspeople came past with no mission but to make sure that the old man had not died. They saw him breathing, even though movements of his chest were slight.

So they came the third day and noticed that the body of Kendred the Wise had shrunk somewhat. His clothing and shawl lay loose around him. On the fourth day, he seemed even smaller, as small as a boy-child of six or seven. Then, when they came by on the fifth day, there was no body at all, just bits of cloth he had worn for years and years.

The deeds of Sir Kendred were no longer known, but the stories of Kendred the Wise were told and retold for generations afterward until the people learned to write and then the stories were put on paper where they are read and studied to this day.

I put the sheets of paper on my lap, not sure what to make of the story.

6

"So what did you think of the story?"

"I'm not sure, Fred."

"Here's my interpretation. The point is that there are some things in our lives, not necessarily dragons in dark woods, that we just cannot control. Or kill. Or get rid of.

"I heard someone talking on the radio one day about the transitions from one presidential administration to the next here in the United States. According to this person, there is a list of twenty-some issues that faced every administration. You know, things like the national debt and Social Security and dealing with terrorists. Well, this individual, and I can't remember who it was but it was someone associated with one of the administrations in the past, said that basically the same list gets passed on from one administration to the next. There may be one issue that gets kind of resolved in four or eight years. But the rest go on and on. So it seems to me there are some problems that just cannot be solved. At least not in the short term. Dragons that can't be slain."

"But we live in a 'can do' culture, don't we? Anything is possible if we spend enough money, time and effort."

"You're right. That's the attitude. So let me give you an example from the medical world. Let's take bacteria and viruses. Medical sciences devotes itself to finding ways to combat infections caused by bacteria and viruses.

Of course, we only want to kill the one that create sickness in us. We don't want to get rid of the bacteria in our mouths and guts that help digest food. But the doctors tell us that this powerful new antibiotic will kill everything and we should be prepared for the trots for a while."

"But we've been pretty successful in fighting infectious diseases, haven't we?" I asked.

"In the short term, sure. Sulfa drugs and then penicillin and now all kinds of new pharmaceuticals designed just to get rid of infections. But then you read newspaper stories about drug-resistant bacterial infections. No one pays much attention to it except for older folks, or someone going to the hospital, or people who get sick a lot. The rest of us, say 'not me.'

"You see, the viruses and bacteria are living things. They are not visitors from another galaxy. They belong here. They have as much right to live as we do. If God had wanted us to get rid of the bad bugs, He would have made them unable to mutate. Or He wouldn't have made them at all.

"Every time a new drug-resistant infection is discovered, we go 'Oh my!' But the bacteria are saying, 'Thank God, now we have a new race that is not killed off as easily by these humans.' We are so homocentric. We really believe the world was created just for us. All other living things are just here for our eating or viewing pleasure. Well that's nonsense. It is a whole world, and every living creature down to the smallest nastiest virus has a right to live."

"Right to life for viruses?"

"Sure, why not? I suspect that every time we develop a vaccine sooner or later there will be a strain of virus that mutates and is resistant to the vaccine. We know that happens with the flu bug. That's why we need to get flu shots every year. Every year the vaccine is a little different."

"But what good is a flu virus? Or some bacteria?"

"See, that's a human question. You are really asking: 'What good is the flu virus to me or my people? What good is that stinking bacteria that gave me food poisoning? The answer is that it has no value for you or yours or the human race. But it has value for itself. I mean, what good is a wolf? Or a butterfly? Or a fly? Nothing. Nada. Wolves, butterflies, and flies have no intrinsic value to human beings. Butterflies are pretty to watch. They do help pollinate some plants, but most of the plants aren't of any use to us."

"So the lesson of Kendred is?"

"That there are some things in life that cannot be killed or controlled or manipulated. You have to take them the way they are. People who can

21

do that are wise. If you keep on trying to kill or control or manipulate, you spend a lot of time and effort with little result. In other words, the thing is controlling your life."

Sayings of Fred
The more you try to control anything,
the more you are controlled by it.

7

"There's another moral to the story of Kendred, by the way," Fred announced later that day. "You can have more effect by going around teaching and telling stories than galloping all over the place on a big horse, dressed in your armor, and flailing around with a sword."

8

We were sitting in front of Fred's trailer. He moved the chairs out from under the tree so we could look at the stars, that night perfectly clear but with a light haze from the town of Moab. Still the stars blinked and shone as they can do only in the clear high altitude air of the west.

"That's way out there," Fred muttered.

"What?"

"Those stars. Way out there."

"Yeah." Obvious to me. Of course, they were way out there. It was the universe.

A long silence, as usual, with Fred.

"Can we change that stuff out there?"

"Of course not, Fred! It's way out there, as you said. How could we change it?"

"Exactly. We live in a universe where a lot of things can't be changed. We are limited by those things. The old business of we can't fly because of gravity. No matter how hard we flap our arms."

He paused again, looked up at the branches and leaves of the tree above us.

"Does that mean our lives are totally determined?"

"I hope not!" answered Fred. "I sure hope not. Because then my life would be a waste. But there is a lot of life that is fixed for us. For some people almost all of life is determined, fixed, rigid."

"Why?"

"Because they chose to live that way. Who they are is dictated by their parents, their teachers and coaches. Their friends. The minister or priest or rabbi. They live out a whole bunch of ought to's. Some of it even comes from the larger society. You're expected to look and act and work in certain ways. If you don't, you are weird."

"So we should rebel?"

"No. That doesn't work either. If you rebel then you are just 'not doing' what is expected. So you are still being directed by all the ought to's. You're just doing the opposite. See that's why so many people who look as though they're rebelling all look alike. They are just conforming to their own rebellious ways."

"The answer, then, is...?"

"There's no answer."

"Okay. So that leaves me nowhere." I was frustrated again.

"Nope. It leaves you with something else."

"And that is?"

"Searching inward." Silence. Fred scratched his stubbly beard, not looking at me. Then he went on. "The opposite of reacting to everything external is to look inside. See what your soul says."

"Oh no! Are we going to get into religion?"

"Nope. We are going to get into spirituality, though. See most mystics – the really spiritual people – seem to believe that everyone of us has something holy or godlike within us. We are inspirited. That comes with being born. Everyone of us probably has some kind of life mission. Something we are supposed to be doing. Problem is we don't listen to the soul messages. They get overridden by all the external stuff we get. They get silenced by all our talking and analyzing and thinking. And if they do come through, we get scared."

"Why?"

"Because those soul messages point us in risky directions. They are not rational. They are not what we are supposed to do. If you listen to those soul messages and follow them, you will appear to be strange. You'll do things that are unusual. You'll go against the grain of society."

Sayings of Fred
Life is a constant struggle to balance all the rules
and regulations of society against the dictates of
your soul.

9

Fred, Barker, and I formed a triangle in the dirt under the large tree. Fred leaned back in his favorite old aluminum-and-plastic-webbing chaise lounge. I was perched on an equally old folding lawn chair. Barker lay on his stomach, his hips rotated to the left with hind legs sticking out that direction, but his head placed on his two front legs stretched out in front. Every time Fred and I had a conversation, Barker assumed that position.

Fred began once again with that simple cross, the equal length vertical and horizontal lines. "Okay. So we have that line," pointing to the horizontal one, "representing a time line. To the left here is the past. To the right is the future. Now some people live in the past. Or they live out of the past. I mean their lives are dictated by what happened to them in the past. In fact, I think that is most people. Programmed by their parents, teachers, coaches, friends, whoever. They live out the programming.

"A very few people live in the future. They dream. Daydream. Fantasize. Always looking for something to happen ahead somewhere. Some of them are good at making things happen. Some try to make things happen and get unintended consequences.

"Does that make sense?"

I nodded. Barker raised his eyebrows and looked at me as if to confirm the fact that I understood. Throughout my time with Fred, with just a few exceptions, Barker checked me out whenever Fred stopped talking or asked me if I understood. I don't think Barker really understood what was going on but just got a cue out of Fred's voice intonation.

Barker dropped his eyes and resumed a watchful position.

"Then there's this other line." Fred redrew the vertical one. "We go from in here," pointing to the bottom of the line, "to out there. In here, inside of ourselves, the purely subjective inner self. Out there is the physical world. But it's also the cultural and social world. It's all those influences that act on us.

"Where the two lines cross is the here-and-now. That's where we actually live. At least, where we're supposed to live. I repeat. Some people live in the past. Some in the future. Some are controlled almost completely by those outside forces. A very few march only to the internal drummer."

He paused and looked out across the yard, across the dirt road, toward the red rock cliffs, the backdrop to any scene in Moab. There was silence. I was a bit anxious.

"The clue," Fred concluded, "is to live in the here-and-now, using the accumulated experiences of your own past and your culture's past, planning as best you can a little way into the future, knowing and understanding the influences on your life in the past, now, and in the future, and being supremely aware of what your inner voice is saying."

He looked at me, frowning. Barker looked up again.

I nodded. Barker blinked and dropped his eyes.

Fred did make a cryptic remark, later. He said that if you go out far enough, in your thoughts, and go in far enough, introspecting to your depths, you end up at the same place. Whether or not the universe bent back on itself, the extremes of human imagination and thought did. And, according to Fred, the journey outward and the journey inward both passed through the mystical.

10

"Now we need to talk about shit."

"What?" I exclaimed.

"You know. Shit. Poop. Feces. Bowel movements."

"But why? We've been talking about philosophy and life and all sorts of high flown things and all of a sudden you want to talk about shit?"

"You bet. Because you need to examine your own shit. I don't mean that metaphorically. I mean look at your bowel movements. They send messages about you. About your health. About the state of your soul."

"The state of my soul? Come on, Fred. This is getting ridiculous!"

"Wait me out. Listen to what I have to say."

"Okay. Okay. But on this I'm really skeptical."

"Did you look at your shit this morning?"

"I guess. I glanced at it."

"What did you see?"

"Geez, I don't know. What was I supposed to see?"

"You should look for two things. First, the color. It should be like milk chocolate color. Second, whether or not it is solid, cohesive."

He paused and looked at me. I didn't have a thing to say!

"If you are healthy, really eating well and exercising, then your shit will be a nice light brown and cohesive. It will look like big logs in the water."

"How do you know this?"

"Personal experience. And talking to some other people?"

"You talk about shit?"

"Sure. I know it's one of those taboo subjects. As kids we're taught that it's not good, not polite to talk about our bodily functions. So we don't. And we're robbed of a great deal of knowledge and insight from that. One of my jobs with you is to open up some of these subjects."

He continued. "We all shit. Even those beautiful models in magazines and those handsome actors on TV. Everyone shits. A lot of people check it out as it sits in the toilet bowl. But they don't know what to look for. So I'm telling you what to look for."

"So what do I do?"

"Every time you shit, look at it. Then check how you're feeling. How well you're doing that day. Think back to what you ate over the last twenty four hours. Here's what you'll find. If you ate well, if you ate good foods with lots of fiber and lots of dark green veggies, your poop will be solid. Oh yeah, you also have to drink lots of water to make it float. Fiber and water. The color and consistency depend on how fast you ate. Take your time and treat your GI tract gently and you'll have cohesive bowel movements. Eat the right kinds of foods, eat slowly and the color will generally be a nice brown."

"You mentioned exercise."

"Yeah. If you exercise, particularly walking, it speeds up the movement of the food remnants through your guts. That helps in creating cohesive, brown floaters."

"Okay. Okay. I guess that makes some sense. But what is this stuff about the soul?"

"Important. You see most people ignore the soul's messages. We've talked about that before. We charge on getting ahead. Making money. Gathering possessions. Creating families. On and on. All of that is dictated by the world outside. Remember the cross, the two lines? Our lives are dictated by that world out beyond ourselves. We develop a kind of personal and social inertia. We just keep doing whatever it is we're doing without thinking about it. Every once in a while something pops up to remind us about what we really want to be. We shove that back down and keep on keeping on.

"That puts our mind and body at odds with the soul. The soul wants us to touch another human being or be held, but we can't because of the social restrictions. The soul wants us to run in shallow surf and kick sand and water. But that is too childish. So we deny, deny, deny the soul's impulses.

"And that affects our bodies. It affects our shit. Deep inside you know what you want to do and be but the conflict with what you ought to be and should be causes a kind of quiet suffering.

"That's why people smoke and drink and take other drugs. It's why they see sex and orgasms as the answer to life's problems. It's why they work long and hard and get so tired that there is no time or energy to reflect and meditate."

I was stunned. Shit is a reflection of the state of the soul! Maybe he was on to something there. This required some time to absorb. I just shook my head, not is disbelief, but in wonderment.

And so the lessons with Fred went on. I started looking at the results of my bowel movements every day.

Sayings of Fred
Check your bowel movements to get an
assessment of your soul.

11

"Let's talk one more time about the 'in here' and 'out there.'" Fred sat forward in the aluminum chaise with its ragged plastic straps. Barker planted himself across from me, giving me one long look before dropping his head to doze.

"Oh no!"

"Oh, yes. Just one more time."

I nodded, captivated and captured, at this moment, in the front yard of the old man.

"There are two 'things' inside of us. One is the soul. We beat that one to death a couple of days ago. But there is something else. That is your awareness of your own body. Only you know what is going in there. Only you can feel your muscles. Your guts. Your headache. Or whatever. A doctor can take your blood pressure and temperature and pulse and respiratory rate. But no doctor can crawl inside of you and feel your pain."

"So? Somewhat obvious."

"Yeah. I want to tie this back to peeing clear and checking your bowel movements. Those are two ways for you to check on how well your body is doing. But you can do more. You *should* do more!"

"Like what?"

"Do an occasional body check. Wiggle your toes. Rotate your feet. Swing you lower legs. Lift your upper legs. Stretch your arms back. Move your head side to side and forward and back. Your body is trying to send you messages all the time…just like the soul. And all of our daily rushing around makes us ignore the body messages. We just override them. It's that outside stuff again. It's always dominating our lives."

"Okay. I guess." I was tired and this wasn't making a lot of practical sense to me. Barker looked at me. I actually nodded at the dog.

12

I was less tired two days later, and Fred stepped me through the body check. We did start with my toes. I wiggled them. I rotated my feet around the ankles. Stood up and leaned forward, against the tree in Fred's yard, to check my calf muscles. Did a knee bend, not too deep but enough to test those big thigh muscles.

Then we started at the other end. I rotated my head. And I felt some of the tenseness in my neck and shoulders. That came on stronger as I rotated my shoulders up, forward, down, and back. Fred had me bend forward and then back so I could feel those long back muscles and the good old abs in front.

The whole process took no more than ten minutes. I knew I was carrying some tension in my neck and shoulders, probably where I always had and in the future would. I found out that my calf muscles were tight.

"See," said Fred, "the body check is easy."

"But my usual question, Fred, so what?"

"Well that tension in your neck and shoulders is a message about how you are living. You are carrying some kind of weight around in your head and on your shoulders. It's for you to figure out what the weight is."

"Couldn't it just be from driving or sitting or sleeping funny?"

"Oh sure. But if you were really in tune with your soul, you would drive differently, sit differently, and sleep better."

He won again. I guess. Later in my journey some of the weight would be lifted, but it took months for that to happen. And lots more experiences.

13

"Okay," I started. "We talked about the world 'out there' and my world 'in here.' Now how do I use this in living? It's all very theoretical. Very flimsy to my mind."

"Yep. It should be. We haven't gotten to the part about living when it comes to the 'out there' and 'in here.' What do you think?"

"Fred, I don't have a clue at the moment. So talk to me."

"Well here's the deal. 'Out there' is a bunch of ought to's, limits, expectations. Stuff like that. It is coming in at you all the time. If you reach out there, you are doing something the psychologists call reality testing. You touch the real world. You find out what your boss expects. You jog or run and find out how tired you get and how fast and how much your muscles hurt in the morning.

"Most people live in the 'out there.' Their lives circle around all the expectations and limits and social norms and rules and all that stuff."

"Yeah, I guess I did that."

"Until you quit your job and took off."

"That's true. And now I'm floundering around. Flopping around in Moab."

"Okay. But that will stop."

"So what about the 'in here'?"

"That's the world of fantasies and dreams. That's the world of possibilities. We don't dream about what we know we can do. In the 1800's people didn't dream about walking. They dreamed about traveling fast on wheels – you know like trains and automobiles – and they dreamed about flying.

"So the world of 'in here' is where we color outside the lines, as that cliché goes. It's what you see when you fantasize about something. It's what comes to you in your dreams, if you can remember them."

"And all this means?"

"It means that a real life, an active effective life is one where you create something out of the limitations. People knew they couldn't fly by flapping their arms so they invented balloons and gliders and airplanes. So if you know you can't be something, you dream of ways to get there. That's one of the secrets of life."

"Okay, so again it's a balance between the inside and outside. The 'in here' and 'out there.'"

"Close, but not quite. It's not a balance. It's an integration of the two. If you balance, you end up half way between dreams and realities. If you integrate them, you end up with dreams that become realities.

Sayings of Fred
Create a life by dreaming and then finding ways
to get around whatever blocks the dream from
happening.

14

"Let me put it another way," Fred started. "We need to live in the here-and-now. But we need to take into account the world 'out there' and listen to the 'voice in here.' In other words, 'here' is where the soul meets the sensuous, where the spirit meets reality.

"And the 'now' is where history meets future. But for your purposes, it is where the 'causes' of the past meet the 'possibilities' of the future."

"So you are living at the intersection of the soul, the sensuous, causes, and choices. At least that is where you should be living. Most people don't. Most people in our society ignore the soul, miss a lot of the sensuous, because they are living out all the causes in their lives and not making any choices. I can't put it any more succinctly than that!"

It made some sense.

Sayings of Fred
The here-and-now is the place where your soul
meets reality and your personal story line meets the
possibilities of tomorrow.

15

The next day Fred had me try an experiment. He told me to focus on my breathing. In the first part, I inhaled and held my breath for a count of twenty and then exhaled slowly for another count of twenty. After the second cycle, I yawned. Fred said that I was expelling the carbon dioxide in my lungs, and the yawn was the final push. I continued the inhale, count to twenty, exhale, count to twenty. The exhale was harder because I just wanted to "whoosh" my breath out. Just like always. But Fred insisted on the twenty count.

After about ten cycles of long inhales and exhales, Fred told me to breathe normally but concentrate entirely on the breathing. He had me repeat a simple mantra: *breathing in the spirit of the earth, breathing out the essence of my soul.* I inhaled on the first phrase, exhaled on the second.

I began to relax. Didn't realize that there had been some tension in my body. And my mind did go blank. I just repeated the mantra, breathed in, breathed out.

"That's one way to get into here-and-now," Fred said after I stopped. "For that brief while, you were completely in the here-and-now. You were totally in this moment and in this place because that is when and where your breathing was."

Thus I learned one of the disciplines that would be useful later in life.

16

"Are we getting anywhere?" Fred turned and looked at me. His dog, laying on the ground between us, looked up at the same time and gave me the usual questioning stare. Was everyone checking up on my life?

"I don't know."

"It's not all that difficult. Your body is sending you messages. Your soul is sending you messages. But when you live in the world, you spend most of your time meeting deadlines and goals and expectations and fulfilling other people's needs. So those body and soul messages are ignored."

"I guess that's true."

"Sure. You're tired and not thinking at full speed. Yet you go to work and do the best you can. You'd be better off resting. Doing something to get back on track. Your body knows when it is tired. If you would stop for a minute, you would know that when your body is tired the old brain doesn't work as well. But you fake it. Everyone does. Well, almost everyone."

"And soul messages?"

"You go to work. You don't hate it but you don't really enjoy it either. It's just work. You make money. You go out with friends. You laugh a lot. But inside you know that this isn't really enjoyment. You have sex with your wife or female friend but it isn't really satisfying. For you or her. You ignore that."

"So what does all that have to do with soul messages?"

"That vague discontent is a message. And I bet that if you or anyone would really listen to the soul messages they would be about what kind of work you were really meant to do. Not what you got steered into by teachers and friends and professors and counselors. And maybe even parents or aunts and uncles. And you'd discover that the kind of people you would really like to be with are not the ones you have as friends. What you'd really like to talk about is not what you get to talk about. And you'd find that there is a difference between making love and having sex!"

"Wow! Sounds scary, just like you said!"

17

"If you follow your soul messages, you'll be a flake. A weirdo. And you may starve do death or at least go hungry a lot. If you follow your body messages, exclusively, you will be the ultimate hedonist. You'll do nothing but exercise, sleep, take naps, eat, drink, and have sex. And you may end up not making much if any money.

"But if you keep on living your life as you have, it will be pretty empty. You will have friends, a job, a lover, even hobbies. At the end of it all, though, you will be one of those people who says: 'I wish I had done…I wish I had been…I wish…I wish.

"So your task is to take your soul messages and your body messages and do your reality testing and come up with a blend that allows you to be whatever it is you were meant to be. And, buddy, it is a task! It is work!"

18

"Now here's something interesting for you to try." Fred almost smirked as he said it. Sometimes he was deliberately irritating.

"All right. All Right."

"We went through the bit about your body sending you messages. Through your urine. Through your shit. And through your muscles. But some of us know that you can also train your body!"

"Oh come on, Fred!"

"No. It's true. You can train your body to relax. On command."

"And how do you do this?"

"Well an old doctor, Jacobsen I think was his name, developed this technique. And it is powerful. Sit back in the chaise there and put your arm on the armrest."

I did, the obedient but skeptical student.

"Now clench your fist on one arm. What you are feeling in that forearm muscle is tension. Relax the fist. Now you are feeling the lack of tension. Or relaxation."

"Okay. I agree. I can feel the difference."

"Continue doing that. Do your other forearm. Then do your upper arms."

I looked at Fred as though he were just giving a lecture.

"No. I mean do it, right now." So I did.

Fred had me tense up each major muscle group in my body: feet, calves, thighs, neck, shoulders, stomach, and back. Each time I tensed and relaxed a couple of times.

"If you do that regularly for a week or two," said Fred, "you will eventually 'teach' all those muscle groups what relaxation feels like. And you will be able to induce the relaxation without going through all the tensing"

I did practice this a few times and it did seem to be working. However, I didn't do it seriously for another year. Then I had the opportunity and desire. I found a simple method for going into a deeply relaxed state that did not involve napping. In fact, after twenty minutes or so of the deep relaxation, I would feel energized rather than the droopy feeling that comes after a nap.

19

"Do you want to go on with this?" Fred glanced at me.

"With what?"

"This adventure you've started."

"I'm not sure."

"We've talked a lot these past few weeks. It's been almost all talk. A few experiences. Now it's time for you to move on to find out more about yourself and life."

"And how do I do that?"

"What do you think?"

"I'm not sure."

"Well, based on all this talk, do you think your life is in balance?"

"No. Absolutely not."

"In what ways?"

"I know that there is something I am supposed to be – or do. But I don't know what it is. And I am pretty sure that I am way over on the side of using my mind, my thinking and analysis too much. Trouble is, I don't know what to do about any of that."

"That's where Fred comes in," smiled Fred. "There are some adventures you can go on that will help. If you're interested, we can arrange those adventures."

"Okay. I guess." At this point I wasn't sure. All that Fred had talked about up to this point made sense in a mad sort of way, but I was still me, still the product of my family, my schools, my friends, and my work.

"Tell you what," Fred spoke softly as he looked down at the red dust around his boots. "Go on hiatus. Let all this ferment in your mind and body and soul. Then if you want, come back. I'll be here."

20

The next morning I stuffed my sleeping bag and clothes back into the Wrangler. Fred had left. Gone. So I drove out of his yard, down the dusty road, and onto Highway 160 heading south. Ahead of me were the Grand Canyon and L.A.

All along the way I kept thinking about creating a life, looking at and smelling my pee, trying to figure out how to listen to soul messages, checking the color and consistency of my bowel movements, and being amazed at the strange combination of spiritual, profane, and intellectual lore of the past weeks.

HIATUS

So I drove south through southwestern Utah. Just out of Moab the road winds and undulates and then traverses a flat plain with the southern LaSal Mountains rising to the south and west, forty five degrees to my right as I looked out the window of my Jeep.

Some months later I would be a passenger in a truck driven by a wonderful woman who would teach me about love.

I bulleted through the canyons and across mesas occasionally noticing red rock formations, but I was targeted on the Grand Canyon. I shot past Monument Valley and gave a nodding, grudging look at its prominences, a quarter mile or so off the road to my left.

I stopped in Kayenta, Arizona at a fast food place, peed, noticed some yellowness, ordered a diet cola and filled my water bottle, and moved on. At Cameron, a Navajo village, I swung the Jeep to the right and headed for the east entrance of Grand Canyon. A little after noon I stood on the canyon rim.

It's too big and grand to really comprehend. There's too much to see. The usual awe of the first-time visitor took over. On the other hand, there was a disturbing background of tourist chatter. In what should have been a cathedral of silence, people laughed, mumbled, hollered and conversed; not a Tower of Babel but a canyon of babble.

I was turned off. I drove to Tusayan, just outside the park's south entrance, ate lunch, and pointed the Wrangler south to Williams, Arizona not realizing what role that small town would play in my later life. I stayed overnight, got up early, and drove due west toward L.A.

That evening I stayed somewhere, now out of memory, and continued to my friends' house in Santa Ana the next day. Surreptitiously I checked my bowel movements and the clarity of my urine. Of course, I didn't mention any of this to my friends.

L.A. treated me well. The weather was mild, my friends congenial, and I was haunted, particularly after going to bed and waking up in the morning, by questions of place and time, of body and soul. None of my bowel movements quite measured up to the standard Fred had set, but I was peeing clear on most days. I needed to return to Moab.

SECTION II

The Soul Quest

1

So I returned from my trip to Los Angeles and Phoenix. I told Fred I would stop through Moab on my way back, but then realized that there was no "back," there was no place to go, no home, no return.

I drove from Phoenix through Flagstaff, on to the Navajo Reservation and Tuba City, Kayenta, and Mexican Hat, then on to Blanding and Monticello in Utah to Moab not knowing whether Fred would be there or not. He wasn't. I checked into one of the older motels thinking that I would go hiking in Arches and Canyonlands national parks for a few days using that time to decide what to do next.

The next day I drove into Arches and wandered along a well worn, densely traveled trail, listening to an occasional burst of a foreign language, mostly German and Spanish. No fun until I struck out on a less used trail around and behind Spectacle arches. I was away from the crowds and could see for miles across the red rock and sand to the created by the Colorado River.

By early afternoon I was back in town and drove past Fred's place, drawn to it. His camper was parked in its usual place under the tree. I backed up, having run a little past the drive, and pulled in. No sign of Fred.

So I sat in one of the old folding chairs, restless and uneasy. Weeks in the urban worlds of Los Angeles and Phoenix infected me, and the relentless drive from Phoenix to Moab, done in a day, amplified the energy level.

Then Fred appeared. He nodded, accepting the fact that I was there as though he had fully expected me to arrive on this day, at this time.

"How was the trip?"

"Okay, I guess."

"Doesn't sound so red hot."

"Well I got to see some of my old friends again. That was good. But they kept asking me what I was going to do. You know, like you aren't someone unless you're employed. Have some kind of job. We had some good times, but it bugged me."

"No wonder. You're a nobody."

"Wait! What do you mean by that?"

"Just what you said. If you don't have a job, you aren't anyone. You don't have an identity. People have trouble dealing with you. See, you're a trouble maker."

"Well, I don't exactly see myself that way."

"Of course not. But you're breaking all the rules. You're supposed to be productive and useful, You're not supposed to be wandering around. You should have invested your inheritance and kept on working. Or at least found another job in another city."

"I guess you're right. Maybe I am a trouble maker. But you are too."

"Absolutely. That's my mission in life. I'm here to make trouble."

I laughed at the old man who didn't appear the powerful revolutionary, sitting under a tree in Moab, Utah. Later Fred would point out to me that the Buddha didn't look like a revolutionary either but had changed the way many people believed and lived.

"Let's follow this train of thought," Fred continued. "See work and activity are anesthetic. If you stay busy and involved, you don't have time to think about anything else. Like what life is really about. What you really should be doing. Who you should be."

"I hadn't thought about that."

"Work can be just as effective as alcohol or any other drug in blocking any soul searching."

"Soul searching?"

"Yep, soul searching. That's a good phrase. Not used too often anymore. But it has meaning. You stop. You dig deeply into that inner self we talked about while you were here before."

"Like therapy."

"No, not like therapy." Fred frowned. "That's a modern idea. Actually you can use therapy as a way to escape what I'm talking about. Particularly what they call the 'talking therapies.' Everything gets converted into words. Experience gets dulled by talking about it. In therapy people 'work on' their lives. I'm pointing to something different."

"In what way? I don't understand."

"It's simple. Like everything I know is simple. If you stop doing, stop talking, stop being totally involved all day, every day, you know what happens?"

"No."

"Your soul starts speaking to you."

I nodded but didn't really understand. Silence hung lightly between us.

"Look," Fred motioned with one of his hands in a kind of circular motion, "when you have a conversation, one person talks and then shuts up while the other person talks. If one person talks all the time, the other person never has a chance. Well your soul is another version of your being. If your active, outer shell keeps on yakking all the time, your soul doesn't have a chance. So it resorts to subterfuges, like dreams. You shut up at night when you sleep, so the soul says, 'Okay, now's my opportunity,' and it sends messages. Of course, most of the time, those messages are ignored."

"So I have to take 'time out' of my ordinary way of living to let the soul speak?"

"Exactly. Want to try it?"

"Right now? Here?"

"No. In a couple of weeks. First we'll have to do some preparatory work. But if you want, we'll give you soul a chance to speak."

"Do I want to do that?"

"Well it ain't necessarily fun. You may get some messages you don't like. It may scare the hell out of you. But it will be real. And you can always shut down that line of communication. You've been doing it for all your adult life. Right?"

"I guess so."

"Think about it. If you want to take a break from life as you know it, I can arrange it."

"Okay." I'm sure my brow was creased with lines of perplexity and maybe a little anxiety. The trip to friends in Los Angeles hadn't done a thing for me. Why not try Fred's kind of trip? As he said, I could always shut down the process if I wanted to.

Sayings of Fred
Your soul talks to you in the pauses in life, and that's why you need to create pauses.

2

I was going to go on a 'soul quest.' That's what Fred told me. He handed me a book, *The Book of the Vision Quest*, and told me to read it at any pace I wanted. And to read it in any sequence. Just look it over. Get a feel for the vision quest process. He did say that he had problems with the idea of a 'vision quest.' That phrase comes from the Indians. But an Anglo can't really go through the same thing. Fred instead called it a soul quest.

So I read. Sometimes perched on one of the old folding aluminum chairs in Fred's front yard. Sometimes under a tree on the road to Canyonlands National Park. And occasionally even in McDonald's where I bought a Diet Coke and sat.

The vision quest was an Indian rite-of-passage for young males. They went off for several days without food or water. The purpose was to give the young man a chance to get a 'vision' of his calling, his place in the world.

Now white people had adopted the phrase and created an experience for people of all ages. This adapted vision quest, Fred's soul quest, consisted of a week or ten days in a natural setting, away from civilization. In other words, out in the wilds somewhere. During the time away, there were three days of fasting. Okay, that bothered me. I like to eat. In fact, I get anxious if I think I might miss a meal. I have been known to bring along a snack if I even think lunch might be two hours late. I don't like being hungry.

Did I want to go on a soul quest? Not at all sure!

Fred suggested we start preparations. I could back out at any time.

I bought a notebook at the City Market in Moab and started a journal at Fred's urging. The first few entries were minimal. Fred handed me a short piece of paper from a notepad one day with suggestions about topics or issues. That helped. I started to write longer entries and began to enjoy the writing.

Then, several weeks after the whole business of a soul quest came up, Fred said I ought to go on a spirit walk. The idea was to go somewhere and walk 'as the spirit moves you.' You don't follow a trail. You don't have a destination. You walk in whatever direction seems right. Stop at whatever interests you. And you are supposed to do this without eating for the day.

I agreed to try it. But I cheated and took along some snack food stuff, just in case.

Fred and I discussed where this walk should take place. The country around Moab is mostly canyons and cliffs. Walking in a canyon pretty much restricts you to walking up and down the canyon, and that's not the idea of the spirit walk. On the other hand, some parts of the desert can be dangerous to go wandering in. Dunes rise and fall. There are few landmarks, and the ones that do exist can't be seen from between dunes.

3

We drove to an area off the main highway into Moab. We needed an area where I could wander without getting lost. Most of the desert around Moab consists of either slickrock, slabs or great mounds of red polished sandstone, favorites of the mountain bikers who flock to the area, or of undulating sand and rock. In the former, there is a good chance of having the cyclists come cruising by which would ruin the whole idea of the soul walk. And in the latter, the wanderer who ends up down in the arroyos between the mounds of sand and rock can easily get disoriented. That's not good either.

So we chose an area that lay a mile or so off of the main highway, bordered on one side by the road leading back to Canyonlands National Monument and on the other by high red rock cliffs. In between was a stand of cottonwoods and tamarisk hydrated by water occasionally collecting along an otherwise dry creek bed.

Fred parked his truck under one of the cottonwoods, and we got out.

"Here's the deal. Stand here and look around. Take your time. In fact, sit down if you need to. Just keep looking around until you see something that 'calls to you.' It will happen sooner or later. Some place in this area will seem to draw you. Walk to that place. Stay there for a while. Then repeat the process. Look around for another place that seems to attract you.

"You'll end up meandering around in here. You can't get lost. Worse comes to worst, you either wander close to the road or the highway or you'll be blocked by the cliffs over there."

"Okay," I said as I began to survey the area. Nothing particularly called to me. So I did sit down facing the cliffs to the south and the main stand of cottonwoods. Nothing.

Finally, I did see one large cottonwood, a grandfather tree, that looked interesting. I walked to it, away from Fred and the truck. The shade of the tree was pleasant on a warming day. In fact, getting hot. I sat under the tree for quite a while without really looking for another place to select.

Boredom set in, and I looked around again. I wanted to go to the edge of the cliffs, where they merged with the sand and rock below. I struggled over in that direction, struggled because of the thick tamarisk and other small underbrush. I arrived at a slope of red sand and rocks, big and small, eroded off of the cliff. The slope created a ramp up to the vertical beginning of the cliffs, and standing there, I realized how high the cliffs really were. I also saw the big slabs of sandstone that had fallen off of sheer wall.

There was still an attraction to walking up the ramp but at the same time a sense of danger, even though the odds were enormously against more slabs falling while I stood there. I climbed. The sand was loose; the slope steep. It took a lot of effort, and I sweated my way almost to the cliff wall. I couldn't quite get there as the slope steepened. But I could stand there and crane my neck looking up at the red wall and the desert varnish, a deeper red, stained in vertical streaks.

I turned and sat looking back down at the trees and shrubs below. This was a good place to be! I was amazed. There was no trail. No markings. I got there intuitively.

For a couple more hours, I meandered around the area. But there was nothing to compare with standing at the base of the red rock cliff, looking up at it and turning to scan the green vista below.

Getting back to Fred and the truck was no problem. I walked out to the road and followed it back to where we had parked.

Fred nodded and got in the truck.

"Boy, that was something. I really got into it…"

Fred shushed me. "Don't talk about it. Just remember it."

I have since learned, from that experience and others later, that sometimes it is good to follow an inner guide, a silent pathfinder, to meander and wander. We don't have to walk along a trail to a destination every time. We don't have to go along a predestined path to some particular conclusion in life either. I also learned, later, the value of not talking about an experience.

4

We, the next day, sat on two flat rocks, forty-five degrees to each other, Fed hunched down, facing the red sand at his feet. I sat more upright. Barker stretched out on his opposite us, in some shade.

"Here's the thing about the soul quest," began Fred. "It is based on the hero's journey. At least as far as I am concerned. When we get back to the trailer, you can pick up the Joseph Campbell book and page through it. Right now I'm going to give you the five-minute version."

"Okay."

"In every culture there is a myth about the hero's journey. There are three basic elements to the journey. First, the hero leaves home. Leaves the normal, day-to-day world in which he or she has grown up. Kids who go to college understand that shift. And you've made a change like that by leaving Chicago, your job, your friends. Leaving home begins the journey.

"The next step is facing tests. Crises. Once the hero crosses the boundary from the usual, conventional world, there are a series of these tests. In come societies, the tests are put on the individual. Particularly if it is a ritual of passage from childhood to adulthood.

"Finally, the hero returns. Having faced the tests, the hero comes back. But comes back changed. And that is the big thing. Instead of returning to the home world as the same person who left, the hero comes back transformed.

"Campbell – I think it's Campbell – has a good image of the returned hero. He – or she – now stands with one foot in the conventional, normal, regular world but with the other foot in a different, unique, special, and maybe spiritual world. The returned hero spans the boundary. Spans the margins of the two worlds.

"In Christian-speak, you are now no longer 'of this world, but in it'"

I didn't say anything as Fred looked up at me. Barker, good old Barker, opened his eyes, questioning me as well.

"Are you curious about how this relates to the soul quest?"

"Sure. Since I'm going out there."

"Okay. When we hike up the canyon sometime in the next couple of weeks, you'll be leaving behind this world of cars, stereos, radios, people, stores, fast food, and on and on. You are going out into the wilderness. That's a good place for a hero's journey."

"Is that the test?"

"Nope. Once we get out there, you will go on a three day solo. You will sit in the canyon for three days with no human contact. You will be alone. That is your first test. And it is a big one for most people in this world today. We are so used to having other people around. Even if we don't talk to them, they are there. You are going out there, and you'll see no one. So aloneness will be one test."

"Any others?"

"The second one is silence. There will be no voices. No music. Nothing to distract your mind. In fact, you will go out with no books or anything to read. There will be no input to your brain. Except of course what you can see, hear, or touch in the canyon. And that will be a big test because we are so used to having some kind of stimulus. In fact, I bet that you are used to having a lot of stimuli. Multiple stuff going on at the same time. Reading while listening to some music. Talking to someone with other conversations in the background. Out there, you'll be facing silence."

"That's beginning to sound a little scary."

Fred went on, ignoring my comment. "And then there's the last test. For the three days, you will fast. No food. You can drink all the water you want to. But no food."

"Now that sounds like a real test!" I muttered. Aloneness and silence were kind of abstract at this point. But no food was real. Really real. I loved food. I was the kind of person who would look at my watch at work or at home to see when it was time to eat again. I looked forward to eating. I liked the taste of food. I liked the feeling of the food going down my gullet.

"Yeah, it's a real test."

A long silence. Both of us sitting in the sun on those rocks with just a hint of a breeze coming down canyon and past us out toward town. Barker was now on his back, front legs straight up and bent slightly, rear legs spread, airing his private parts.

Fred went on. "So those are the tests. You will face silence and aloneness. You will fast. And when it is all over, you may find that you have changed in some way. You may not know how. But you will probably have changed. It may take a couple of days or a couple or weeks or even a couple of months, but at some time you'll find out that you are no longer who you were."

I nodded.

5

Fred suggested another adventure in the desert, one that sounded like fun and mildly risqué. Once again we bounced out of Fred's yard, this time in my Jeep, and into town, then north, again to the turn off to Canyonlands, and drove along that road for several miles before coming to a dirt road to the left.

"Turn here," Fred pointed.

I turned and drove no more than a mile. We were well out of sight of the Canyonlands road.

"Okay. I told you back at the trailer this was going to be nudist day. Now, I'm not social nudist, so you go off over that way and shed your clothes. I'll do the same over here. We'll take half an hour or so and wander around buck naked.

"I'll take my whistle with me. When I think we've been out here long enough, I'll toot the whistle. We don't want to get sunburned buns!" That was a premonition of something that would happen later – to me.

I walked away from the truck, turned and saw Fred walking the opposite direction, and I walked until I was out of sight of the truck. Obeying a deeply ingrained modesty, I found a clump of three junipers and stood inside their triangle. Getting the T-shirt off was no problem. I dropped my jeans and forgot that they wouldn't come off over the boots. So I sat down in the sand and unlaced and shed the boots. And pulled the jeans over my feet and socks and off.

I could stop right there, I thought, and Fred would never know the difference. I waited a couple of minutes. Oh what the hell! I slipped my shorts off and stood naked, except for my socks. I decided that putting my boots back on was wise, and did it.

It was easy to stand there between and behind the junipers. Fred had said we should walk around a little. I finally moved away from the trees into the open.

And I was delivered of the most liberated, free-feeling state of my life. No, I wasn't going to become a nudist, a social nudist in Fred's words.

But I sure could get used to walking around with no clothes in the great outdoors like this. A little breeze came up and tickled my butt and testicles. A new sensation. This was fun!

I wandered a little farther away from my pile of clothes until I heard Fred's whistle. I wanted to stay naked a little longer but couldn't. I slipped the boots off again, put on the shorts, T-shirt, and jeans, relaxed and tied the boots and walked back to the truck.

"Don't talk about it!" Fred said as I approached. "Just remember it."

6

"You know," Fred started, "what we were talking about the other day, the business of being between two worlds, is not all the uncommon."

"How?"

"Well, the children of immigrants, the first generation Americans, live in two worlds. They live in the American culture. They watch TV. Listen to the radio. Talk with their friends. But the parents are still from the old culture. Maybe Hispanic. Or Slavic. Or Japanese. Whatever. These kids have to learn to live in between the two cultures. To jump back and forth depending on where they are. With whom they are dealing."

"And others?"

"Sure. There are lots of people living on the margins of society. We think everyone is mainstream. Not true. Talk to folks who live in rural settings. It's a whole different kind of life. I met a guy last year whose family, his wife and kids, live out on a ranch with no electricity. It would cost a fortune to run power lines out to his place. So they make do with lanterns and candles in the winter. They heat the place with a wood stove. But his kids go to school in town for five days a week. They board. And they live between those two worlds.

"The other example are the Native Americans. They have their own culture. Many are trying to hang on to that. But they also live in this modern Anglo world. The adults and kids lives between two cultures. They have to adapt.

"Sometime in the next year or so, maybe you'll have a chance to experience those kinds of people. Their kind of existence. And not for just a day or two. I hope it would be for a couple of months, at least."

I nodded, not knowing that in the following summer, I would be living in a small cottage on a lake in Michigan, learning from and about people I couldn't have imagined.

7

Before I went out on this intriguing but anxiety-inducing soul quest, Fred asked me to write out, in my journal, a brief summary of my history, not a chronological listing of events, but rather my inner history. How I had been formed. My values and where they came from. He also suggested that I write out, as best I could, how I saw my future.

This is the only case, in this book, where I will provide excerpts from my journal. A journal is private and ought not be revealed or published. It's not written for consumption by anyone. It is not a message to someone else or to an audience. However, I believe that what I wrote in this case is useful in understanding the later changes in me and my life as a result of the soul quest.

"I have always been a conforming, 'good boy.' I tried to make my parents proud of me or at least not to be ashamed. Certainly I did some goofy and strange things in adolescence, but they were never malicious and fortunately were never revealed.

"I always believed that hard work would get you ahead. There may be people who are political and manipulative and some of them will be successful, at least in a financial sense. But I believed and still believe that ultimately merit is rewarded. Good people can be successful and have the advantage that they do not have to regret or hide their actions.

"I have been an idealist. The most important book in my early years was the story of King Arthur – The Once and Future King – and I took from that book Arthur's mantra that 'Right makes might' rather than 'Might makes right.' Somehow you would always be rewarded if you did the right thing even if it did not pay off immediately.

"Later, in my college years, I was infatuated with the story of Don Quixote, particularly the musical, Man of La Mancha. I memorized the lyrics to 'The Impossible Dream' and can still recite them.

"Sometime later I discovered the film The Graduate and the ending to that story also struck a responsive chord in me. When the lead character charges into the church and rescues the bride from the marriage that was wrong and he takes her off on a bus, I really liked that idea.

"However, when I went to work, I found that the 'real world' was not up to my ideals. I never compromised very much. Sometimes I had to. I worked on some PR campaigns in which I really didn't believe. I worked for some clients who were real jerks. But that came with the territory. I never got cynical. In fact, what happened is that I numbed out. I just ignored what I was doing, that is, for whom I was doing it, for what I was doing it. I distanced myself from those things.

"There were a few projects I worked on that I really enjoyed. They were fun, and I believed in what I was doing.

"My romantic nature took over in personal relationships. I had several relationships with women before I married Andrea. In every case I idealized the woman. Of course, the reality was that they did not and could live up to my idealization. Maybe they did the same for me.

"With Andrea it was different. For one thing, she came closer to meeting my ideal. And when she didn't, I found something else in her that made up for it. So that relationship went on for quite a while and then we got married. I think maybe that was our mistake. We had a real hard time dealing with all the little issues that came up.

"I have always tried to look on the positive side of things. Somehow I could always get up off the mat and go on. When I would get depressed, I usually knew why. If I waited long enough it might go away. Or I could work my way through those times.

"I was an avid reader all my life. I love books. Particularly good literature. I like novels that tell good stories with real characters. For some reason I have gotten really enthused about some South American and Central American authors. They write fascinating stuff.

"I also love the outdoors. That was one of the things that Andrea and I had in common. The problem was that there was very little time to really get outdoors. To go hiking. Or camping. Whenever I am outdoors I feel really, really good. That is why I bought the Jeep Wrangler, so I could get out into the back country more often and more easily. Again, there really wasn't much time."

- - - - -

"I'm not sure what to write down about my future. I think I may go back to Chicago and back to some kind of work after I get this current 'itch' out of my system. That's what I think it is. Just an 'itch.' If I scratch it, it will go away.

"I have no strong desire to get ahead in the usual sense. I don't want to run a PR agency. I enjoy the 'doing.' The writing, editing, and all that stuff. I don't see myself as a manager or entrepreneur.

"I would like to have the opportunity to be outdoors more, so I guess that is part of my future. I don't want to get into another job where there is a lot of weekend or late night work.

"As far as relationships go, I would like to meet someone who is compatible with me. Maybe I could let go of my idealistic version of a woman and learn to accept her for what she is.

"I don't see myself as having a lot of friends, but I would like to have a few very close friends.

"That's about all I can think of in terms of my future."

8

"There's a caveat on this soul quest thing," Fred announced as we sat, this time in his trailer with showers occasionally dampening the yard, western "dust wetters," but just a little too wet to sit in.

"And what is that?"

"You may run into demons out there. Dragons. Witches. Devils."

"Like they are running around in the canyon?"

"Nope. Not real life, solid beings running around the canyon, as you say."

"Then what?"

"Demons in you. They may come out. It is one of the warnings the mystics talk about when they introduce someone to meditation. You see consciousness keeps those demons at bay. That is one reason to work hard, keep thinking, inundate yourself with noise, watch television, and all that stuff. It keeps the demons down."

"I still don't understand."

"Everyone one of us has some darklings lurking inside. There is a side of you that you don't want to deal with. I have one. Everyone has one. The psychologists call it your shadow self. If you sit quietly long enough, some of that shadow shows up.

"And there is something else. All of us have done things we don't like. Maybe stuff we shouldn't have done. Stuff to feel guilty about. Instead of sitting around and feeling guilty all the time – which would be really unhealthy – we park that stuff somewhere in the back of our minds. But if you don't keep the old mind occupied, as we say, those bad things come back.

"I just needed to warn you. It may not happen to you. The three or four days may not be enough. But if a demon visits you, you'll have to figure out how to deal with it."

"Sounds a little scary. But I don't think it will happen to me."

"We'll see. The pause for the soul to speak may involve other voices."

Sayings of Fred
The real demons and devils are inside of you.

9

The soul quest trek began in Fred's front yard. We shouldered our backpacks and walked up the road, away from Moab, and up Mill Creek Canyon. The road ended at the site of the old mill. A small dam made a waterfall. Beyond that the road turned into a trail hugging the right side of the creek alongside a low canyon wall.

We waded across the creek four or five times as it meandered back and forth across the canyon floor. We hiked along the creek sides avoiding the ledges and cliffs on either side.

Then we emerged from a stand or tamarisk to confront a solid wall of rock twenty feet high. Fred unsnapped his pack belt and slipped the shoulder straps off.

"Here we do a little rock climbing. Nothing too bad, though." This created a little anxiety in me. I didn't see any way to get up the wall.

With that he scrambled up a crack running diagonally across the face of the rock from right to left with a few scrub bushes growing out of it. Fred found good handholds and at one point had to hang on to the roots of one of the bushes. He ended up on top of the rock and pointed down to me, "See if you can hand up my pack."

By climbing a few feet up the crack and with Fred laying on his belly over the edge, we got out hands within three feet of each other, and the pack was a little more than three feet tall.

"Okay. Now you do it. But first hand up your pack." I did.

The climb wasn't as difficult as I had worried over. I made it up and to the flat table that stretched ahead for a quarter mile or more.

We reshouldered our packs and went on.

After a bit more than an hour, we found ourselves at a wide section of the canyon where the creek flowed along the right or east side along towering red sandstone cliffs. A grove of big cottonwood trees grew along the creek providing shade and shelter. To the west, there was a rising section of sand and sandstone, lifting toward the cliffs above which were the slickrock areas beloved by mountain bikers. Down where we were prickly pear cactus populated the open areas. And a few juniper trees spotted the landscape.

Fred set up his tent underneath the cottonwoods, and I followed his lead. We camped just a few yards apart. I slipped my self-inflating mattress into the tent and unstuffed the sleeping bag from its sack. The down fluffed quickly. My few personal items – flashlight, pocketknife, bandanna, and stuff sack with shaving gear and sunblock – took up the two pockets sewn to the inside the tent. I rigged the fly over the tent even though there didn't seem to be much chance of rain.

With that, Fred and I collaboratively set up our kitchen – two burner stove, pots and pans, larger dishwashing pan, and our two mess kits with rudimentary stainless steel flatware. That done, Fred sat down leaning against one of the cottonwood trunks and motioned me to do the same. I did.

"Okay, here's the deal," he took a stick and played with it drawing random lines in the sand. "We're going to spend a day or two getting used to the canyon. And getting you ready for the solo. After that we have to find you a place to go on your solo. Right now, let's just sit for a while."

10

That afternoon, late and just before evening, Fred and I set up eight big rocks to form a circle about twenty feet in diameter. I had no idea what it was for.

After a light dinner cooked on our two burner stove, Fred took me to the ring. "Start walking around the outside of the circle," he said. "Just keeping walking until you feel one part is more comfortable to you. You'll know when it happens."

Another form of Fred's craziness. What was this, anyway? But I did as told and started walking the perimeter. Nothing happened. I walked and walked. Somewhere, however, around the fifteenth trip I did notice that one area of the circle did feel different. So I walked another four or five laps. Each time the feeling of that one place got stronger. I finally stopped there.

Fred came over to me. "This circle represents the four directions and the four seasons. From Native American lore. Each segment of the circle has certain qualities. They can indicate something about you."

"Like what?"

"Well, where you have stopped is the part of the circle that is associated with wisdom and intuition. The opposite side…" he pointed to the other side of the circle…"is related to knowledge and reason."

I continued to stand there. "This is something you may want to think about. It is saying that your life may be more satisfying to you if you focus on what we call wisdom. And if you use your intuitive powers as much as you can."

That came as a surprise to me. I had been a "success" in my professional life mainly because I was always organized, thought things out, and could produce plausible reasons for what I was doing.

11

The next step in the soul quest process had a major effect on me, although I can't describe all the details here.

Fred laid out the general plan for the activity. I was given a handful of small slips of paper. On each I was to write down something from my past that I wanted to leave in my past, that is, leave it behind and not have to think or worry or feel guilty or be concerned in any way about it. After the writing, we would build a small fire, and I would put each slip of paper in the fire saying: "This is no longer a part of me."

Fred handed me the slips of paper and sent me off to do the writing. I chose a seat between the roots of a large cottonwood tree on the bank of Mill Creek. And I sat. For an hour nothing happened. Nothing came to me. Then I wrote down one event in my past that had occasionally bubbled into consciousness, particularly as I would be waking up in the morning. It was an event that troubled me.

It took me most of the afternoon to complete my assignment. At the end, I had eleven slips of paper with writing on them. I will not reveal them here. Frankly, I have forgotten most of them. So the process did work to that extent. However, for those I do remember and even the ones I don't, they are highly personal. I chose not to reveal them here. Besides, the specifics are not important. The process was.

I burned each slip of paper, pausing after each. I did say: "This is no longer part of me." After the eleventh bit of paper and part of my life went up in flames, I did feel some sense of relief. The ritual worked to that extent in the moment. It worked even better through the years.

As I slid into my sleeping bag and lay back that night, there was a lightness to my mood. Perhaps I could put parts of my old self away and have a new beginning.

12

Fred asked me to go off and think about what I would want as an epitaph, what should be written on a gravestone. I wrote down a dozen or more possibilities. The one I chose was:

He worked hard and was a good man.

It didn't seem like much of a statement about an entire life. Fred made no editorial comments. He just grunted and handed back the sheet of paper.

13

The next day started slowly. We got up a little after sunrise and cooked up some multigrain cereal. The conversation was desultory. About the weather, the rocks, the cacti, and other trivia.

After cleaning up the pot we used for the cereal, our two metal bowls, and stainless spoons, Fred pulled a small sketch pad out of his pack. He handed it to me.

"Here's your assignment for the next hour." He pointed to the sketch book. "Draw anything that comes into your head. Go over there under that cottonwood, and just look at the paper. Then draw anything at all."

"But I'm not an artist."

"Don't have to be an artist. Just put down some lines. Do your best. You're not going to be judged on how good the sketches are." He pointed to the cottonwood, and I, obedient as ever, went over and sat down.

I stared at the first blank page. And stared.

The first thing I drew was a book. It was a thin book, and I did my best to draw the cover and spine. A few lines showed the pages.

I turned the page and stared some more.

Nothing at all. Blank. A cipher. Zero. Nada. Nothing. I wanted to get up and take the book back to Fred. I looked up, and he was gone. Oh well.

So I stared again. I sketched a sheaf of papers.

Then, turning the page, I drew my own crude version of an old quill pen with an ink well next to it.

Again a blank mind and a blank page.

I doodled some simple designs: a spiral, four interlocking rings in a quadrangular arrangement, a set of nested squares and rectangles.

Another page. I tried to draw a tree. Not too bad. It looked like a tree, more or less. On the next page, I did my interpretation of a small prickly pear cactus. Then, quickly, I managed to fill several more pages with inexpert attempts at mountains, cliffs, and canyons.

At that point, Fred showed up. "So what's happened? What have you got there?"

I showed him. A few pages with a book, sheaf of papers, and a pen and ink well and then more pages with outdoorsy, landscapy kinds of things. "Interesting." That's all he said.

"So what does this tell you?"

"No. What does it tell you?"

"Not much."

"Okay. Then we'll leave it for a while." Fred walked back over to our campsite. I followed.

14

"Tomorrow is solo time." Fred looked over at me. "Think you're ready?"

"Yes." I felt confident at this point.

"We'll find you a place to camp out for three days. Tonight we'll fix our dinner. Your last supper!" He grinned over at me. "At sundown, we don't talk anymore. And no talk in the morning. We start our fast. You pack up your tent, sleeping bag, and stuff and move to the solo site. I'll stay here."

I nodded.

"For safety, we'll use written notes once a day. Tomorrow afternoon you'll leave me a note that you're okay. I'll pick it up before dark and leave you a note that I'm okay. We'll do that through the third day. On the morning of the fourth day, you pack up and come back here."

"Okay. I got it."

"Then let's have you look for a site." He stood up.

I uncranked my body, and we walked, single file, farther up the trail, Fred following me. "Keep looking around. Stop every once in a while and look around. Do that until you find a place that looks inviting."

Nothing looked particularly inviting where we were. I moved on slowly, stopping occasionally. The trail wound along beside the creek, the canyon narrowing ever so slightly from where we were camped. After fifteen minutes of slow walking, I arrived at a place where there was a shelf of red rock above and to the left of the creek, a shelf maybe six feet higher than the trail which was ten feet or more above the creek. I clambered up onto the shelf and looked around. This did look like home, at least as much as home could be in this canyon. There were several big juniper trees, one or two twice as tall as me.

I pointed. Fred was still down on the trail. "Does this look all right?" I asked.

"It's up to you. I only came along to find out where you would be."

"Okay, I guess this is it." I looked around and then returned to the trail and checked the area. I wanted to be sure that this was where I ended up the next morning.

As a final step we found a rock next to the trail roughly half way between where I would be camped and Fred's site. That was the place we would leave our "OK" messages. It tuned out that wasn't necessary.

15

Morning arrived, and I felt hungry. I felt hungry because I knew that there would be no breakfast for me. This was the beginning of the three day solo and fast. Clumsily, a little angrily, I took down my tent, stuffed it in its small bag, and rolled up my sleeping bag. That took more effort to get into its bag. I pushed, shoved, shoveled, and finally sat on the bag to get it in. The drawstrings on the bag drew the top closed.

There was no sense in taking along a dish, spoon or fork, or anything else needed to 'dine.' There would be no food. I did pack two quart bottles of water together with the filtering pump I would use to fill the bottles over the next three days.

Cheating, I stashed two fruity breakfast bars into one pocket of the pack.

I was ready. I visualized my solo site. Fred was up before me, sitting cross-legged in front of his tent. He had a small drum and a rough stick with a leather lump at one end. He nodded to me and started to beat on the drum, very slowly. He motioned me up the trail.

I shouldered my pack and trudged away, the beating of the drum sounding like a dirge. I walked until I couldn't hear the drum anymore and shortly was at the solo site.

I set up camp quickly. There wasn't much to do.

Then I sat under the nearest juniper and assessed my combined feelings of boredom and hunger.

The hunger was more a longing for something to taste than the real gut-empty hunger that might come later. I just wanted to munch on a potato chip or taste a couple of red grapes. Anything!

I knew I had that stash of breakfast bars but at this point I was intent resisting the urge. A little like not smoking a cigarette for someone quitting the habit. I was in the process of quitting eating for three days.

16

The boredom was worse. There were sounds. Subtle natural sounds. A bird call. The breeze in the juniper. And even a high-flying commercial jet somewhere overhead. Other than that, though, total silence.

I did miss hearing the voices of people. I did miss music. I even missed the sound of cars and trucks.

The sun moved steadily upward, and I figured it must be about noon. I had left my watch behind, on purpose, figuring that clock-watching would be worse than just getting through the days. If it was about noon, it was about time to have lunch. But I wasn't going to have any lunch. I sipped on my water bottle again. It was now about one-third full. The water did chase away actual pit-of-the-stomach hunger. It didn't do a thing for the 'want' of something with taste. Sugary taste. Fried fat taste. Anything!

Nothing moved in the canyon other than a few ravens circling overhead. No animals. Certainly no humans.

No humans? No one to see me. No one to care about what I did.

An impulse. No nudist, I was never interested in walking around naked with a bunch of other people. But here I was in the middle of nowhere. No one around. I slipped the T-shirt over my head, arms out of the sleeves. My khaki shorts dropped quickly once the belt, snap, and fly were undone. I stood up in my briefs.

What a feeling of freedom! What the hell! I slipped the briefs off and stood there buck naked except for my boots and socks. The breeze slipped between my legs, airing out buttocks, scrotum, and penis. This was great!

I walked a short distance, for the first time since somewhere in early childhood with no restraints on my torso and no restraints on my activities. So I dragged the sleeping back out of my tent, spread in on the ground in front of the juniper, and laid down.

Boredom and hunger, temporarily, were set aside from the feeling of absolute freedom. I laid there for a while. How long? I don't know. No watch. No cares. No one around.

I did, at last, get up and put on the briefs, shorts, and T-shirt. I prepared dinner. That is, I made a several-minute ritual out of getting the water bottle, looking at it, opening the top, sniffing the odorless contents. I spent minutes sipping, savoring, enjoying my dinner of water. That was it.

Within half an hour I was hungry. It really hit. There was a hole in my gut. I drank some more water. The sun set slowly beyond the rim of the canyon, but I took the sleeping bag back into the tent and got ready to lie down. Even if I didn't sleep, I could lay there and try to not think about food.

It was hard.

17

Somewhere in the middle of the night I knew I was in trouble. My entire groin area including my penis was on fire. Oh shit!

Smart guy! Sunbathing in the nude, so free and wild! Now I had a fierce case of sunburn on the one area of my body that had never before been exposed to any sun, much less the still effective autumnal sun of the desert.

What to do?

Every time I moved, turned, or even twitched my piece, my partner, my penis roared back at me in anguish. The inside of my thighs, right in the crotch, were hot and painful. My buttocks were burned. My lower abdomen almost glowed in the dark where now there was red scorched skin.

Great! Here I was on my noble soul quest, seeking from the inner voice some direction for the future, and instead I was a stupid idiot with a char broiled butt and penis. I couldn't lie down, sit up, or even walk with any degree of comfort. I couldn't put on my briefs. And it was something like three o'clock in the morning.

There was no way I could walk back to where Fred was camped out, almost a mile back down the trail. Shit! Damn! Shit damn!

So I endured, sleepless in the canyon, until the first hint of daybreak. Then I headed down trail, in T-shirt, sweat shirt, socks, and boots, naked from waist to mid-shin. Fred was up, sitting, faced to the east, watching the sunrise. He saw me. He fell over backward with silent laughter. He couldn't stop.

I was madder than hell. I wanted sympathy, not ridicule. It took him minutes to get over his mirth. "So what now soul quester? Did the sun give you a message yesterday?"

'Shut up, Fred. I'm hurting."

"Well there's a cure for what you've got. At least there's temporary relief."

"Well tell me what it is. I need it now."

"Go sit in the creek!"

"What? Don't you have some kind of ointment or salve or something?"

"Nope. Besides, it wouldn't do you much good. That cold water in the creek is your best bet." He pointed to the water gurgling twenty yards below us.

I waddled down and started to lower myself into the water. It was freezing! "Sit down!" hollered Fred.

"Damn, it's cold!" I shouted back.

"I know it. But that's what's going to help."

I hesitated between the pain of the sunburn and the pain of the cold water. Reason won. I sat down slowly. The burning, of course, diminished. The pain went away. It was replaced with a creeping numbness in my buttocks and crotch. My testicles withdrew until I thought they might end up somewhere near my rib cage, and my burned penis shriveled to a pathetic inch or so.

When I got out of the water, just ten minutes or so later, I felt better. Of course, I knew the burning pain would return, and I would have to douse it in the creek.

And that is how I spent the second day of my soul quest.

There were no more days in the canyon. We hiked back to Fred's place. I wore pants with no brief and managed to survive.

Sayings of Fred
Never get sunburned on your genitals.

18

Sunburn on skin never before exposed to sunlight takes a while to heal. I spent five days soaking my private parts in an old bathtub Fred had sitting along one side of his yard. I didn't care whether or not people would see me get naked before I got into the tub. Pain overrode modesty. And fortunately no one walked by as I was going to and from the tub.

Then I went through another week of itching and peeling. I won't go into the messy details. It wasn't pleasant or pretty. I recovered from my stupidity having learned the obvious lesson.

19

We set out again. This time I knew what to expect on the hike back into Mill Creek Canyon. By midmorning we were back at the campsite. My healed groin and lower abdomen pained me momentarily, my body's memory of a bad experience.

I didn't bother to make a big deal out of setting up my camp. I would be going back out on solo in the morning. No sense in getting too much out of the pack only to have to restow it the next day.

20
Solo Day One

I wake to the beginning of the day, the lightness of morning glows on the eastern horizon, a few stray clouds, lost from the mother formation, slip slowly across the sky near the horizon, the horizon defined by the red rock cliffs above me, the sky a pale blue over the cliffs and still deeply dark on the opposite side of the canyon as a hunger creeps into my belly, a hunger arising from the knowledge that I would not eat this morning or today or for the next three days and that knowledge, filtered through a too active brain, affecting my gut which did not yet understand the extent to which there could be hunger, a realization that would come in another day and a half. Anxious and fatigued I take down the tarp and roll it to fit along the lower formed metal frame of my backpack and my clothes are stuffed quickly into the upper cavity of the pack while it takes me a long time, a seemingly long time, with much jamming and pushing, to get my sleeping bag rammed into the pouch on the pack, and then I stand up and the light on the horizon has brightened and I see Fred standing next to his tent looking at me and then he points up the trail so I shoulder the pack, chin and jowls grizzly, mouth pasty, and eyes half clouded over, I shoulder the pack and start up the trail winding along the creek, rising here many feet above the water then dropping down, short green bushes tugging at me when the trail nears the water. Then I am climbing again, dreading yet exhilarated by the advent of this fasting solo in the desert. I am thinking and not thinking at the same time with random images and bits of phrases slinking through my mind, I begin to repeat "Boutrous Boutrous Gali" to myself over and over in rhythm with my footsteps and then I see my place in the desert, the not-so-carefully selected place next to a juniper tree on the rock shelf above the trail, the place surrounded, I now find, with prickly pear cactus and an occasional patch of cryptogamic soil so that I will have to step carefully when leaving or returning, the strange soil resulting from decades of biological activity and which is destroyed instantly by the wanton step of the unaware human treading a path of nowhere here in this desert canyon, so I step carefully up to the sandy place in front of the tree, the place which will be my home, moreso than I can now imagine, for three days, the place which will become mine, spiritually, forever but which now is just a sandy place in front of a juniper tree, a tree to which I can tie one end of the rope which will serve as the backbone of my house, the trap laid over the rope forming a crude tent with no front or back, just a tarp hanging on a piece of rope, soon secured along the side with some rocks, a tarp tent that suddenly looks very open to sun and rain and varmints and insects and anything else which could make like unpleasant here in this part of the canyon.

Red rock everywhere, darker red desert varnish spilling over the edges of the canyon walls, imagining people up in Arches above the western canyon wall, visualizing those people driving and looking and chatting and not realizing that some poor idiot is sitting in the canyon down below, alone, without a clue as to what he was doing there, with nothing to do, no books, nothing to write in, just a tarp, sleeping bag, some clothes, and a water bottle.

Boredom, instant absolute boredom, hanging over and around me, nothing to do, so I get up and walk down to the creek where the two-foot wide, two-inch deep creek is simpering, and I walk back up to my campsite and go beyond it to a rock wall on the ledge above and behind the campsite and I walk along the ledge and seven steps along the ledge I hear the creek sounds coming out of the rock, not from the creek below. I know I am already hallucinating until I look more closely and move around and find a concave dish in the rock wall is reflecting the water sounds, a perfect and natural parabolic dish, not receiving satellite signals but just bouncing back the incessant gurgling of the creek.

I sip some water and wonder what is going to happen to me out here, not that I am afraid, but filled with curiosity, and okay, some anxiety, because I have never been alone outdoors for any length of time and certainly not without food at which point I realize from the position of the sun that it is lunch time but I don't have any lunch, so I take another sip of water, and the hunger really grabs me. It is a mouth hunger, a flavor hunger, more than deep gut hunger, and I want a hamburger or a triple-decker turkey, ham, and cheese sandwich, and I want a diet soda, and I want, I want, I want, and there is nothing to satisfy the want so I pull the sleeping bag out from under the tarp and lay down on it in the shade of the tree. It is beginning to get hot out here in the desert, and I wonder how bad it would be if I just went back to Fred and said to hell with it, but there is a macho part of me that won't let that happen, so I suck it up and lay there and drowse a little bit until some kind of little flying bug buzzes my face and no matter what I do I can't discourage the little bastard, and I am getting angry, I'm hungry and hot and bored and there is nothing to do, nothing at all, so I sit up and try to concentrate on studying the prickly pear cactus, scrub oak, and whatever kind of grasses, most of them greenish-brown, surround me, and I want to write down some kind of description or something but there is nothing to write with, so I lay back down on the sleeping bag and the little bug has gone away. I drowse again until I realize that the sun is beginning to get a little lower on the western side of the canyon so it must be dinner time but I don't have anything to eat and I get up and walk back down to the creek, take a couple of big slugs of water from my water bottle and pump some water from the creek into the bottle through the absolutely guaranteed filtering system.

So I watch the sun set and there is a three-quarter moon so there is not total darkness and I can begin to see the brighter stars and all I can think of is going to sleep so before the end of twilight I am stretched out under the tarp, falling asleep and waking and finally just conking out.

21

Solo Day Two

The day begins slowly with the sun gradually sliding up across the eastern wall of the canyon and eventually reaching my crude shelter. I don't want to get up because there is nothing to do. That is, there is nothing to eat. I sip water and its tastes strange, the first time I have ever bothered to notice the taste of water. I can't figure out a way to kill time here. Time is here. It can't be killed. There nothing to murder it with. No radio. No books. No writing materials. Not even an instruction manual on how to inflate an air mattress which I don't have anyway. So I walk around a little but feel lethargic. Noon comes and goes. At least the sun goes as high as it is going to go.

I lie down on the sleeping bag under the tarp in midafternoon and it is hot but I doze off in my torpor and get uncomfortable laying on my back so I roll over one side where my shoulder and hip produce pressure so I rotate back onto my back and fall into a restless sleep.

In that sleep I have a dream that I remember vividly as I come back into consciousness and the dream is like this: *I am walking down a street in Chicago carrying a suitcase or backpack or something full of clothing and all my little mementos and accumulations and I am leaving Chicago heading out of the city but something strange is happening because as I look back over my shoulder the big buildings of downtown, around the Loop, are disappearing,*

62

they are getting shorter and shorter and sliding into the ground, and there is no dust as from an implosion but the buildings are, one by one, going away, and the farther I walk the more buildings dissolve and the ones closer to me are doing the same thing; it is as if the city is evaporating from the inside out, from the inner core out to where I am walking which is not some kind of park or green space and when I look back there isn't much left of Chicago, the skyline is gone and all I can see are some trees in the near distance and then I am walking on a dirt road under an intense blue sky and that is the end of the dream.

I come awake and am very depressed and the depression seems to be the result of Chicago disappearing even though it was just a dream and not reality. So I get up from the sleeping bag and slide out from under the tarp and stand up and walk a short distance but the depression weighs me down so I sit down and feel like crying but I have never cried as an adult male and can't do it now.

Then I find myself getting an erection out here in the middle of nowhere and virtually starving to death, I get an erection and I find that I need relief, somehow I have a strong sexual need and so I masturbate and it is easy and afterward I feel relaxed and satisfied.

So I stared at the red rock walls of the canyon splattered and dripped with desert varnish, and it is like a huge Rorschach test because there seem to be all kind of images on the walls. I stare at one stretch for a while and then I see the face of a monkey clearly outlined in the varnish, a small smiling monkey with one eye kind of closed in a wink so I look at another section of the wall and then turn around and stare at the opposite side of the canyon and suddenly there emerges from the rock relief and varnish a set of three baboons, all in different poses and I become conscious of my own projections onto those rock walls and all the images disappear.

Torpor from lack of food sets in and I sit without thinking or doing and there is nothing to imagine and my mind goes into a resting state and I can't remember what day it is and how long I have been out here until I get hungry and thirsty and take a long pull of water from the bottle and realize that I need to go down to the creek and get some more which I do and then come back and the sun is beginning to set so I walk around a little and now there is a slight chill in the air because a breeze is blowing down canyon making me put on a sweat shirt and sit down against the low rock wall which is still warm from the afternoon sun.

22

Solo Day Three

I sleep fitfully, dreaming, turning over, the ground hard under my sleeping bag and foam pad, my hip pressing against the dirt-rock underneath the ground cloth tarp spread out under the crude shelter, my shoulders turned, my neck bent at a strange angle; moonlight glowing through the front and back of my tarp-tent; I wake to some sound nearby, a footstep, a creature rummaging through the cactus and Gambel oak, I don't know what it is and drop off into my dream-filled sleep, now no-sound wakes me up so used am I to the sounds of civilization, of even small town Moab, that the quiet is unsettling. I turn over trying to get comfortable and it works for a few minutes, then the pressures and strains reappear; I begin dreaming again and this time it is a nightmare: *I am sitting at a computer keyboard in a small room trying to write something; I can't seem to get started; I type in a word or two and they disappear from the screen; I am very frustrated because I want to put down more words but I can't type them fast enough and the computer keeps erasing whatever I write; so I begin to punish the keyboard by slamming down words as fast as I can and now they appear but also the words I had typed before show up in the middle of the ones I am writing and the whole thing makes no sense when I read it over; I am creating nonsense writing; then the computer printer starts printing something so I stop typing and the printer just keeps on printing, spewing out sheet after sheet of words; when I pick up the sheets of paper which the printer dumps out onto the floor, I read sentences and paragraphs the seem very profound but I can't remember typing them; I look back at the screen and now there are words appearing on the screen even though I am not typing as if some spirit is creating a document without my help; I feel completely helpless and out of control; the printer just keeps on churning out the pages and the computer screen flashes words and sentences and paragraphs at a higher and higher rate until there is a flash of light from the screen and it goes dark and a puff of smoke comes out of the printer and all the paper in the printer is on fire.*

At this point I wake up and I can remember the dream very vividly; I am afraid; I feel a fear as strong as I have ever felt; I sit up and shake my head but the dream images stay in my brain; I don't know what it means but the dream is accompanied by the feeling of frustration I had while dreaming and then it is combined with a sadness, a depression that flows from my gut to my lung and face and my head droops on the neck so I crawl out of my tarp-shelter into the night with the moon draped near one wall of the canyon and stars hanging in the night sky, tonight neither sparkling nor shining, just hanging there reflecting my feelings; and I sit against one of the rock walls near my tarp-tent trying to clear my thoughts and feelings, and nothing works so I sit in a daze until the first sliver of dawn wedges itself between the sky and the canyon wall.

That day I am visited by a raven, circling and floating overhead, and I call to the raven – come here raven, come here raven – but I do the calling in my head not out loud yet the raven hears me and circles closer until it eventually lands in a juniper tree not too far away and looks at me with those dark eyes until it is bored and takes off and that is my whole social life for that day.

23

The final morning dawned brisk, but I didn't. The lethargy of fasting continued. I took down the tarp, slowly. I rolled up the sleeping bag and tried getting it back in stuff sack. It was hard work, and I got frustrated and angry. Finally, I got the damn thing rammed into the bag.

As I stood up to leave, I had a sudden sense of grief. I was leaving this place that had become my home for the last three days. No, more than my home. I "owned" this place is an entirely different way than anyone who could buy property. I had become intimate with this place. I knew a great deal about that small space I had occupied, walked around in, and looked over. It was more familiar to me than any apartment or condo I had ever occupied. More than the room in my parent's house.

I loved this place. And I didn't want to leave it!

How silly. I wanted food. I wanted to get back to Fred and to Moab. I wanted to hear voices, talk to people, tell about my experience. But I didn't want to leave here. I wanted Fred and those people to come out here and bring food so I could show them my place. I also realized that was foolish, because if they did come, it would no longer be 'my place' because I would have to share it with them and that would destroy the whole thing. In other words, I was like a possessive jealous lover.

So I walked away, disciplining myself to not turn around and look.

Within minutes I was with Fred who had the little propane stove going. He nodded to me. "I'll cook up some hot cereal for you. Just don't each too much too fast. In spite of how good it looks and tastes and how hungry you are."

"Okay." Suddenly I didn't want to talk all that much.

So I sat and ate my cereal while Fred talked.

"A couple of things to think about. We'll be heading back into town in an hour or so. You are going to find it kind of hard to get back to all that noise and commotion. At least it will seem like noise and commotion.

"The other thing is that whatever happened to you out there can't be assessed right now. It will take a while. Maybe weeks. Maybe months. Sometimes it takes years for it all to sink in. So don't be in any big rush to talk. Or analyze. Just get back into that world back there in Moab."

24

So no real demons appeared, at least not the usual kinds of demons, during my three day solo, but the image of Chicago disappearing was upsetting. The computer and printer that spewed out words I hadn't written still created fear, foreboding in me. I survived the three day fast. It turned out to be not as difficult as I had thought. Partly because of the lethargy that set in on the second day. I began to not care all that much. All I wanted to do was rest.

Fred sat me down when we were back at the trailer and, after feeding me a light meal of rice and veggies, began one of his brief lectures.

"We talked about this a little bit before you came out here. The idea of the soul quest and the three day solo is to give your soul a chance to get its messages out to you. Being out here was a kind of pause in your life. But it wasn't necessarily real calm and leisurely. Right?"

"Yeah, that's true."

"You see this kind of experience is a test. Most people can pass it. It's not a real tough test. But it is a test. It's harder than just continuing the usual daily routine. It is supposed to be hard, difficult.

"That's the whole point. People grow up, become real when they undergo some kind of test. A few folks, and there aren't many, manage to get through life without much of a test. If you meet them, you find out there isn't much there. It's like the lyrics of that song from some musical: 'Without a hurt, the heart is hollow.' I rephrase that to: without a lot of pain, the person is hollow.

Sayings of Fred
Without a lot of pain, a person is hollow.

25

Coming off of the soul quest the noise of Moab was deafening. People seemed to be talking very loudly. Cars and trucks roared. Music blared. This was the price of the transition from the solo and the dialogues in the canyon to the world of everyday life.

I hated it. I wanted to run back to the quiet. But there was no turning back. I had to reenter the world of people, vehicles, radios and CD players and all the other usual sounds of life.

It took about three days. The quiet of the canyon remained locked in my mind, but I learned to cope with the world in which I would live out the rest of my life.

26

It came to me slowly, not in a flash of insight. Leaving Chicago and driving out west had been a decision. An intuitive and not very rational decision. Fred would say it was a soul decision. Some kind of spiritual thing had moved me to take advantage of inheriting my parents' money and to leave behind my old world. I could easily have stayed in Chicago, invested the money, and just kept on keeping on. I didn't.

Now I had a level of anxiety that had never existed in that other life. It was a low level, continuous anxiety. Why?

Because now I had to make conscious decisions about what to do next. Who to be in the future. I couldn't be carried along by some kind of professional or relational inertia. Instead, there were a huge, almost infinite, number of possibilities. I could go anywhere, do anything, be anyone.

Oh sure, I still had my life history behind me. There were some things that were highly improbable or unlikely. I wouldn't become a musician. I lacked the musical background. But there were thousands of potential scenarios about the rest of my life.

I mentioned this to Fred. Once again he drew that crazy cross on the ground. In here. Out there. The past. The future.

"Here you are," pointing to the center, the intersection of the two lines. "You have a history. There are limits on you from the society you live in. You can't just be anything you want. But you have 'tuned in' to your soul, your inner spirit. And you have found something that you didn't expect. At least I think so. And here is the future, stretching out in front of you.

"Remember what I said some time ago? *You create the future.* It is not foreordained. It is not totally determined. And that means choices. You know what? Making choices – having to make choices – produces anxiety. We don't like to do that. It's easier to get into routines. It's easier just to follow rules. It's easier to rely on what other people expect you to do. But now you don't have any of that. I don't have any expectations for you. No one else here does. Some of your friends may have expectations, but they aren't around.

"So what you are feeling is completely understandable. And it may be the demon that you unlocked on the soul quest."

I nodded.

Sayings of Fred
It's easier to live a life without choices.

27

"One final thing we need to discuss," Fred announced. "And that is becoming a shaman."

"Do I want to be a shaman?"

"No. Not in the traditional sense. There's a lot of confusion among modern white people about the role of the shaman in traditional societies. We have made the shaman into a healer, someone who uses some kind of magic or some traditional herbal remedies to heal people."

"So what is a shaman according to you?"

"Not according to me. According to David Abram in his book *The Spell of the Sensuous*. He lived with and worked with these kinds of people. His take is that the shaman is an intermediary between the community and the more-than-human beings around the community."

"Community? And nonhuman beings?"

"Not nonhuman. More-than-human."

"Oh."

"Yep. You see the shaman in traditional societies lives near a village or town. A community. Each village has its own shaman. And the more-than-human beings or spirits include the living things likes the trees, animals, insects, and so on. It includes the spirits of those beings. The shaman interprets what those spirits are saying. What they need. And how that will affect the community. Of course, that also includes the spirits of the herbs used to heal. And all that stuff. But the healing part of the shaman's role is only a small part. Not the whole thing."

"So I'm supposed to become some kind of go-between between the other-than-human world and my community?"

"No. That's tough in this day and age. We don't have nice small, cohesive communities. So you'd play hell trying to do that."

"What am I supposed to do, then?"

"Become a shaman to yourself. You can always do that. What you can do is stay in touch with your own spirit, that spirit which is other-than-human. Which may come to you through your soul, that part of you that is related to some higher level of consciousness or, if you like, God. You can stay in touch with your body and what it is telling you. And you can stay in touch with the natural world around you. The air, the ground, the trees and animals. All those natural things around you."

"This assumes that those things are around me."

"They will be. Now that you have been on the soul quest and after you go through some other experiences, you will find that you have to live somewhere where you can stay in touch. With your soul. With the natural world. That will be your soul place."

Sayings of Fred
Everyone has a soul place where they really belong.
The problem is in finding it.

28

So what did I learn from those weeks in Moab? From the three day solo and our many conversations?

Looking back at the sketches I had made the first time out in Mill Creek Canyon I was able to figure something out. The first sketches were of paper, books, and pens. All about writing. After that the sketches showed natural settings, canyons and mountains. Maybe that was the change that was happening to me. Shifting from writing and words and thinking to just existing in this new world where I now lived.

I also learned that sometimes it is good to test yourself in ways you've never been tested before. To deliberately create painful, difficult, challenging situations and survive them. I realized the truth that life really is difficult.

As Fred said one day while we were hiking through slickrock country, "Making choices is the hardest thing in the world. It's no sweat to just keep on keeping on. That's inertia. The tough thing is to sit down and consider options and then pick one and go with it. That is hell on earth. It is painful because you have to live with the consequences. And the only person to blame is yourself. But it is also the only way to get where you really ought to be."

Sayings of Fred
You have to go through hell to get to heaven.

29

Epilogue

The insights from the soul quest came slowly and long afterward. I describe them here in one place but they occurred over months, during the time I was with Venus and after that in the hiatus I took for the late fall, winter, and spring of the year.

The vision of the monkeys and baboons was fairly easy once someone told me to consult some of the books on symbols. Of course, it did occur to me that monkeys chatter, and we use, some of us, the phrase "monkey brain" to describe the constant chatter that occurs in our heads as we move through the day. So monkey has a negative connotation. Monkeys are also seen as flighty. In Christianity, the monkey definitely has a negative implication: it is the human sunk to its lowest depths, depraved, animalistic, greedy, lustful, and vain. The latter perhaps because monkeys spend time grooming themselves, as most of us have seen in zoos.

But the very negativity of the Christian view can be translated into positive traits. The monkey represents the sensual, that is, the enjoyment of the senses: touch, smell, taste, hearing, and vision. This would become a theme in my subsequent journey with Fred and others. Our society is almost completely focused on the mental, intellectual, analytical, and verbal, to the extent that most of us are unable to truly enjoy the sensory experience, the sensuous.

So I took the vision of the monkeys and baboons in its positive light as the following year progressed. Someone pointed out to me that I had a need for sensual enlightenment or else I would not have had my monkey-and-baboon vision.

There is another meaning in the ape, monkey, baboon images: sexuality. This was hard for me to accept at first. Again, I grew up in a society in which there were all kinds of sexual scenes, innuendoes, suggestions, and explicit displays on TV, in movies, in books, in advertisements, and almost everywhere I looked. At the same time, there was a taboo against talking about sex in 'polite company.' Everyone knew it was going on but no one talked about it.

Part of my problem was that I saw sensuality and sexuality as one and the same. I would learn the difference in the months to come.

The dream of Chicago disappearing wasn't that difficult to figure out. It was the first insight I got from the soul quest. I had left Chicago behind. The dream was simply a way of closing that chapter in my life. For my purposes, Chicago had disappeared. Of course it still existed physically for the millions of people who lived and worked there, but for me it was gone. The nice thing is that is dissolved, evaporated. It didn't blow up.

Several years after the soul quest I reread my description of the dream about the computer. First I have writer's block, can't write anything. The computer isn't helping because it erases the few words I am able to write. I write faster and faster but can't keep up with the computer. Suddenly, there is a drastic change and words I had put into the machine start appearing in the midst of the ones I am currently typing and they make no sense at all. The next change occurs when the computer starts creating words on the screen without any effort on my part. I found two significant features of that final part of the dream. The first is that when I read the words (in the dream) they had a profound meaning, something I had never attempted in my life. Writing wisdom was the last thing I had ever considered. The second important feature, to me, was that the computer was typing "as if possessed by a spirit." In other words, there was something beyond me doing the creation. Again, a foreign feeling and thought for me.

All of this resulted in a feeling of helplessness, being out of control. That was frightening at the time because I was one of the regular members of my culture who always wanted to feel in control. Suddenly, I was in a situation in which a computer, inhabited by a spirit, is creating words of wisdom and I am not in control.

Years later I realized that the kind of writing I always wanted to do was, to some extent, not controllable in a conscious way. The words, the message, the meaning arose, sometimes from sources that I couldn't identify or understand. As if I were possessed by a spirit.

Writings from the Soul Quest

Waiting

September
Mill Creek Canyon
Moab, Utah
Sitting in my place
on a rock shelf
above the creek
below the canyon rim
I learned waiting.

Without clock or meals
to time my day,
marking minute-hours
by the sun dawning, rising,
peaking, falling, setting
I learned waiting.

Peacefully, with spirit full
and stomach empty
warm at day
cool at night
I learned waiting.

When coming back
someone may ask
Waiting for what?

I do not know.

Waiting-for happens
when there is an Expected.
In Mill Creek Canyon
there was no Goal.

And that is how
I learned waiting.

Raven

Come here Raven!
My spirit sings.

Raven circles.

Have you heard me Raven?
My soul asks.

Raven circles.

I open my eyes
and reach out to Raven.

He flies away.

Spirit

Spirit is pure white and holy,
A misty apparition
A state of simple being.

Where are you spirit?
Speak to me.

Instead the sun-warmed rock wall heats
my back at sundown.
Sand and dust invade my every pore.
I drink so much and pass water through.
And Body, not spirit, tells tales of being.

I came to find Spirit
and in that quiet place found my body.

Farewell to Place

Now I must leave you, Place.
Three days and nights I have lived with you
And slept with you
And learned to love you.

I know where cactus plant waits,
where delicate desert-earth must be
stepped over.
I sat in the shade of your juniper tree.
I borrowed your rocks to steady my canvas
home in the wind.
I watched you awaken each morning
and drift into slumber at night.

I wanted you to be my Place, alone,
to belong to me
to own you
as any lover would.
But you simply wanted to be a Place,
Available as a friend to anyone.

Now I must go, Place.
Even though I belong here.

SECTION III

Venus

1

The bookish narrator of *Zorba the Greek,* Zorba's "Boss," looks at his wasted life and yearns to learn all the arts of the body. Swimming, fishing, hunting, running. He needs to fill his soul with body but also his body with soul. The two, body and soul, are antagonists in Kazantzakis' tale. For the narrator there is only mind, not even soul. He thinks and analyzes and writes. He plots, plans, and manages and is incapable of feeling, sensing, being aware of either the body or the soul. Zorba, on the other hand, is pure body and soul. No mind, no thinking and analyzing for that Greek. Zorba tries to teach the narrator -- without success. That is what I read out of the story of *Zorba the Greek.* The narrator does not accept his own Zorba, the one inside of him and the sensual, animalistic one inside of all of us, but tells us his story.

When I met Fred, I was the modern American version of the narrator. The stay in the desert, alone and hungry, opened my inner eyes to possibilities. Still I thought too much. Worried about tomorrow and what I or we were going to do. I needed to plan ahead, to know what was coming. In the midst of whatever it was, I thought about what it meant and what was next. Or was I trying to figure out how it related to my past. I was a long way from being Zorba.

I needed to find the Zorba in me. He -- or the female equivalent, a Zorbette -- resides in each of us. Where? Buried deep under the cultural teachings and parental warnings.

The talkative intellectual meanderings of the narrator, who Zorba calls Boss, are too much for the intuitive and earthy Greek. One night, in their conversation, Zorba responds that, yes, he feels that he has six or seven demons in him, and the Boss outlines his argument that there are three kinds of men. The first eat, drink, make love and a lot of money, and become famous. The second concern themselves with the lives of all men not just their own. And the third devote themselves to the entire universe, all things living and dead, here and long gone, here and far away. All men are engaged in the struggle of turning matter into spirit.

Zorba, a simple peasant, is perplexed, and he throws back at the Boss: If only you could dance what you mean, then I would understand it. Such a beautiful suggestion! Dance your ideas so that another being can understand them. Stop talking and dance!

Sayings of Fred
Learn to dance your ideas.

On another night Zorba and his Boss sit by the sea and talk. Zorba believes that this widely read man beside him knows a great deal. So he asks the most basic and important question of all: Why do men die? The narrator, Boss, has no answer and feels inadequate. He talks abstractly and elegantly. Zorba does not understand. His response is simple: I think of death all the time; I am not afraid of it; but I do not like it.

So right at the end of the story of Zorba the Greek, he and the Boss watch their mining scheme collapse, physically disintegrate in front of them. And they dance. Zorba teaches the Boss, and they dance. Zorba shouts at the Boss: To hell with words and paper! to hell with plans and profits! to hell with mines and monasteries! They dance and Zorba says he has never loved another human being as much as he does the Boss and now they can communicate everything to each other because they can dance!

Fred had me read *Zorba the Greek* when I returned to Moab. The beginning of my next lesson in life. For years I was tutored and mentored in the arts of thinking, writing, speaking, calculating, computing, programming, planning, assessing, analyzing, evaluating, and taking action. I was a good citizen of a culture devoted to designing and controlling. The soul quest opened up another kind of world, one inhabited by demons and spirits in which intuitive messages, encoded by the soul, emerge during long periods of solitude and silence. I had experienced the domain of the mind and discovered the realm of the soul. Now I would embark on a different kind of learning.

2

This part of the story begins innocuously enough. Two days after I finished reading *Zorba,* taking sporadic breaks, a Toyota truck pickup rolled into Fred's yard in the early afternoon. Fred was in the trailer, again either napping or meditating.

A young woman slipped out of the truck with a smile on her face so broad and radiant that I couldn't help wrinkling my face in response.

"Hi, I'm Venus!" she announced, and I use that verb advisedly. She made a proclamation, not just an introduction.

I introduced myself.

"So what are you doing here?"

I retold, in minutes my meeting with Fred and the vision quest. I didn't say anything about the teachings, the past and future, the inner self and outer world. And I minimized the soul quest, making it sound more like a Boy Scout camping trip than a spiritual adventure.

Venus nodded. "Sounds like good old Fred is at work again!"

Just then, Fred stepped out of the trailer. Venus ran to him and they embraced in a way that made me jealous even though I had just met her. They loved one another. And I wanted a hug like that from someone, preferably Venus.

"So you've met, Venus, huh?"

I nodded. "Just now."

"Well Venus is one of my dearest friends. We've known each other a long time."

Strange since Venus was one-third Fred's age.

Venus looked at me and smiled again. That expression was utterly contagious. It was as if all the humor and happiness in the world resided in this one woman and came out in her smile. I felt happy for no reason at all.

She was Woman. A prototype. The essence of Woman. And, strangely, not very feminine, at least in the usual sense. An Earth Mother.

I stole glances at this woman. She wasn't pretty or beautiful. Wholesome came to mind, but that seemed a little hokey. Natural. Primitive. Sensual. Yes, something like those native women in Gauguin's paintings. Primal. That was another good word. Basic woman.

Venus was large. She had real hips and big breasts, evident even under the loose denim shirt she wore. Her waist was smaller than hips or shoulders but not tiny. There was a definite small protrusion to her belly, evidence of the uterus that lay within. Her feet, stuck into sandals, were tanned and toughened from exposure to sun and sand even though they were not dirty. Her toenails were not decorated but trimmed evenly. Similarly, her fingers were thick without being pudgy. There wasn't much fat on this woman but there was a lot of her.

Then we sat in three of the four folding aluminum chairs in Fred's yard, under the tree, letting the warm breezes blow over us and using the shade to stay cool. Barker lay on his side next to Venus who directed her conversation to Fred, telling him that she had been to the Sierras, had visited Morro Lake in California, hiked in northern Nevada, and had just recently settled in to live in Flagstaff, Arizona.

I watched her with a wide-eyed fascination. Her long black hair was pulled back into a ponytail with elastic bands spaced inches apart. She had a high forehead and dark eyes framed in equally dark lashes and brows. A hint of Navajo or Hispanic genes somewhere in her genealogy.

Her face and neck were tanned as were her arms and hands extending from the rolled up sleeves of the blue denim work shirt. I couldn't tell about her legs covered by worn light blue jeans.

In small gestures and voice inflections, Venus gave off energy and vigor and health. I'd never met such a woman before. All my experience was with women who worked indoors, engaged in self-development workshops or reading self-improvement books, and got their exercise in health clubs. Venus filled up more space than she occupied physically. Some refer to women as radiant, but Venus radiated – outward, encompassing everyone and everything around her.

I was immediately attracted to this Venus. She violated all the stereotypes of the beautiful woman in magazine ads and TV shows. Venus was an ample woman. She was big-boned. Certainly not fat. In fact, as I would learn a little later, she was physically fit.

This woman, this Venus, was powerful. Not with a physical, destructive power, but a personal, soulful, and spiritual power. If ever anyone were centered and grounded, whatever those words meant, this woman exemplified them.

I wanted to know her better. I wanted to find out who she was and how she had become this person. Strangely, I didn't want her, at that moment, sexually. In fact, I was - hard to admit - intimidated. Not a good way to arouse sexual feelings.

As abruptly as she arrived, Venus stood up and said she was staying with her friend Cheryl here in Moab. Then she turned to me and said, "How about a hike tomorrow?"

"Sure." I felt like a high school nerd who has just been asked to the senior prom by a cheerleader. I spent so much time watching and so little time listening that I was surprised she even remembered I was there. "You bet!" I said, rebounding from my stupefaction.

3

The next morning, over breakfast, I asked Fred about Venus.

"Who is she? And how did you meet her?"

"Well, you will find out who she is. That is the least of your concerns. Venus is one of the easiest people to get to know. As for how I met her, I can't quite remember. It seems to me that we struck up a conversation somewhere over in the Escalante area when we met on a trail. Shit, I can't remember! Don't ask an old man that kind of trivia."

And that ended our conversation about Venus who showed up a little after eight. "Ready?"

"Oops. Not quite." I wasn't used to impromptu greetings and arrangements. We hadn't agreed on any time.

"Okay. No problem. Get your stuff together and let's go whenever you are ready." She lowered herself into one of the folding chairs, stretched out her legs, and looked up at and through the leaves of the tree.

4

Once again I was walking up a canyon, this time Negro Bill canyon east and north of Moab. In single file, Venus leading, we marched along the sandy trail, the small creek several feet below us. There was no reason to talk. The sun was warm, through a sky splattered with curved cirrus clouds that someone had told me were nicknamed mare's tails. They foretold a change in the weather, probably a cold front moving in from the west or northwest.

There is a sensual pleasure, I now realize, in plodding along on a trail. Eyes and feet and legs, through some magical circuitry in the brain, function autonomously. As long as the eyes focus on the trail, leg muscles plant feet in the right places to avoid rocks and plants. No thought required.

We went on this way for close to an hour, silent, absorbed in the process of walking, occasionally looking up at a hawk or raven circling overhead. I felt comfortable with Venus.

Our resting place, which turned out to be our destination for the day, was in the shade of the red rock cliff under an old cottonwood tree. The sand was soft. It was windy out in the open, but next to the rock wall and under the tree, all we got was an occasional small gust.

We had eaten our lunches in silence. Again, I was comfortable with that in the presence of Venus. With most women, I would have needed to talk and be talked at. Not with her.

I lay back with my poncho and a sweat shirt bunched under my neck, looking up through the cottonwood branches and the cirrus clouds skipping over the canyon. Venus reached over and touched my arm. I was startled, but in good male fashion, didn't flinch or react. She stroked the small blond hairs on my left forearm and then moved her fingers down to my hand. There she traced them over the tendons and veins leading to my fingers.

"Your hand is awesome," she said.

"What?" I was startled, and this time couldn't hide my reaction.

"Your hand is awesome. Have you ever really looked at it?"

"No."

"You should. Look at this." She moved her index finger first over the tendon running from my wrist to my index finger, then to the next one over leading to the middle finger, and then over the next two. "Isn't that incredible?"

Of course, those tendons and fingers had been with me for my entire life, and I tend not to look at my body parts as particularly marvelous.

"I guess so," I answered dubiously.

Venus moved her finger back across my hand and felt that web of flesh between the thumb and hand. She massaged it gently. Then she pulled her hand away and lay back in the sand.

"You see," she started, "we get so used to our own bodies that we don't see how awesome they really are. And that's sad. Each of us is a miracle.

Look at how all those parts work together. Isn't it amazing that we could walk in here without stumbling? That we could stride and balance. That we could adjust our walking to the sand and rocks. I think it is absolutely amazing."

"I think you're amazing," I responded.

"Ah, but we are all amazing. And wonderful. And awesome. That's what I had to learn.

"You see," she went on, "I have a belief, a very strong belief, that we should approach each other with awe and reverence. Instead of with all of the other 'stuff' we bring to relationships with people. And with animals and trees and rocks.

"Look around us here. All of this is awesome. It's much more awesome to me than some huge cathedral built by people. Or some skyscraper or some big old dam. There are a thousand little miracles right here."

I turned to her. She was looking straight up and speaking with emotion.

"Here is what I think. Each of us is a creature, and you know, that means we are the product of a creator. I happen to believe the creator is the Universe, some kind of Great Plan, that I don't understand. You may believe in a God, I don't know." She turned to me and looked me right in the eye.

"Honest, Venus, I don't know what I believe." And that *was* honest because I could be no other way with her.

"That's okay. But we have been created. You know the Christians believe we are created in the image of God. Well then each of us has a little God in us, and that deserves to be approached with reverence. Some people believe we are creatures of a Great Spirit, and that also deserves reverence."

"But most of us don't approach other people that way," I stated the obvious.

"Oh, I know. That's because we are bundles of needs and wants and expectations. So we see other people as need satisfiers. We see them as someone who either meets our expectations or doesn't. If they do, we like them. If they don't, we don't like them.

"And what's really funny, is that we like the people who are most like ourselves. People who are different are strange and sometimes even enemies. Heck, we ought to encourage cloning because that way each of us could clone ourselves and then we would have the perfect friend and partner!"

She smiled at that. It amused her, I think, to visualize every human being having a clone alongside.

"So how do we approach other people with reverence?"

"That's an abstract question."

"Oh, I know! I'm good at those."

"Ask me how you and I can approach each other with reverence."

"Okay, how can we?"

"By trying."

Now that made me feel stupid and a little angry. Again, she looked over at me.

"Now don't get upset at that. Here's what I mean. We have to work at it. It doesn't come naturally. We take other people for granted. There are a lot of them. And then when we get to know someone, we take for granted who they are and what they feel and believe."

"Well I'm still not sure what you mean by trying."

"I just did it a little while ago. I found your hand awesome. That wasn't an exaggeration. I didn't say it in order to impress you. I didn't say it so you would fall in love with me and marry me! Oh god, no! I said it because when I looked at your hand, I saw something that was utterly marvelous. Here, look at it!"

She grasped my hand again, and, of course, I looked. She was right. That appendage I had taken for granted over the years was impressive. It had all kinds of levers and wires and energy supplies. It could move in really miraculous ways. Okay, I guess I could get excited about my own hand.

"I guess I see what you're getting at."

"Okay, now let me say this," she went on, "I find you to be awesome."

That struck me as ridiculous. If there was one thing I wasn't, it was awesome. I wasn't exceptionally big or strong. I wasn't a nuclear physicist or a neurosurgeon. On the contrary, I was pretty ordinary. So I said that.

"Oh but you're not ordinary, my friend," and she reached over and patted my cheek, a maternal gesture. "You are exceptional and awesome."

I couldn't ask how or why. Too egotistical.

"I feel awe in your presence," and she continued, thankfully, without me having to ask, "because you are a complete human being, a marvelous blend of body and mind and soul. Look at you! Look at yourself! Just being alive is a miracle! And having all your physical parts working together is a miracle! And having the ability to think about yourself is a miracle!"

"But I'm just another ordinary human being."

"No, you are not 'just another ordinary human being.' You are a human being, made in the image of something or someone, created by some greater power. You are an extraordinary human being. Just like all the other human beings."

That didn't make me feel good. I wanted to be special. So I said that.

"And that's our problem. We are constantly judging ourselves against other people. Am I stronger? Am I richer? Am I smarter? So only the strongest, richest, and smartest people can be awesome. Everyone else is 'ordinary.'

"Let's change how we think and believe. Management people have something called zero-based budgeting. Instead of creating the budget for next year based on this year's, they start over every year. They ignore what was spent last year. Well let's use zero-based comparisons for you and me. Let's start with 'not being' at all. That's zero for us. We're alive. We can feel. We can think. We can hike. We can talk to each other. All of those are pluses. All of those are miracles."

She was making sense. Instead of comparing myself to Gordon, the guy with whom I was competing back on the job in Chicago, I needed to think about where I was right now. I was sitting in a beautiful canyon in Utah talking to a marvelous woman about really important issues. A marvelous woman! Yes! She was marvelous. I remembered the awe I felt in her presence that first day in Fred's yard.

I think she saw the light dawn in my brain. She smiled and laid back.

"Thank you," I said turning to her.

"You're welcome."

"I think you are marvelous."

"I believe we are both marvelous."

Sayings of Fred
Approach every human being with awe and reverence.

5

I must have passed some kind of test because three days later Venus and I set off on a camping expedition. We slung our tents, sleeping bags, stuff sacks, and other camping gear into the back of her pickup. Venus whipped the truck around, and we slid out of Fred's yard onto the dirt road.

I wanted to ask where we were going, but I knew that I might as well shut up and enjoy the ride. It didn't matter where we were headed. I was going camping with Venus.

She drove us out onto the main drag of Moab and pointed the truck north. Miles beyond the town limits, we turned left onto a paved road, the one to Canyonlands National Monument where I had done my spirit walk. Over the first few miles, we traveled on a flat and straight section of road. Then it made a quick turn to the left and up a switchback. From that point on the pavement wound and meandered to the top of a plateau.

Looking intently ahead, Venus finally pulled off to the right onto a rutted dirt road, outside of the National Monument boundaries. We bounced our way across the high desert landscape for another several miles. A cluster of junipers appeared on the left, and Venus drove to them. This was to be our campsite for the next few days.

The trees were just tall enough to provide shade during the day. Several were big enough that we could pitch our tents under them shading us all day long.

We talked little and went about setting up camp.

6

That evening we built a small fire in the metal fire pan. There is never is a need for a roaring bonfire. A flickering gentle flame is better and uses less wood. We sat in silence, staring at the flames, occasionally looking upward at the darkening sky and the emerging stars.

Venus began to clap her hands in a steady rhythm but very softly so that at first I was barely aware of the sound. She maintained the beat while resting in her folding camp chair. Her arms rested on her thighs, and her hands came together softly and regularly.

I joined in. The repetition was hypnotic. For minutes at a time I went into a meditative trance, more effective than any of my meditation practices.

Slowly, Venus uncurled her body upward. She didn't stand up. She grew and unfolded upward until she had both feet planted and began swaying in time to the rhythm of our gentle hand clapping. Her shoulders rotated and moved forward and back. Her spine bent forward and then undulated backward and then forward again. Her hips slid sideways.

I stopped seeing a woman there in the darkness with her and the campfire light swaying, shifting together. Venus melded into the air and sky and firelight and became, just for a brief time, a part of the scene.

And then she moved, again slowly and deliberately, toward me and, I swear, pulled me up in a soft swirling motion so that I didn't even feel my leg muscles push me erect. I stood opposite her at first just swaying sideways and then gradually joining in the dance.

So we danced, not to the beat of a drum or the rhythm of an orchestra but to an inner cadence. We didn't touch. We didn't move our feet much or far. We just swayed and rocked, locked in synchronized movements dictated by internal pulses.

Strangely I didn't get tired from this dancing. In fact, I was energized by it. I think I could have gone on for hours, but we slowed until we stood opposite each other in the dark, lit by a gentle glow from the fire.

We doused the fire and went to our separate beds without saying a word. I felt as close to Venus as I had to any human being in my existence. As I lay in my sleeping bag, starting to doze off, I realized that I had danced a feeling to another being. I had said something without words, Venus did the same. Yes, Zorba! I danced a feeling! There was hope for me yet.

Sayings of Fred
Find someone and dance your feelings for one another.

7

The next morning we made our multi-grain cereal and dried fruit breakfast, sat in silence watching the sun jump above the horizon, heading for its zenith later in the day.

After the meal, Venus pulled her sleeping bag out of the tent and motioned for me to do the same. We laid the two side by side underneath the biggest of the junipers. Venus created something between a chaise lounge and a bean bag chair by putting a couple of stuff sacks filled with clothes under her back and head. I chose to lay horizontally, at least for the first hour or so. When my back started to get stiff, I rolled to one side but eventually copied her lounge.

"Okay," said Venus when we were settled down and the morning air warmed, "Let's talk some more."

She put her fingers to her lips. "You don't have to agree! I've got you trapped out here!" With that she laughed deeply. I had to join in.

"So you're a city guy who is looking for a change in your life. Well, that's good. Now you've met me, and you have a bunch of different feelings. Here's what I am guessing. For one, you want to have sex with me."

I started to say something, the usual denial, of course.

Again, she shushed me. "That's okay. You're a normal man. You should want that. You get horny. We are out here alone, and you keep looking at my legs and butt and boobs. Hey, I've been watching you!" Again, that deep laugh, not sarcastic or angry, but thoroughly enjoying the situation.

"And," she went on, "you are curious about me. You want to know more about who I am and where I come from. What I 'do' for a living. You are curious."

A pause. "Then you think you are falling in love. You want me as partner in addition to being a lover. You want us to be a couple. Am I right?"

Yes, she was right, and I had to admit it. "Okay. You're right."

"Well, there are some things we need to get squared away." She looked at me with a smile, but this time a serious smile.

"Like what?"

"I've got a friend up in Buena Vista, Colorado. Fred will probably take you up there sometime to meet him. His thing is words. I learned a lot from him years ago."

It was hard from me to believe that Venus, maybe in her early thirties, could have learned anything 'years ago.'

"So let me expound for a little while. The two words 'sex' and 'sensuous' mean the same thing to a lot of people. Not me. We'll talk about sex in a little while. Right now let's deal with sensuous. What we're going to do here for a few days is explore sensuousness with each other. Face it, the word means something about focusing on the senses. Like touch and smell and taste. We all see and hear. Probably too much."

I looked over at Venus and wanted to talk about sex. I wanted to have sex! But I listened to her.

"Now, what I mean is that we see things and hear things and then we talk about the sights and sounds. When we start talking, we lose the sensations. We substitute words. If you get to Buena Vista, you'll hear more about this.

"There is also the word 'love.' I don't use that word much. It is abused. It means all kinds of things. From sex and horniness to caring about someone to a reverence for God or some Great Spirit. Do I love you? Yes!"

My heart leaped, to use that old cliché. I wanted her to love me!

"I also love Fred and my friends at home. I love all kinds of people. I am getting to know you, and so far I like what I have found out. So I love you that much. But don't think that that means I want to have sex with you. Anyway, that is a guy thing, isn't it? 'I love you, Sarah' means 'I am saying this so you will have sex with me.' Once the sex is over, the guy finds out her doesn't love Sarah quite as much.

"That's not cynical. It's true.

"Now here's something important. Good sex, really satisfying sex, comes after two people have really gotten to know each other. After they have experienced sensuousness together. After they have known each other intimately. And that word, 'intimate,' is another one that gets converted into physical intimacy, touching and foreplay. But we can be intimate soulfully. Without touching.

"Remember, I said the other day, that sometimes we act as need satisfiers for other people. And we look for people who can be need satisfiers for ourselves. Well, what would it be like if we approached each other with awe and reverence, not with a bunch of needs to be fulfilled? Including sex? Seems to me, that then sex would be really great. See, it would be spiritual."

I nodded. This, frankly, didn't make a lot of sense to me. Spirituality and sex were opposites in my thinking.

"Okay, so you're having trouble with that. Right?"

I nodded. "How did you know?"

"Well anyone born into this culture would have trouble with it. It's built into everything we are taught. It's built into novels and TV shows and movies. Spiritual people are like Mother Theresa or some monks in a monastery or a solitary Buddhist sitting on a mountain. Sexy people come on to each other. They dress to attract the opposite sex. They talk in innuendoes. Can you imagine Mother Theresa talking about sex, much less having it? And can you imagine the hero or heroine of a TV sitcom involved in some deep spiritual meditation? Of course, not!"

I nodded, this time agreeing more fully. What she said was true.

"You see," continued Venus, "there are some folks who believe that the sensuous including sex are spiritual. And that spirituality involves the sensuous. To our puritan Western civilized way of thinking, that is absurd."

Sayings of Fred
Look for the spiritual way of making love.

"Yeah, it certainly goes contrary to what we get taught about religion."

"Absolutely! And to go farther, this whole business of sex is the great hidden secret of life in our world. Have you ever noticed that in novels and movies people go to war or go on long travels and never have sex? What do they do? Are they sexless people? Of course not! They masturbate. They find someone to have sex with. Or something."

"That's true. If you think about it, sex disappears from the story in those books and movies."

"On the other hand, sex is promoted and displayed everywhere. People joke about it. TV sitcoms hint about it. There are TV shows that show young women with deep décolletage in skimpy bathing suits. It's everywhere. Yet we can't talk about it in polite society!"

8

"Let's talk about intimacy…" Venus began our next dialogue "because that is the key to a lot of things in relating to people. What's intimacy mean to you?"

"I guess it means 'getting intimate.' Well…" I hesitated "getting…I mean touching someone else."

"Back to sex again, huh?"

"Well yeah."

"But see it also means getting close to someone emotionally. Here's that old body-soul distinction coming up again. You and I have become intimate. We've found out a lot about each other just by talking about our histories. About who we are. And we haven't been intimate physically. Right?"

"Not that I remember!" I joked.

Venus smiled. "Well, you remember correctly if you mean sex. Except that we did get intimate physically by exploring each other's hands. Remember that?"

"Oh yeah. I remember." Of course! That had been very intimate. And our conversations had been very intimate. But we hadn't had sex, and I wanted to!

"So let's just put a whole bunch of stuff together in one big lump here. We can be intimate emotionally. And we can be intimate physically without having sex. We can be in awe of each other because each of us is a unique and special being. In fact, each of us carries with us something spiritual and mystical. So we can have reverence for each other. And you know what?"

"What?"

"That is the key to making love!"

9

So for four days we hiked in the mornings and late afternoons, ate our meals together, talked about life and our lives, and slept in our separate tents. We hugged. We explored each other's hands and arms, feet and legs, gave each other back rubs and scalp massages.

On the second afternoon, Venus turned to me: "You must be getting really horny! This has to be driving you crazy."

"Yeah, I admit it."

"Well look, why don't you go off in the truck and find a place somewhere around here and take care of that! I mean masturbate. Let's not pretend that no one ever does it! It drives me crazy to read books where men and women go for weeks with no sex, and the only sex the authors deal with is intercourse. Or maybe oral sex. We all masturbate. It gets rids of the itch!"

So I got into the truck and drove off a mile or so. Using a bottle of Vaseline, I managed to get rid of my itch in a few minutes. When I got back, Venus was in her tent. As I started to look in there, I realized she was taking care of her itch.

By reducing the glandular imperative, I could treat Venus as something other than a way to satisfy my need.

Sayings of Fred
If you have a need, satisfy it. Just don't make someone else responsible for your satisfaction.

10

"I'd like to show you my homeland." Venus glanced over at me.

Could I refuse? Would I refuse? Of course not!

She lived near Flagstaff, Arizona, and we drove there from Moab on a cool day with clouds hovering near the red rock rims. Instead of the usual scudding and slipping clouds, these billows held fast so that the tall La Sal peaks east of Moab were hidden and, in places, the cliffs bordering the highway were faint outlines.

South of Moab the highway rises to a high dry plateau. For the first hour, the clouds hung low and as we dipped into one basin the car was wrapped in fog. The scenery disappeared. We were wrapped in a white shroud of moisture able to see the white center line only a hundred yards ahead. Venus drove carefully at a slower speed.

Then, rising out of that valley, we broke into absolute clear with the sun grinning at us from the east to our left, and it was time to put on sunglasses and to lower the sunshades over the windshield. The high desert country undulated; we passed over rises and then dipped into brief valleys and later canyons. The road turned as it dipped and rotated as it rose so that the colors and views and shadows cast by the sun changed smoothly but erratically.

The Abajo Mountains, a short range, really nothing more than a couple of peaks, came into view. Far away to the west the Henrys lay low on the horizon.

Monticello lies due east of the Abajos, a small town but the beginning of an agricultural section of southern Utah. We passed green fields. Crops grew in the fields, and we would see that again in the stretch of highway before and beyond Blanding. In between Monticello and Blanding was more dry desert. A truck driving along a back road raised a trail of dust a couple miles east of the highway.

Just beyond Blanding we passed the turn-off to Hite Landing at Lake Powell and staying on the highway headed for Bluff. The black asphalt dove through rock walls twice before we slowed for the two miles or so of Bluff, Utah announced by a sign: "Use of Engine Brakes Prohibited." No roar of semis decelerating! Out the other side we could begin to see, as Venus pointed out, the higher features of Monument Valley.

More dry desert zipped by. The next landmark was Mexican Hat, with the 'hat' a big flat stone perched on a high stone pillar, both eroded by wind. At the south end of Mexican Hat the highway turned left sharply across the San Juan River and then climbed quickly to another high plateau. Big fleecy clouds drifted over the landscape, and we raced through the shadows they slid along the red dust and rock. The clouds drifted eastward and we drove relentlessly southwestward.

Bits of blue wove themselves into the tapestry of clouds as we droned at sixty miles an hour toward Monument Valley and Arizona. Monument Valley itself lies astride Utah and Arizona, a part of the Navajo Reservation. The highway skirts the buttes rising majestically from the desert floor. To our left, eastward, multiple monuments, varying sizes and shapes, stood silently as they had for eons.

We didn't talk. No need. The desert was not, as show in movies or books, a barren wasteland but a palette of earth colors. It had to be appreciated without words.

11

Venus lived in a two bedroom house, in the midst of a pinyon-juniper forest, with the San Francisco peaks rising, peeking, looming, or simply standing, depending on the day and the lighting, outside the living room picture window. To my surprise, the furnishings were masculine. The furniture was simple and functional. Venetian blinds covered the windows. The only drapes were across the big picture window in the living room.

The couch was set back from and facing that window, two big unmatched overstuffed chairs on either side. Sitting in the couch or either chair presented a view of the mountains.

Behind the couch, along the back wall of the living room was perched, on a stone slab, a wood burning stove. Split aspen logs were stacked neatly alongside. A basket of kindling perched on the other side of the stove together with a short stack of newspapers.

I learned very quickly that the residents of Flagstaff center their lives around the mountains, even if subconsciously. First thing in the morning, they glance at Aggasiz and Humphrey's, the two tallest, to look for clouds or snow. All day long, driving through town or sitting in a restaurant, folks looked up at the peaks. Arriving back in Flagstaff from a trip to Phoenix, the mountains appear and welcome returnees miles out on Interstate 17, and they can be seen from the Verde valley, from Camp Verde, fifty miles south. Coming in from east the peaks stand tall as sentinels, visible from seventy or eighty miles away, particularly from the east. Just west of Williams on Interstate 40 the peaks peek over the forest.

So Venus oriented her daily life toward the peaks. Not only the living room but the adjoining kitchen and dining area provided a view of the mountains. Cooking, washing dishes, preparing food, eating, talking, reading, or just sitting in any of those rooms featured the San Franciscos.

One large Ansel Adams print hung on the wall to the left of the picture window. In the dining area, two topographical maps had been framed and suspended behind the rectangular table surrounded by four chairs. There was no tablecloth on the table. There were no frills at all in the house.

The master bedroom, occupied by Venus, was dominated by a large rustic bed centered under one of the two windows in the room. From the bed, its occupant could see the peaks. Two small chests of drawers stood against adjacent walls. A closet with sliding doors completed the room. The only decorations were three black and white photos: mountains, a small stream in a canyon, and a saguaro cactus. There was a picture of Fred, at repose in one of his chaise lounges, standing on one of the chest of drawers.

The other bedroom, which I would use, was small. A queen size bed took up most of the room. It had neither headboard nor footboard. A single chest of drawers stood in one corner. And a small closet with bifold doors took care of one wall. There were two windows in the room. One overlooked the back yard of the house. The other presented a pleasing view of the pinyon-juniper forest behind the house but no mountains.

Venus' house stood on an acre of land backing up to a National Forest boundary. But there was no fence or any other sign of a boundary. Walking a few hundred feet behind the house, across a dusty yard with scattered native grass plants, lead directly into the intermixed juniper and pinyon. Any time the sun shone warmly enough, the scent of the juniper wound through the woods.

So we walked, sometimes silently, sometimes talking softly, among the trees, not following any trail, just meandering to patches of sunlight or toward a particularly intriguing pinyon. Those hours in those days were the most comfortable and serene of my life. I have not been able to clone them since, except in a few rare instances, but they remain a vivid sensory memory and a state to be sought again, sometime, somewhere.

12

"One of these days we're probably going to make love," Venus said as she turned to me.

I wanted to. I wanted to for a long time. But this was a different way for a woman to deal with me. Usually there were games to be played, hints and flirtations, approaches and withdrawals, until a meeting, a culmination took place. Not today.

Poised, composed, and ever-cool, I stuttered: "I...I...I think so too!" Inane response! First kiss and then pet and finally have sex. With Venus there was no game playing. We were going to make love.

"Before we do," she continued, ignoring my blithering male idiocy, "we need to talk about making love and sex."

"Okay." I didn't have the vaguest idea about what to say or do.

"Here is what I feel and believe. Our glands produce hormones. When they build up we get horny. Then we need sex. We need relief. But there is a difference between sexual relief and making love."

I was silent, dumb.

"Our soul produces a longing for contact with another being, a human being. We want to touch and be touched, to be held. We want to be nurtured and held. When we do those things we love each. I mean that in a physical sense. We provide love to each other. When you touch me and hold me, I feel loved.

"So it seems to me that making love happens when we need sex and we long for contact at the same time. Our body demands relief. Our soul asks for contact."

That made sense to me, but I was a little disappointed because it meant that sex could only occur infrequently. It would depend on both people having the physical need and the stirred soul.

She read my mind. Actually, she probably just predicted the response of a typical male.

"That doesn't mean two people only have sex on the rare occasions when they both need relief and both get a soul message."

Thank god!

13

On a cool bright Tuesday morning, Venus climbed into her car and drove, with me as passenger, to Walnut Canyon National Monument. We paid our five dollars each to enter and walked out the back of the Visitor Center. Below was the canyon, steep walled and narrow, lined with two kinds of rock, a lower rounded layer and an upper stratified lamination. Sandstone and limestone, the same formations, that covered all of this part of the Colorado Plateau.

Venus led the way down twisting, winding stairs, a metal railing on the outer side, without stopping to let me read the signs along the way. She had a goal in mind, and we stepped out toward that goal.

At the bottom of the steps, the trail made a quick right turn through a notch in the limestone and then descended another dozen or so stairs, with a turn to the right, and then onto the asphalted trail. We walked past two remnant walls of a cliff dwelling, then past another set of walls, until we reached a large outcropping of rock.

"We'll sit here," Venus said as she motioned me onto the rock.

Facing north we could see a group of cliff dwellings across the canyon as we sat perched under a big evergreen of some sort.

"What are we doing?"

"Listening. There are spirits of the Old Ones down here. Spirits of the ancestral Hopi. So let's just sit and listen."

Which we did. A soft breeze was interrupted, occasionally, by a gust that moved the needles of the pine ever so slightly. There was no sound at all, unlike the rustle of leaves in the woods where I hiked as a kid.

We listened. Occasionally a group of canyon visitors walked by, talking to each other, commenting on the cliff dwellings, the depth of the canyon, and the ruggedness of the life of the people who had lived there. That is mostly what I heard. Not the souls of the Hopi ancestors but the monkey brains of the intruders.

I wanted to come to a place like this when there was no one else around.

Venus just sat and stared across the canyon.

"I guess they're not here today." With that she got up and coaxed me back on to the trail. We walked around the trail, looked at and in some of the cliff dwelling rooms, and then ascended the stairs to the Visitor Center, taking three short breaks to catch some of the thin air.

"Sometimes they're there. Sometimes not."
I nodded.

Sayings of Fred
The spirits do not appear on command.

14

In one short conversation, Venus made an important point, for me, about sex. Two people can be horny at the same time. They both need sexual release. If they are willing to talk about it, they can have sex and get the release. But it is little more than mutual masturbation. It does have the advantage of touch and sensuality that masturbation does not.

15

"The ideal," said Venus, "is to make love." There was a long silence broken only by the cawing of an upset raven somewhere in the woods.

"Our body tells us we need sex. We call that horny. It can be strong or weak in us. Depending on our physiology, our wellness. Our soul tells us we need to be loved. We need to be cared for...cared about. We need someone to be with. When both happen at the same time, the body needs sex and the soul needs to be loved, then we can make love.

"Making love is beautiful because it means we have accepted both the needs of the body and the desire of the soul. I don't believe there is any higher pleasure.

"You see, so many people talk about wholeness or holistic living. Well making love is the ultimate testament to wholeness. It is the body and soul getting together with another body and soul."

Many times after that day I found that I was having sex but not making love. Venus held out an ideal that happened very rarely. In fact, I believe that it cannot be planned. It happens.

16

"Today," she announced at seven thirty in the morning, "we are going to take a field trip!" And she smiled. "But I'm not telling you the purpose of the field trip 'til we get there."

"Okay." I was ready to follow Venus on a field trip, trusting her and unaware of the incredible experience that would follow.

We threw some fruit, cheese, and bread into a plastic grocery sack for lunch. We each picked up a well used, clean, and thick sleeping bag from her garage. With those provisions, and only those, Venus lead us out into the pinyon-juniper woods behind the house, at least half a mile back into the woods, well away from any of the U. S. Forest Service roads winding through the area. She picked a place within a circle of trees, a place that had both sun and shade, but totally hidden from the view of a stray wanderer.

We spread the sleeping bags on the ground and hung the grocery sack from the limb of a pinyon a few feet above the ground so that the food was in the shade but readily accessible to us but not squirrels or other small critters.

Then Venus untied her boots and slipped them off, followed by the grey woolen socks. Without hesitation, she lifted the t-shirt over her shoulders and head and along her arms and hung it casually on a limb near the grocery sack. She motioned to me to do the same.

I untied my boots, cranked them off, and slipped out of my socks and then shed my t-shirt. What was going on here? Were we going to have sex? Who knows with Venus?

"Come here," she said. I did.

She took hold of my hands, just as she had done previously in Negro Bill canyon, and held them. Slowly she moved her fingers over my hands, not massaging but simply touching and feeling. Then, in a quick movement, she tucked her hands under mine, and I began to feel the tendons, ligaments, bones, and even veins in her hands. I looked at them, fascinated, understanding now the marvelous human hand, the incredible mechanical complexity, and at the same time the warmth and tenderness and, yes, even love that was communicated by those hands! Love? Yes, love. Not infatuation or sexual desire or needy holding. Simply love. A caring for and caring about. Transmitted by two hands holding the two hands of another being.

She moved her hands back around and moved them slowly up to my forearms and there repeated the gentle, probing exploration. Venus was studying me in a sensuous way, not provocative, but with great sensory awareness and great feeling. Yes, feeling! A strange two-meaning word in English. She was feeling my forearms with her hands, and she had feelings about those forearms, gentle caring emotions, which I could sense.

Again we reversed, and I explored her forearms, feeling the light hair on them, the muscles, good strong muscles, but now relaxed, under the skin. I looked down at those arms, tanned but still smooth, and -- strangely -- began to understand her arms. Understand her arms? Those were the words that popped into my consciousness. Before this I would have used 'felt,' 'touched,' 'sensed,' or synonyms. Today, I appreciated her arms; I understood them.

Venus raised her arms slightly so that my hands moved upward, crossing over her elbows, to the biceps and triceps of the upper arm. Still there was silky hair but less sensation of tendons and bones, more of muscle. There was more to touch and feel.

We switched again, and Venus softly studied my arms. I could sense through her touch something about her, about the essence of Venus, that would have been impossible through words or activities. She probed with her thumbs the muscles of my upper arms and brushed the skin and hair to get a sense, I believed, of me.

Then she startled me. Venus reached under each armpit to feel the hair. I reacted by putting my arms down, unfortunately gripping her hand exactly where I didn't want them to be.

"Let me," she said.

"But that's kind of gross," was my reply.

"Oh no. Only if you think so. That hair is part of you. As much as any other part of you. You showered this morning. You're clean. Let me touch your there." Which she proceeded to do, gently forcing my arms up.

It still felt strange and gross to me -- for a while. Then, after a few minutes, I got used to it. Of course armpits are parts of the body, as much as any other part. If you are going to experience a body, you need to experience all of it, not just selected, expurgated parts. So I let her touch me where no other human being, except maybe my mother touched me as child while bathing.

And I touched her in those same places. She had shaved, but I could feel the slight stubble. The flesh in the armpit is soft and wrinkly, a totally different feeling from the skin on the arms or legs or torso. I could also feel that small ridge of tissue which is the beginning of the breast on a woman, and strangely, the sexual side of me did not rise up.

Oh yes, I said to myself, here is the sensuous without the sexual. A learning! Another learning! Oh God, I was learning, slowly but surely.

Sayings of Fred
Sensuous doesn't mean sexual.

17

As the sun approached it's zenith, not overhead but somewhat to the south, Venus got up and retrieved our lunch. We divided up the apples, grapes, cheese, and bread and sat there, half naked, warmed by the sun, hidden from view, and began to eat.

Venus took a small bite, a very small bite of the cheese. "Look." she said, "take the tiniest bite you can. Savor the flavor! How's that for a marketing slogan! But seriously, let's eat very slowly. Let's enjoy the taste of every little bit of what we eat."

So I took a small bite of the cheese in my hand, leaned back, and kind of rolled the cheese around in my mouth and then chewed it lightly. The taste flooded, truly and honestly, flooded my mouth and taste buds. A tiny bit of cheese, and it was one of the most flavorful moments in my life. So I did the same with the bread. And I tasted, totally, the "breadness" of the dough. It wasn't just something to carry the butter or cheese or meat, but it was a taste treat in and of itself.

This was getting to be fun!

18

What a strange day! My friends in Chicago would never believe it. In fact, no one would believe this. An entire day, touching and being touched by an attractive woman, finally completely nude, in the woods, and no sex! And there was no need for sex. There was comfort, liking, love, caring and being cared for. Far more important to me, now as I grew up, than having sex.

But there was the certainty now, that we would make love sometime. Sometime soon.

19

"Fred, I am sure," Venus began, "has talked to you about the life struggle between the demands of society and the impulses of the soul."

"Yeah. We've gone over that a few hundred times!"

Venus smiled. "Well Fred does like to reiterate his main points!"

Then I smiled.

She continued. "Here's something we all need to think about. If you live the 'normal' life, then you can only have sex when your schedule and your partner's schedule permits. For most people that usually means in the evening or on weekends. Problem is that most of us get tired working all day so the evenings are not a good time. Particularly if you have a demanding stressful job. And weekends may not be any better. That is when we have to catch up on errands. All that stuff. And for some people there is even work on the weekends.

"So people end having sex without making love. It's like I was saying a few days ago. Both people are horny. They get together for a quick roll in the hay. And then back to work and the social life and errands and whatever else there is to do. No wonder so many relationships end up disappointing and finally fall apart.

"The problem is that making love involves the soul. It involves being ready to love someone. Care for them. And you can't do that on demand. You can't do that if you are hassled and stressed. You can't do that if there are things to do. So most of the time people have sex but don't make love.

"I don't know what the answer is. People have to make a living. They have to live the world as it is for them. We can't have everyone dropping out. But I really truly believe we have created a sick society when we can't take the time to make love."

20

We took off at midmorning for a hike. Venus bumped along the rutted dirt road leading from her home to the narrow paved road and then out to US 89, the main artery out of Flagstaff heading north to Utah and Colorado, the highway we had traveled some weeks before coming from Moab.

At a forest road sign, Venus turned left and we climbed upward around the northeast flank of a mountain. In places, the road was narrow with a sharp drop to the right, and we met two vehicles coming down. Fortunately, local people in those situations drive slowly, and we passed with no problem.

Then we traveled, briefly, through a forested area with not much view in any direction and emerged at a small meadow. A few parties were camped around the meadow in National Forest camp sites. We drove to a parking area.

Venus climbed out, and I followed.

"This is the Inner Basin trail," she pointed to a trailhead thirty feet directly across the parking area.

We started up the wide path, obviously well tramped by hikers over years and years.

"This inner basin," Venus explained, "is actually a caldera, you know, the inner part of a volcano. Some millions of years ago, I guess, the volcano blew."

She paused for several steps before going on. "What you see as mountains, the ones I've showed you, Humphries and Aggasiz, are actually high points on the rim of the crater. There's also Fremont, named after a territorial governor who wasn't very good. Before the big blow, this mountain was probably over fifteen thousand feet high. Now Humphries is just a little over twelve thousand."

When we returned to her house, Venus took me by the hand and pointed to the mountains. "If you follow the slope of the mountains up, imagine if they continued. That is where the peak would be." After that, I couldn't help but see the ghost of a bigger mountain rising above the San Francisco Peaks.

We continued up the trail and passed through several groves of aspens, large in diameter and height. "Look over at those trees, "Venus pointed. "See the carvings in the bark? Those were put there around the beginning of the last century by shepherds. They used to graze sheep up here. And the shepherds would carve stuff into the trees. In Spanish. In fact, some of the stuff is pretty raunchy, from what I've heard."

We walked upward, the trail occasionally steepening and inducing some quicker, deeper breaths. "You've heard of petroglyphs, right?"

"Sure, symbols and stuff carved into rocks. Some are in the rocks around Moab."

"Right. Well those carvings in the trees are called 'dendroglyphs.'"

So I learned another little interesting fact, useless but interesting, from my friend Venus.

Sayings of Fred
It would be a pretty dull world if every bit of
knowledge had to be useful.

21

There are rare days in mountain and high desert country when the air temperature is in the 50s or low 60s but the heat of the sun warms any creature standing or lying outside. It was a day like that when Venus and I drove from Flagstaff to the Grand Canyon. We went the 'back way,' up highway 89 and then to the west to Desert View, the east entrance, and beyond.

A slab of polyurethane foam and a sleeping bag lay in the rear of the truck, all the better to lie on. We had a mission: making love on the rim of the Canyon. A few weeks before Venus had taken me to this same place where, finding a secluded place, we lay naked in the sun enjoying the sheer sensuality of the warmth and the view.

The parking area had one other car. We saw where that couple, a man and woman also, were sitting with a small camp stove and lunch. We avoided them.

A dim track through pines lead to the edge of that enormous slash in the earth, the Grand Canyon. It was not visible until we got within ten feet of the rim and then it spread out below us, as always a stupefying sight.

Venus led me several hundred yards to the west of the trail, well away from any likely explorers. I unfurled the three-inch thick foam mat and then rolled out my down sleeping bag on top of it. We were right on the edge of the canyon so that, lying on the sleeping bag, I could see over the edge and down onto the enormous stone tables, called temples by whoever had named those features in the past.

I shed my T-shirt and Levi's after untying and dropping my hiking boots. The sun and slight breeze stroked my torso and I stood there. Venus followed suit, raising her T-shirt over her head and then slipping out of her khaki shorts. In one brief flipping motion she unsnapped her bra and let it drop next to the sleeping bag. And so we stood admiring each other and the day.

As usual we began with gentle massage. Venus paid particular attention to my scalp and neck, and I fell into a sensuous reverie becoming oblivious to everything but her hands, the sun, and the canyon. I did not become lost in thought. I lost all thought.

Then, in a natural transition, she turned and I ran by fingers up and down her back, crossing between her shoulder blades, up and over her shoulders, down along the margins of her back, into the cleavage above her buttocks, and then back up and around again. She purred

We slipped from the sensuous into the sexual without conscious effort or the need to speak. We kissed and held each other. We stroked and caressed. We kissed the parts we caressed. The onset of sexual excitement was slow but certain. I hardened. She responded to my touch.

We spiralled our way down to the sleeping bag, entangling our arms and legs and torsos, raising the pitch of our excitement. Our bodies slipped and rolled over one another until it was time, and then I entered her.

We stayed enmeshed in sexual union, moving slowly and gently, escalating and subsiding for a few moments, until there could be nothing but the orgasmic explosion foreordained by our foreplay and our caring for one another. Venus reached climax first, arching her body against mine, and then, within seconds, I detonated.

The usual ecstasy and release flowed through me as we parted. I rolled over to my right as Venus watched -- and then I started to slide over the edge of the Grand Canyon! I was falling into the Grand Canyon! I dug my fingers into the sandy dirt laced with a few rocks and couldn't hold on. I slipped farther and started to roll. My momentum increased. "Oh shit," I though, "I'm going to die!" The sliding and rolling continued. I bounded over a small ledge and the entire Canyon loomed below me. Twenty feet down I got hung up in several small pine trees. The needles punctured my naked rump and back, but the pain was excruciatingly beautiful because I had stopped. Venus – naked and eyes popping – looked over the edge.

"Oh my God," she called down to me. "Are you all right?"

"I think I am." Getting back up to Venus was going to be a bit of a problem for this naked, scared, and sexually exhausted male. I managed to squirm into a position where my feet were pointing down toward the Colorado River and my nose was aimed upward. Gingerly and carefully, and I can guarantee that I have never moved as gingerly and carefully in my life before or after, I began to move up toward Venus. The process took several hours according to my mental clock, although in all likelihood only ten minutes of real time.

At last, I rejoined my friend, my lover Venus. Then I started to laugh. The jolt of adrenaline kicked in. I was shaking and laughing, and she joined in.

"Can you imagine what would have happened if you hadn't stopped," she smiled at me. "A search and rescue party of park rangers would find your body later today and report a dead naked man with a smile on his face a thousand feet below the rim!" I visualized my own naked body slumped across a ledge far below with a gentle smile on my lips. I laughed all the way into my clothes and back to the jeep. Venus drove back to Flagstaff.

Sayings of Fred
Be careful when you roll over after making love.

22

I had fallen, not from grace, but from the rim of the Grand Canyon after sex. It took a week for all the little scrapes and bruises to heal. Venus assisted in that healing by gently bathing the scratches with warm saline solution and then putting some kind of scented salve on them. She tended to the bruises, as soon as we returned to her place, by cooling them with damp cloths.

She loved me. I mean that she cared for me. And that launched us into a discussion of love and orgasms and ejaculations.

"I'm going to suggest something to you," Venus began, "that I know nothing about as a woman. That is, I don't know anything about it through experience. But I have learned to listen to men…and to be sensitive – bad word – alert to their reactions right after sex."

"This sounds like something serious."

"Well, it's not earth shattering. It won't end wars or stop killing in the streets. But it's something that we should know about. 'We' means both men and women."

"And it's about orgasms and ejaculations?"

"Yep. So let me just say it short and sweet. There is a big difference between orgasms and ejaculations. You can ejaculate without having an orgasm. And I think you sometimes can have an orgasm without much of an ejaculation. Or maybe even none. Does that ring true?"

"I'll have to think about that for a minute or two here. Yeah, I guess I know what you are talking about. If I'm really horny but also kind of uptight, I can have an ejaculation without an orgasm. I think most men know what that is all about. But an orgasm without ejaculation?"

"Keep thinking about it. Maybe I'm wrong, but I think that does happen every once in a while.""

So instead of the usual discussion of female orgasm, we spent those few minutes on the male experience. And I learned something, became aware of something, that was part of my own experience. Venus was a good teacher – in many ways and of many things.

23

Sometime later, Venus added a thought. She said that her experience paralleled what she had told me. There were times when she had sex including an orgasm but the result was not really satisfying. There were other times when the sex was less electric but ultimately more satisfying. And, she thought, it all had to do with the soulfulness of the encounter.

24

We drove into the Coconino forest around 10:00 one morning, back to one of our favorite places, away from the highway, a place where we could walk back away from the single lane dirt road and be in an open area yet hidden from anyone except the nosiest.

I was relaxed. Except for making an occasional entry into my journal, I had nothing to do in Flagstaff, in Venus' company. The days flowed by. The northern Arizona sun shone nicely. An occasional cloud built up or drifted by. The landscape itself was resting and restful. In the ponderosa forest the feeling was similar to what I would have later in The Pinery in Michigan. Tall and straight, limbless for their first twenty feet or so, the overarching evergreens created a natural cathedral.

Venus parked just off the dirt road, and we unloaded the sleeping bags and blankets. The forest floor is soft with pine needles even if underlaid with limestone. And walking on those pine needles creates a gentle crackling as the dried spindles break underfoot.

We walked, softly, into the forest, turning back occasionally to see if Venus' truck was still in sight. Eventually it was hidden from our view just as we would be hidden from the sight of anyone driving along the road. We laid the sleeping bags side by side with the blankets rolled up to act as pillows. Both bags in a patch of sunlight, ten degrees warmer than in the shade of the trees.

I knew; I sensed the mission of the day. We were going to make love. We had kissed in the morning, soft gentle kisses after breakfast, kisses full of promise. Without discussion we packed the truck and Venus drove into the forest. Now we stood there looking upward at the long ponderosas, seeing hundreds of pine cones under each tree, pine cones ranging from brown-black, aged through years on the ground, to newer lighter colored cones, ones fallen just in the previous year.

Venus unclothed herself. She didn't undress. She didn't strip. In a simple ceremony, Venus revealed herself. Until she stood, naked and glowing, in the sunshine.

I followed in my own version of the ceremony. No hurried unbuckling, unzipping, dropping but rather a slow ritualistic shedding of the societal covers until I, too, was naked.

There followed the most amazing sexual experience of my life. We loved each other. We showed caring in our touch. It began with a simple embrace. Then we repeated the sensuous touching of weeks before, feeling the texture of our arms, legs, necks, faces, backs, and torsos. We didn't dive right into sexual foreplay but engaged in soulful, sensual foreplay. I didn't even get aroused during this part of our encounter.

Of course, we ventured further into sexual arousal, alternately touching, kissing, helping each other to become a fully sexual being. Then we made love.

For the second time in my life, I made love. Venus and I combined the soulful and the sensual and the sexual in one act. Then I understood what she had been saying. I understood more of what Fred had been saying. I understood it mentally and my body understood it as well.

25

Three days later we ventured in the juniper and pinyon woods near Venus' home. This was not a day for making love but rather for exploring sensuality in a different way. Venus explained that to me before we left.

She brought along her one-burner camp stove, a small pan, two quarts of water, and several washcloths. We parked the truck in a secluded area off of one of the Forest Service roads, and Venus set up the stove, poured some water into the pan, and allowed the water to heat over the low flame. She unloaded her sleeping bag from behind the seat of the truck and unrolled it, this time in a shady area because the day was beginning to get hot.

Without saying a word, Venus approached me and pulled my T-shirt out from under my jeans. She lifted it off of me and gently pushed me to a seated position on the sleeping bag.

Then I was washed, cleansed, bathed. Venus took a washcloth and dipped it in the water heated on the stove, and with it, she began to wash my back. Her touch was gentle. The cloth was wet and warm. And I began to sink into a meditative trance.

Venus washed my arms, my chest, neck, and face. She lay the warm cloth on my face and left it there for a few minutes. The trance went on. It was the most sensuous experience of my life to that point.

She untied my boots, slipped them and the socks off, and then undid my jeans and slid them down over my hips, as I laid back on the sleeping bag. The washing continued. My legs, front and back. Then Venus removed my shorts, and I lay there completely naked as she bathed my groin and lower abdomen and penis.

During this time I didn't become aroused. It was not a sexual experience. It was pure sensuality. So I learned the difference between sexual and sensual again, not in words, but in experience. A lesson that cannot be forgotten, and if not talked about too much, that lives on as a set of sensation-memories.

26

A strange gaunt figure walked up the road and toward Venus' house. I called out to her. She walked into the kitchen and looked out the window.

"Oh, that's Ruben Mahoney!" As if I might know who that was.

"Ruben is a character. You'll meet him in a minute. He stops here every once in a while."

"Who is Ruben Mahoney?"

"Well it takes a little explaining and some story."

He looked like a homeless person with a bedroll and long hair, except that, up close, he was neat and washed. No ordinary homeless person this! Ruben cam up to the house and knocked lightly. Venus opened the door and motioned him in. She introduced me to Ruben who simply said "hi." A man of few words as I would discover that day.

Venus fixed breakfast for Ruben Mahoney who sat quietly at the table, ate slowly, and consumed everything on the plate.

"So what have you been up to, Ruben?"

He glanced down at his hands. "I've been up to the Hopi mesas learning some things about dry land farming."

"Such as?"

"Well," Ruben looked around the room without establishing eye contact with either of us, "I learned that you need to plant corn in clusters instead of rows. You plant eight or nine seeds and wait for them to germinate. Then you thin out the cluster to may four or five plants."

"Why cluster?"

"That was very interesting. For one thing, if the plants are in a cluster, then in the morning the plants on the west are in the shade of the ones on the east. In the afternoon, it's just the opposite. Also, the clustered plants sort of hold each other up in strong winds. It all makes a lot of sense."

There was a long silence. Ruben looked down at his hands.

"Those people up on the mesas know a lot about the natural world. About how to grow things without irrigation. At least without much irrigation."

And that was the extent of the conversation with Ruben Mahoney. He got up, thanked Venus for the meal, and started to the door.

"Wait!" said Venus. She went to the kitchen cabinets and got down some dry boxed foods, macaroni and cheese, pasta, and several small boxes of raisins. "Here take these."

Ruben accepted them graciously, slipped his small backpack from his shoulder and stowed the food item. He nodded and was out the door carrying the bedroll under one arm.

"So who is he?"

"We're not sure. He wanders around the southwest. Always seems to be able to get someone to offer him food. Sometimes he talks more. Probably a little shy with a stranger like you in the house."

"Sorry."

"No. That's all right. Ruben doesn't expect much from anyone. He gives a lot though."

"Like what?"

"Well…he gives wisdom. I know that sounds crazy. But he dispenses wisdom. Really simple and direct stuff. I met him at Fred's. Where else, huh? The first time I met him he talked about 'soft walking.' He had noticed that all the trails that nature lovers and outdoor adventurers take are beaten down. The reason, he believed, was the fact that everyone wore hard soled boots. So he bought some moccasins, the kind you can get at almost any gift shop, Minnetonka or something like that, and started walking in those. What he found out was that you have to step much more carefully because you can feel every little bump or rock or even a clump of grass. You end up walking a lot more softly. Instead of tromping around, you step carefully and lightly.

"Another time we sat down and talked for a couple of hours. It was amazing. He zeroed right in one who I was and what I ought to be doing. He told me to quit screwing with all the little jobs I was taking on. He knew that I had an annuity from my parents. He pointed out that if I didn't live too lavishly, I could live on the annuity and do whatever I wanted to do. Up to that point, I had taken the payments from the annuity and invested them. So I did what he suggested. And here I am today!"

"And what is it that you do, Venus?"

"I try to teach. Not formally. Not in a classroom or workshop. I meet up with people, and we interact. Like you and me. If I think I can have some kind of impact, I go on. If not, I move on."

And that was all Venus was willing to say on that subject.

27

Sometime later Venus handed me a few sheets of paper. "Here's a fun story. Read it, and then we can talk about it."

The Adulterer's Cake

Suzy Jackson was cute, slender, medium height and what men would consider "built." Suzy did not consciously flaunt her attractions. In her late twenties, Suzy could still get away with wearing her blond-streaked hair in pigtails that went well with her freckles and pert nose. She was married to Curt Jackson, a civil engineer working his way up the corporate ladder. They belonged, at her insistence, to the Fairmist Bay Community Church. Suzy was active in the church, mainly in the women's group. Curt was not active. His work took him away from Fairmist Bay frequently and sometimes for periods of several weeks. Projects on which Curt worked were located all over the United States and even in Asia.

Every two months the Fairmist Bay Community Church Women's Group held a bake sale. Every two months Suzy Jackson brought a devil's food cake, a perfectly baked and iced devil's food cake. The reason the cake and icing were perfect is that Suzy, upon joining the church and the women's group, practiced baking devil's food cakes. She did this compulsively. One week when Curt was gone, Suzy bought eight packages of devil's food cake mix and all the ingredients needed to ice the eight cakes. She spent most of that day and some of the next baking eight cakes. By the sixth cake the outcome was perfect. But she baked and iced an additional two just to make sure.

At the bake sale a strange thing happened. As soon as Suzy delivered her cake and it was put on a table, Martha Wingate purchased it before the sale opened... Martha Wingate was in charge of the bake sale. She was more matronly than Suzy even though only ten years older. Martha was larger, taller, and wider than Suzy and wore her hair in a more conservative style, medium length, carefully tinted and then prodded into shape each morning. Martha was also "built," but no man would ever comment on her physique. Too imposing.

After Suzy delivered her devil's food cake she left since the sale was well staffed decade-long members. With Suzy out the door, Martha grabbed the devil's food cake exclaiming "I will not have that woman's cake on this table!" She was agitated. Perhaps for good reason. So she put five dollars into the cash drawer, took the cake, and placed it in a plastic supermarket bag on the floor. At the end of the bake sale, Martha took the bag to her car, deposited it in the trunk, and drove off.

All the women knew why Martha performed this every-two-month ritual. It was well known or at least well rumored that Suzy, cute and pert Suzy, occasionally met a man at a state park twenty-two miles to the north of town. She had been seen there. Once. Maybe twice. Then the word spread.

Suzy drove to the park in her van, dressed in athletic clothes and running shoes. She went regularly on the weeks when Curt was out of town and always on Wednesdays around noon went to the park to run. In excellent shape, Suzy ran three or four miles each time. However, at the end of a run she was accompanied by a man, not Curt but some other man, and they would stand a talk for a while outside the van. Then, quickly the two would dart in through the sliding side door of the van. Some time later, usually less than an hour, the man emerged and walked to his car. Suzy appeared a little afterward, slipped into the front seat, and drove off.

The men Suzy met at the park invariably were from Fairmist Bay Community Church, most married. It being a nice church with very polite people, no one was willing to confront Suzy about her activities. And the women whose husbands might have been seen at the park were never told. Thus Suzy came to be known among the women of the church as The Adulterer, and that was the reason Martha Wingate excommunicated the devil's food cake at each bake sale. She would not, definitely and absolutely would not, have The Adulterer's Cake on her table.

There was no doubt that Suzy met men at the park and did something with them in the back of her van. Martha Wingate and the other women of Fairmist Bay Community Church had no idea as to what actually happened in the van. In reality, there was a certain amount of unbuttoning, unzipping, and untying and a certain amount of kissing, rubbing, and sometimes even pawing. However, there was never any sex. No intercourse. No oral sex. And for good reason.

Suzy Jackson, young and naïve Suzy Jackson, didn't need sex. She did need to touch and be touched and to be in the company of a man. Her husband, away for many weeks, was available only occasionally. Suzy only wanted sex with her husband. Well the men who met Suzy at the park didn't know that. They had heard about her running and her van and the other men. So each one of them managed, somehow, for several weeks at a time to get away from the office during lunch hour and be at the park on Wednesday when Suzy finished her run. They met her with great anticipation and went into the van. But they didn't get to have sex. After a few weeks each man would give up in frustration muttering "tease" and even worse. Of course, they, being members of the church, never talked to each other about their sinful dalliance. Besides, no man would admit to have been seduced into nothing.

Martha Wingate knowing knew full well that her husband would never go to the park and meet Suzy. He wouldn't dare. Martha still felt it necessary to eliminate The Adulterer's Cake from the bake sale table every two months as a way, it seemed to all the other members, to avenge all the wives whose husbands had strayed. All the women in the women's group believed that Martha Wingate took the cake to her home, removed it from the small plastic bag, put it in a large black plastic bag, perhaps even threw it in upside down, messing up the perfectly smooth icing, and deposited it in her trash can so that, later that week, the waste disposal truck would come and maul and crush and destroy that damned Adulterer's Cake. They were wrong.

Martha Wingate, upon arriving home, took The Adulterer's Cake and put it in a round clear plastic cake box and then placed it, very carefully, on the top shelf of her closet, a closet she did not share with her husband. Also on the shelf were an old china plate and a fork which she washed in the bathroom sink after use. Every weekday Martha Wingate, as soon as her husband left for work and the children took the bus to school, went to the closet shelf, took down the container, cut herself a small piece of The Adulterer's Cake and ate it. With great hope for some future pleasure from having ingested the daily dose of sinful chocolate. She made it last for several weeks. Martha Wingate, once a week on Thursdays around noon and dressed in running shoes and shorts and a tee shirt, drove her van twenty two miles to the state park, walked a mile or so, and waited. And waited...

I sat back and smiled. A funny story indeed. The point? I wasn't sure.

Venus came back into the room. "So what did you think?"

"I thought it was pretty funny. All kinds of people with mistaken ideas and misplaced values, I guess."

"Yeah, that's the obvious stuff. But look at what it says about our attitudes towards sex. I know this is my 'thing.' But it drives me nuts to think about all the stuff that goes on because we hide sexual stuff behind some kind of social curtain.

"Look. Here the point of the story. At least for me. This young woman wants to be held and touched and kissed. She doesn't want sex. The guys do. So they sneak around and meet up with her. When there is no sex, they can't talk about it for two reasons. One is that they are guys and would never admit they hadn't 'gotten it.' The other reason is that they all are church members and aren't supposed to be engaged in adultery. On the other hand the older woman condemns the 'adulterer' and her devil's food cakes. But she also wants to be held and touched and kissed. Apparently she does not get that from her husband. So she goes out and tries to get it. But she assumed she is going to have to have intercourse in order to get it. Everyone is totally screwed up!"

I nodded.

28

I was raised, quite obviously, in the American culture, a culture stretching back to the days of the Pilgrims and the multitude other religious immigrants. That culture, for whatever reasons, had a whole series of strong religious beliefs about sex and sexuality. Even about sensuality. Dating back much earlier than the pilgrims, the Greeks divided the human being into the body and soul. So I grew up with the notion that the spirit or soul was good and the body, maybe not bad, but certainly not the equal of the spirit. The sacred stood above the secular. The holy above the ordinary, the profane.

Now I had to unlearn all of that. The body and soul, according to Fred and Venus, were all one. I was a whole human being, not fragmented into a wonderful soul and a mundane body. Bowel movements could reflect the state of my soul. The sex act could become a matter of making love if two souls met at the same time as the two bodies collided.

Venus had fun with me one day. She brought out an old Bible and opened it. "Now here's something you won't hear being read in most churches today." At this point, she began to read a few phrases from the open Bible: 'Graceful legs like jewels; navel a rounded goblet; breasts like two fawns; breasts like clusters of fruit.' Then it goes on to describe how this woman is tall and slender like a palm and the writer goes on to say he will climb up the palm tree to reach the fruit!"

Venus looked up at me. "Can you imagine that being read at a Methodist church service? For that matter, any kind of church service? This is one of the best kept secrets of the Old Testament."

"What is it?"

"The Song of Solomon. You know, Solomon the wise. The one who made all the very best decisions. Well old Solomon had some real neat poetry written!

"Actually, the Song of Songs – that's the way it is titled in the Old Testament – begins with these words: "Let him kiss me with the mouth – for your love is better than wine."

So it turns out that the Bible itself is not quite as dry and austere as I had been lead to believe. No one, in any of the few church services I had attended, had ever read the words to the Song of Solomon to a congregation!

29

Controlled love-making is an oxymoron. I really believe that after my time with Venus. Too many books and videos focus on technique. As if there is some magic button to push. A lesson from many experiences always comes back to me. I discovered it in my high school days while playing tennis. And the lesson holds true in every athletic endeavor. It also holds true in work.

No matter what the situation, the harder you try to do something, the more you work at it, the tougher it is to accomplish. I re-discovered this in my work. If I had to get a project out and the project needed some kind of fresh look or a creative input, it almost never happened. Unless I relaxed, sat back, and let the answer come to me.

In tennis it was exactly the same way. I really struggled for a year and got lousy results. The reason was that I was "pressing." I was trying to think and bully my way through matches. I was trying too hard to make strong shots in the right places. My coach finally got me to back off. It was the old slogan: Go out there and have fun. When I just hit the ball, I started winning more.

Venus taught me that lesson about relationships, particularly sexual relationships. There is no sense in trying to impress the other person with your sexual prowess, your technique, your vitality. The idea is to have fun. That and approach the other human being with an attitude of awe and wonder. Not in the sense that the woman is a goddess or the man a god, but that the other person is *wonder-full.* That the other person may want to have fun, too.

She taught me that lesson one day when we visited Oak Creek, south of Flagstaff. Venus shed her boots and socks, rolled up her jeans, and waded into the shallow creek. I followed, of course. I hadn't waded like that since I was a kid. We were in a pool, and Venus started to run and kick the water and splash. It was childish. Pure fun. We both kicked and skipped and ran with water flying all over the place. We even splashed each other with our hands.

When we stopped, there was an exuberance and abandonment that I wanted to feel again, many times, in the future. We didn't make love there that day. Too close to the road. Too many cars.

Later I realized that part of the magic of making love with Venus was that same sense of abandonment, of complete though temporary freedom from all social constraints. Let the world dictate the rules before and after, but during the interlude give up all thinking and memories. Be in the moment, in the cliché of the spiritual seekers.

Sayings of Fred
The harder you try, the harder it is to get hard.

30

We lay on the king sized bed in Venus' bedroom, blinds raised and curtains pulled wide to see the juniper and pinyon trees just beyond the end of her lot and beyond the trees the snow-dusted San Francisco peaks rising in sacred majesty. Both stripped to our underwear. Ready to make love. Talking softly.

If anyone wanted to play voyeur, he was more than welcome. We were nearly naked on a bed with windows uncovered. A delicious sensuality embraced me.

Venus raised her hips and slipped the underpants down her hips, over her buttocks, and the quickly along her legs until she gripped them in one hand with a crazy smile on her face.

"Look," she said and flung the underpants up toward the four-bladed ceiling fan above the bed. The underwear fell back onto her stomach.

"Oh crap!" She tried again and this time the underwear draped itself across one blade of the fan that began to turn slowly from the impact.

"Hah!" A smile of enormous self-satisfaction planted itself on her face as she turned to me. "Your turn!"

Before I could react, she rolled over and stripped me of my briefs in one quick move. "Here!" She handed them to me.

I couldn't believe this! Here I was naked in a woman's bed trying to throw my underwear so that they would hang on the blade of a ceiling fan! Unbelieving or not, I flung the briefs up -- almost directly over my head so they fell right back on may face! Venus roared! She laughed in spasms, and I couldn't help laughing at myself -- after removing the shorts from my face.

I flipped them up again -- and again -- and again -- while Venus curled into a ball laughing. On the fifth try I did it! Not only did I get them to suspend on a blade, but somehow I actually got a fan blade through one of the leg holes!

We laughed and tears streamed down our cheeks. An utter childish joy filled our hearts and bodies, a shared raucous sensual joy.

Then we made love.

31

We have completely split the soul from the body. People who revel in the body have trouble with positive feelings toward religion. And people who are deeply religious cannot talk about, much less act on, the instincts and processes of the body. I was learning. Fred showed me how the state of my soul was reflected in my bowel movements. Now I was learning about soul and sex, and if ever there was a dichotomy, a chasm in the beliefs of western civilization, it was that sex was profane and dirty while soul was the epitome of puritan.

"Love me!" commanded Venus.

I knew exactly what she meant. I wrapped my arms around her as we stood in the living room. I snuggled her. I used my right hand to softly massage her back. And I listened as she purred, yes, cat-like, she murmured and I heard that sound and I could feel it through my finger tips on her back.

She loved me back. She cared for me, communicated with touch, gentle, soft, nurturing touch. And I loved her in the same way.

Instead of the hurried, even frantic, love making of my past and the kind they show in movies, this was a slow passion, like the soft deep bass sounds of a symphony orchestra, not climbing toward a crescendo, but flowing smoothly, undulating, inducing a swaying of the head and shoulders, melodic without being syrupy, penetrating the soul.

We cared for each other in a simple, physical way. It required no words. No lovey, dovey cards. No 'sweet nothings.' No candy or roses. We were simpatico. There was no question, no doubt about our love. Unspoken because words are always limiting. This was not a meeting of two needs, two wants. It was a joining of two beings, body and soul.

That was the final lesson from Venus.

32

Venus drove us back to Moab on a windy, dusty day. The horizon was indistinct. Mesas and buttes hovered in the distance, their bases blurred by the blowing sand and dust.

I knew my time with Venus was over. She didn't have to say anything. We were heading back to Moab. She was on her way back east, to the Midwest and Great Lakes states. I was on my way to Fred and my Jeep Wrangler.

Strangely, I didn't feel depressed or upset. I knew that Venus cared about me. And it didn't matter whether she was sitting next to me or in bed or alongside during a hike. She would always be with me in one way or another.

I thought I ought to feel jealous or depressed or something. But I didn't. The human mind and emotions work in a strange way. There was the 'should' based on a lot of prior relationships and experiences. I 'should' be upset. I 'should' be begging Venus to stay or to take me with her.

Instead, I sat watching the landscape of northern Arizona and southern Utah flow past. My feeling state? It dawned on me: serenity.

33

Looking back, I realized that Venus and I had not made love all that many times. It seemed more than I could actually count.

So what had happened? One more lesson. My own. A few beautiful experiences, totally satisfying, both physically and spiritually, were worth hundreds of "rolls in the hay."

Sayings of Fred
It's not how often you make love but how well.

We stood and held sparklers of tenderness
and the burning fireflies of love feel all around us
In the morning, the thousand burnt holes in your sweater
testified to that strange ritual.

Give me some signal
So that I will know
when to respect your solitude
and when you need me.
I understand both aloneness
and intimacy.
I, too, am both poles
of the human magnet,
attracted and repelled,
needing and afraid,
Moving toward you and wandering
off in confusion,
Creating an erratic drunkard's walk
on the checkerboard of caring.

The Earth Mother stood
in the field,
naked from the waist up,
her breasts white in the
morning sun,
a testament to fecundity.
And God was pleased.

No moon rose that night,
the stars blinked out
one by one
leaving a black canopy.
Unseeing, I stumbled
on rocks;
crushed the young flowers.
Then something stepped on me,
and I was dead.

Hiatus

Fall came slowly to Moab after I arrived back at Fred's place. Autumn is the best time of year in the west and southwest. The days are clear, the nights cool.

What now? Fred had other "things to do." He didn't tell me what. I sat for several days in front of his trailer. Fred didn't suggest anymore adventures or activities. So I finally asked one day.

"I think it's time for you to take a long hiatus," he said. "Like over the winter. Then we can work out something for you starting next spring. I have an idea. I know some people who own a cottage on a small lake in Michigan. You could go there and live for the summer. They are looking for someone to 'cottage sit' while they are off traveling in Europe. You could do some simple maintenance and enjoy the water. How's that sound?"

"Interesting. But what do I do in the meantime?"

"That's up to you."

"Don't you have something for me to do?"

"Nope. I've done all I can this year. It's time for you to take off and take control of your own life for eight months. Go find some work somewhere. Go visit someone. Come back in May."

I felt rejected. I had let Fred take over my life for the summer. Venus had taken me to Flagstaff and then dropped me off. Suddenly I was depressed. I wanted more adventures. And Fred was having none of it.

So I packed my gear in the back of the Wrangler on a cool Tuesday morning. Fred had taken off several days before. I closed the door to his trailer and walked to the Jeep without the slightest idea as to where I would go.

I had changed over the last few months. The changes weren't obvious to me, encased in my own life-shell. I found out how big the changes were in the visit to Chicago. I drove, slowly, back to the Great Lakes. In Nebraska, I stopped wherever there seemed to be an interesting little museum or some kind of tourist attraction. It took me seven days to creep along the Moab-to-Chicago route.

Ralph and Bud were two good friends, both former co-workers. We worked and played together during my time in Chicago. The guys were the same as far as I could see. Bud had moved on to another firm, but he was still Bud. I was the one who changed.

I stayed with Ralph. My possessions now were a sleeping bag, jeans, T-shirts, running shoes, sweats, and generally a simple and worn collection of very casual clothes. Gone were the slacks, shirts, jackets, and suits. Gone were the wingtip shoes and loafers. Ralph noticed.

"Where are your clothes, man?"

"This is it!" I toted my wheeled suitcase and large athletic bag up the stairs to Ralph's condo.

"Jesus! You aren't the cool guy who used to show us all up with your clothes!"

"No, guess I'm not."

That night we met Bud and went to a local pizza place. Beer and pizza. Standard meal of my past. It still tasted good. And we talked.

There were big gaps in the conversation. Lulls. Ralph and Bud brought me up to date on their jobs and careers, Bud being particularly enthusiastic about his new position. More money and more autonomy.

When it can time for me to tell them about my life, my experience, about Fred and Max and all the other stuff that had happened, I tried. It just didn't work. There was no way I could explain being naked in the desert or getting sunburned on my penis and butt. I couldn't talk about seeing monkeys and baboons on a canyon wall. Or dancing my feelings to a woman. And particularly not falling off the rim of the Grand Canyon after making love. I also couldn't possibly get into a discussion of the difference between having sex and making love or the distinction between sensuality and sex. I now occupied a different world from my former friends.

That night, lying in the guest bedroom at Ralph's, I realized how much difference there was between the old me and the current me. I couldn't go back to who I was or what I was. I could pretend, but it was no good. The pretense was a lie, and I didn't want to lie. I wanted to be who I was and to be able to talk to people like me. Those weren't Ralph and Bud.

I moved on the next day, a Sunday. I made the excuse that I had to get back to Utah to see some people there. Ralph didn't protest. He knew that we were no longer moving in the same direction.

So I called Andrea, my ex. She was home that morning. I asked to stop by. Andrea had moved, so I got the new address and drove the Jeep through the canyons of Chicago and managed to find a place to park only four blocks from her apartment. We were still friends, and she greeted me like a friend. A hug, warm and good.

"So what have you been up to?"

"First tell me about yourself. What is going on in your life?"

She filled me in. A new job, better pay. Several abortive attempts at relationships. Nothing that worked. Andrea was learning to live by herself and be herself. I complimented her on that.

Then I started on my story, beginning with meeting Fred in Moab. I left out most of the stuff about Venus. Andrea, being the good person she was, listened, asked questions, and kept me going. We drank tea and nibbled on bagels. I managed to cover the adventures in a couple of hours.

"Well, I wish I could have the kind of life you are leading!" Andrea smiled wistfully.

We had talked, in the past, about living in the West, hiking, climbing mountains, camping. But the demands of jobs always got in the way. We were both so busy with our jobs and careers that there was little time left for relating, much less wandering out west. And we were so busy and involved that we got tired, spent our nonworking hours just trying to handle chores and keep our little household in one piece. In the process, our relationship ended up in several pieces.

"You've changed!"

"Yeah, I guess I have."

"You're better this way…" Her comment trailed off.

"Thanks. I think I feel better. But I'm lonely. I'm living between two different worlds. I don't fit around here anymore. I spent a day with Ralph and Bud, and I'm not one of them anymore. But I don't have anywhere else to be, either."

"You're in transit!"

That was the best response I could have gotten. Yes, I was in transit. Just like an immigrant moving from one country to another, one culture to a different one. Someday I would land somewhere. It would be good.

I thanked Andrea. She hugged me again. Should I invite her on the journey? No. Impossible. This was my voyage, solo, alone, to an unknown destination. I cared about Andrea, I now discovered, and she cared about me. But we were not destined to be a couple again.

Sayings of Fred
Very few people are in transit in life.

I left Andrea standing in front of the building where she lived. She waved. I waved. And I set out on another long drive, this time north out of Chicago into Wisconsin and then west through South Dakota. Fall had arrived. The weather was getting much colder, particularly across the Great Plains. Clouds scudded low over the hills. There was rain mixed with snow one day.

What was I doing? Where was I going?

I wanted to go back to Moab and Fred or Flagstaff and Venus. Neither option was open. So I continued west into Wyoming and then south and west to Utah. I drove with a new sense of the scenery. I had become more sensuous, aware.

Every evening I took out my journal and wrote in it. Sometimes in a local fast food place. Sometimes in a motel room. Occasionally, I began writing a little earlier and sat in the Jeep before sunset.

My meanders took me back down through Utah, but this time I avoided Moab and picked up Interstate 70 west and then ducked down through Capitol Reef and finally into southwestern Utah. I stayed a few days in Cedar City exploring Zion and Bryce Canyon National Parks. I shot down Interstate 15 to Las Vegas.

Of all the unlikely places for me to spend my next few months, I landed in Las Vegas, Nevada and managed to get a job working for a small public relations agency. I met some nice people. I worked diligently but no longer in the frantic, get-ahead-at-any-cost pace of my previous life. My work was appreciated, and I didn't need to impress anyone beyond that.

I avoided The Strip and all the touristy noise and confusion of Las Vegas. A small efficiency apartment was enough for my new life style since I knew that I would be returning to Moab in the spring. I cooked some meals and ate out fairly often.

Several women expressed an interest in dating, and we went out a few times. I knew how difficult it would be to make love so I acted strange and distant. I was a foreigner in Las Vegas, a temporary resident, someone in transit, and it showed.

My journal occupied an hour a day most days. I did drive out into the desert whenever time allowed. I found I could go somewhere and just sit for hours, enjoying the sun and dryness.

In late April, I told the owner of the public relations agency that I would be leaving and heading back to Moab, Utah. She wished me well. I handled a few more assignments and then left. The hiatus had been a true pause. I have no strong memories of the people or places or events. It was an intermission, and now I was going back to continue the story.

SECOND YEAR

SECTION IV

Stanley Lake
Springtime

1

We rolled out of Moab, beginning our tip to southwestern lower Michigan, up to and the following Interstate 70 across Colorado and after passing through Denver, using I-76 to intercept I-80 in Nebraska. Fred's camper pickup and my Wrangler, in convoy, kept within five miles an hour of the speed limit, five miles over, of course. We stopped every hour and a half or so, depending on the distance between towns or rest areas, and we switched vehicles at least once a day to relive some of the boredom.

Our first stop was in Idaho Springs, Colorado at the Peoriana Motel, after a long day through western valleys, along mesas, and then up and over Vail Pass and through the Continental Divide tunnels.

Day two an equally long haul but diagonally across northeastern Colorado, sparse high desert with only a few cattle alongside the highway up to Interstate 80. that night we stayed in Kearney, Nebraska and began again the next morning through the remainder of Nebraska, flat wheat fields, into Iowa, lightly rolling country to Grinnell, home of the college with the same name, the trip now consisted of a tight focus on the road ahead, watching the mileage posts and counting the miles and hours to the next pit stop or the destination for that night.

The fourth day was a long push, for us, from Grinnell to Kalamazoo, Michigan where we spent our final night on the road. I felt strange driving right past Chicago on I-80 where I had spent so much of my adult life, but I was changing and Chicago was in the past.

During all those hours of driving I listened to whatever radio station was available, most country western music through eastern Colorado, Nebraska, and Iowa. As we approached Chicago the choice became wildly diverse and familiar.

Now I was anxious to see this place where Fred had invited me to spend the rest of the spring, summer, and early autumn. It was a lake, Stanley Lake, located in Barry County, Michigan. That was our destination this last day. Fred led me up US-131 to Plainwell and then on a winding, complex route to Orangeville, passing through onion farming country. Later in my stay, I would drive through that area during harvest with the pungent smell of onion hanging in the humid air.

Stanley Lake, forty-five acres in size, allowed a good swimming to cross it easily. It as much too small for any boat with a motor of more than ten horsepower, and, in fact, the residents, year-round and summer, had an informal covenant to limit motor size to just ten horses. We turned onto a dirt road that passed under an archway of oak trees, providing deep shade even on this sunny May day. There was a slight washboard to the road, particularly on the upsloping sections, which rattle the Jeep, me, and my limited belongings. We turned again and followed another mildly rutted dirt road, ignoring a best to the left, and down an incline. Stanley Lake was not marked with a sign on the road, by agreement with the residents who wanted to maintain their privacy. Technically any resident of the state could use any waterway as long as there was some public access. There was no public access to Stanley Lake. Nonetheless residents kept it a secret.

We drove another quarter mile and Fred pulled into a flat sandy parking area below a cottage painted dark green. We got out and stretched. Then Fred led me up to the twelve wooden stairs, around the cottage, and to its front where we could see the lake. The cottage was mounted on a bank thirty feet above the water lever, one of the higher points on the whole lake. The water was calm. There was one small boat drifting right in front of the cottage, an older man fishing diligently, occasionally pulling out a small fish and stringing it one a line that he then slipped back alongside the boat.

Barker leaped out of the cab of Fred's truck and ran to the front of the cottage, down the embankment, and tiptoed his way into the water. His tail wagged vigorously as the dog looked right and left.

"Barker chases fish," Fed explain. That's when Barker jumped forward and splashed the water with his right paw. "He never catches them, though."

Back around to the rear door of the cottage, Freed pulled out his key chain, picked a long, large, and old-fashioned key, unlocked the door. We entered. A must smell hovered in the room, a smell of unused air, old cooking odors, and the aroma of both wood and kerosene, the latter from the oil stove used for heat.

This would be my home for the next five months. Fred rented the cottage for a small amount from friends who were going to sell it the following year. We would have the use of it for the summer at that minimum cost if we maintained it and did some simple repairs.

2

After unlocking door, opening windows, and airing out the stale smells our first job was to get water running. We need to be able to flush the toilet.

Water came from a well, really just a pipe driven some forty feet into the ground next to the cottage, below the water table, in fact, ten feet below the level of the lake. Fred pointed out to the well pit. A small slab of concrete held a round iron cover that we pried off. Inside was the pump. My job was to get down into the pit that was about four feet deep and only two feet wide. Then I would have to bend over and pour water into the pump to prime it. We'd get a bucket of water from the lake to do it. That was the actual first step. I was delegated, went down to the shore, and dipped the bucket without getting my feet wet.

The preliminaries were finished. A switch on the wall of the kitchen controlled the pump. The bucket of water stood next to the well pit. Then Fred drilled me on the procedure.

"Unscrew the pressure gauge there on top of that pipe. That's where you pour the water. It will go down into the pump and that should prime it. Once it is primed the pump will start pushing water up through the pipes and it will come out of that hole where the gauge fits. You need to slap the gauge back down in there and screw it back"

Sounded simple to me. Fred went into the cottage, and I slipped into the well pit and pulled the bucket toward me. The pump started to hum as Fred flipped the switch. He re-emerged from the cottage as I started pouring water down the little hole. Of course not much water went into the one-inch hole and most of it cascaded over the pump and pipes onto my feet. My old running shoes got wet in a hurry. I kept pouring water with no effect.

Just as I was about to give up because there wasn't much water left in the pump, the prime kicked in. Fred had said that the pump would start "pushing water up." Well it did more than that. It spurted water up onto my crotch and splashed to my chest. All this time I was fumbling for the pressure gauge thoughtlessly laid on top of the pump.

I felt the gauge, gripped it tightly, and, feeling the threaded lower end, tried to jam it into the hole. This had the same effect as holding your thumb over the end of a hose: a smaller sharper stream of water hit me in the face. Reflexively I pulled the gauge back out.

Fred stood a couple of feet back from the well pit bent over with laughter. Barker sat on his haunches behind his master with, I would swear, a smirk on his face. The situation was funny and frustrating at the same time to me. I was wet and getting wetter, and I still didn't have the gauge in place so the water spewed out of the hole in the pipe and slowly built a pond in the bottom of the well pit.

Now I knew what to expect, so I slammed the gauge into the threaded hole in the pipe and created a momentary gusher before twisting the gauge in place. The water system going! At least so I thought.

Sayings of Fred
You learn more by getting wet than by reading an instruction manual.

3

Getting squirted turned out to be only the first half of the story of getting water out of faucets and filling the toilet tank. We walked back into the cottage where all the faucets had been turned on in the previous fall when everything was shut down and drained. The faucets coughed and regurgitated for a couple of minutes until they flowed freely in both the kitchen and bathroom. The toilet tank filled. We turned the faucets off thinking the job was complete.

There was still-running water. Where? We found out shortly with a drip-drip from the ceiling. The plumbing system was a nest of pipes running through the attic since the place was built on a concrete slab with no ground level plumbing. We had a leak in an attic pipe!

Fred turned the pump switch off and hollered at me to open the faucets to drop the pressure in the system. That done we got the old step ladder stored outside next to the back door and put it under the trap door into the attic. Up to the attic we climbed, Fred first. We crawled across the one-by-twelve board and small sheets of plywood to find the leaky pipe. According to Fred the system hadn't been completely drained in the fall and water remaining in the pipe froze, expanded, and split the copper tubing.

We found the split copper pipe and made the repair quickly. There was a hack saw, some lengths of green vinyl garden hose, an old rusty screwdriver, and a dozen hose clamps stored right next to the trap door. I cut through the copper piping on both side of the split while Fred cut a section of hose and four hose clamps. We slipped the hose clamps and hose over the ends of the pipe, tightened the clamps down, and prayed that the fix would work.

Back down on the main level, Fred started the pump again, we closed the faucets, and we waited. Fifteen minutes later there were no sounds of running water and no drips from the ceiling. We had running water, and it only took an hour and a half to get it.

That was my introduction to a more basic way of life.

4

In the past, my needs for water, heat, and electrical power were provided, magically and almost unfailingly, by something "out there." Occasionally the lights went out, and we wondered what had happened. One time I read in the paper the next day that a squirrel fell onto a transformer and shorted out the entire substation. Most of the time, the lights went out and then came back on without explanation.

The waste products of my home, the garbage and toilet flushings had gone somewhere down and out and into something called the sewage system, buried beneath the ground.

At Stanley Lake, my connection with water was clear and definite. I experienced it. The water was sucked up out of a forty-foot well. I had primed the pump and watched the water start to flow. I could see the pipe leading into the ground next to the well pit and emerging in the attic of the cottage.

The electrical energy came down three wires to a box at the back end of the cottage, and as I drove along the dirt road, the power lines paralleled it all the way as far as I could travel. I knew where and how the electricity traveled. After a storm, I knew which tree limb fell on which part of the line and caused the outage.

Heat came from the oil burning stove. Oil flowed from a big tank outside right behind the kitchen through a small copper tube and into the stove. When I turned on the valve, oil spread along the firebox. I could see it. No magic.

And what we flushed and rinsed and put down the drains then directly into a septic tank and leach field. The location was obvious because the grass grew a little greener and a little longer above the septic tank.

In my urban life, connections with the sources of light, heat, water, and waste were mysterious. We took them for granted and were disconnected. It's as if we were floating in a space ship with "the infrastructure" providing for all of our needs. When they failed, we noticed them. Then we were upset.

The bond between me and power, water, and waste disposal was tighter in the cottage. The electricity failed more often. Water sometimes spurted with pockets of air from the faucets. And one time the septic system regurgitated back into the cottage.

But because I knew what was happening, I had more power, more control. There was no imagined Wizard of Oz haphazardly turning things on and off. I could control the flow of oil into the stove. I could go out and check on the pump in the well pit. I could even, if needed, start up a little gas generator and provide enough electricity to turn on a couple of light bulbs and maybe even cook on a hot plate.

There was, of course, a more intimate connection with the earth as well. The cottage walls were thin, and the sounds of wind and water came through to me every day and night. I walked out onto dirt every morning, not a sidewalk. I floated on the water of Stanley Lake in a rowboat. In Chicago, I was isolated from the earth, walking on concrete and asphalt, living above ground in an apartment insulated from natural sounds, riding to work in a bus, and never, ever touching the earth or anything natural for days on end.

Here, I was connected to the sources of light, heat, and water. I was connected to the earth. And I never wanted to go back to the old way.

Sayings of Fred
Honor your connections.

5

Simplicity. That's what I needed. To cut down on the complications of urban and even town living. Get back to basics.

The first step for me was to assess how the complications happened in the life left behind. Looking back I knew that I had owned too much, too many things. For some reason, I owned and drove two cars. The Jeep Wrangler, my current companion, and a Honda Accord. The Honda for driving around town, saving on gas, and for "nice" events and times. The Jeep was my soul car, the one I really wanted, the one that symbolized how I wanted to live, the one that was the exact opposite of the life I was then living.

Two cars meant two oil changes, two washings, two sets of license plates, two sets of new tires, two tune-ups, two of everything involved in car ownership. Too much.

In the apartment I had two TV sets, one in the living room, the other in my bedroom. Two clock radios, one in the bedroom to wake up to, the other in the kitchen for no known reason. A stereo with all its associated CDs and tapes stood in the living room.

On and on. My kitchen, a bachelor kitchen, had a microwave, toaster, toaster oven, and food processor, even when I only ate at home once every two days.

My closet held too many pants, jackets, suits, and shirts. Too many ties. I dressed in half the clothes I owned. The rest were "somedays." But all those clothes needed to be maintained, dry cleaned or washed, pressed, and hung up. Then I had all of the clothes I needed to relax in, to go camping or hiking, and the "grubs" to clean, paint, or do other dirty jobs.

Now, at Stanley Lake, I was down to three pairs of jeans, about ten T-shirts, the same number of turtlenecks or long sleeved T's, ten pairs of socks, and two pairs of hiking boots. I had a heavy parka for winter wear and a lighter weight wool jacket for cool days. I had only what I needed.

So I once owned too much, had too much to take care of. Added to that, too many interests, too many possible things to do. That is the advantage and at the same time the burden of the big city. I belonged to an athletic club where I worked out to stay in shape. I went to movies and plays and concerts. I belonged to five different groups involved in civic and environmental projects. All this on top of a job that required fifty to sixty hours a week.

Sitting here at the lake, my projects were to cook meals, launch a boat, put in a new dock, and go to town occasionally for food. I had time to listen to the wind, watch waves on the lake, and look at the stars at night.

And, finally, I had too many acquaintances, too many relationships to keep track of. Each person needed time and energy from me, and I enjoyed their company but only now realized that drain they represented. They were good people. They brought some good into my life. But I knew, now, that I had never known any of them very well. We related on a nice but superficial level.

So far, at Stanley Lake, I knew Fred. There was a possibility of getting to know one or two other people. But here my best friends were the lake, the sky, the wind, the fish and birds and turtles.

By stripping down to essentials, there was time to listen to my own soul and to the voices of the natural world around me. And that is what I did that spring, summer, and early fall.

Fred left me to my own devices for a while.

6

A large rowboat was angled well up onto the shore, pulled up the previous fall, protecting it from the winter ice alongside a Sunfish sailboat. A three-seater, made of galvanized sheet steel, flat on the bottom, a curved pointed prow, and a flat stern with a well-deteriorated piece of wood bolted in place to hold an outboard motor. The boat showed few signs of weathering besides the rotten board on the stern.

The boat was big; the exterior painted a bright yellow. It became, in my private voice, the big yellow boat. Planning a trip on the lake, I say to myself "Let's take the big yellow boat."

One seat spanned the stern where I could start the outboard and steer. Two additional seats were set forward and aft of the middle of the boat. And a small fourth seat, triangular in shape squeezed in at the bow. That seat was just big enough for a medium-sized child.

With all its seats, the big yellow boat accommodated up to five adults, two on each of the middle seats and one in the stern. Now there was only me.

That spring the big yellow boat rested on the shore, steeply inclined shore and covered with rough grasses and weeds, with its stern a couple of feet above the water and the bow angling up toward the cottage. I had to get it into the water. I tried to drag it back down the same way it had been beached in the fall. No luck. It was heavy. High friction between boat, dirt, and weeds.

I stood back and looked the situation over. I couldn't slide the big yellow boat back into the water by myself. There was no one around to help, and, being male, I wouldn't ask for help anyway. A way had to exist.

I spotted a length of yellow rope tied to a ring at the bow, the anchor rope. The anchor, a round cast iron fishing boat anchor, rested under the small front seat. I pulled the rope out and found that I could swing the bow of the boat around toward the water. That solved the problem. The bow came around easily. In fact, the bow was in a few inches of water.

Stripping off my boots and socks and rolling up my jeans, I stepped into the frigid water. My feet and ankles went from instant cold to instant numb. I yanked and strained on the anchor rope, inching the boat into the water. As the bow began to float, pulling got easier. The big yellow boat floated.

I smiled. A success! I solved a problem. I got something done. It took some strength, brains, and a little bit of luck. But I got it done. What a great feeling! Better than any I ever had in solving a professional problem. A simple exercise in launching a rowboat, and I was feeling good.

The Sunfish, lighter and with a curved bottom, didn't resist my tugging at all, it floated easily, so easily that it almost slipped away into the lake.

7

Max came over the next day carrying a twenty-two rifle. Max, the old man fishing of a few days ago.

"Goddam chipmunks!" His greeting. "And goddam squirrels. Chew up everything. Chew up the siding on your cottage if they're hungry enough." I understood some of his anger a few months later when a chipmunk sneaked into a cupboard where cereal was stored!

"Max!" he stuck out a gnarly right hand, callused, bony knuckles, one finger bent sideways. His grip was tight and short. "Mad Max they call me." He grinned showing yellowed teeth with small gaps between the front uppers and lowers.

"Good to meet you Max. I saw you fishing the other day. When I got here."

"That was me all right. Got to get your priorities straight. Eating, drinking, sleeping, fishing, and screwing. That's what life is all about. Only reason to work is to get enough money so you can eat, drink, sleep, fish, and screw."

I didn't know what to say. So I pointed to the rifle.

"Gonna shoot those sonabitchin' chipmunks. And squirrels. Eat the siding off your cottage if they're hungry enough." That was a Max cliche. "Just wanted you to know what the gun shots were when you heard 'em."

"Thanks." Here was a man totally different from Fred, me, or any of the people I knew.

"You buy this place?"

"No. Just renting for the summer."

"Good thing. The sonabitch needs a lot of work. Isn't worth shit."

"I know. I'm supposed to clean it up and fix it up."

"Take you more than this summer to do that. Even if you was a real good handy man. And you don't look like one."

He had me pegged there. "Well, I'll do what I can."

"You fish?"

"No. Not yet."

"I mean, you ever fished?"

"Not really."

"Hell, come on out with me sometime this week. I'll show you how to catch forty, fifty little sonabitchin' bluegills. Might get yourself a perch or two along the way. Hell, need that many bluegills to make a meal."

"How long have you lived here Max?" I changed the subject.

"Oh Christ, I dunno. Probably twenty years. Lost count somewhere. Don't matter either. Just live day to day. Eat, drink, sleep, fish, and screw. Don't worry about how long ago or how much longer to go."

A different life style. Here was a man not the least concerned with the spiritual life, with transformations, with the meaning of life. Well, actually he had his version of the meaning of life.

Just then Max swung around and ripped off a shot at a squirrel in one of the oak trees next to the cottage. "Sonabitch! Missed him." He squinted up at the tree trying to spot the furry ball, but no twitching tail was in sight. Smart squirrel, got out of the line of fire.

"Come see me sometime. We'll drink and talk. You know where I live?"

"No."

"Four doors down. Barn red cottage."

"Should we set a time?"

"Shit boy. Come whenever you feel like it. This isn't the big city. If I'm there, I'm there. If I ain't, I ain't." With that he turned and stalked off.

Sayings of Fred
Learn from everyone you meet.

8

There are many ways to prove your manhood. One of them, around Stanley Lake and a cottage, is mechanical. Directly in front of the cottage, lakeside, perfectly aligned with the door on the screened porch were two sets of two support posts for a dock. Every cottage had to have a dock reaching from the beach out far enough to allow one or two boats to be moored.

Fred showed me the posts. They were too high. Years before the lake level was two to three feet higher, and the posts were positioned so that a sailor or piscatologist could step off of the dock directly into the boat. (Piscatologist, I was informed, labeled any avid fisherman.) With the lake level lower, the dock was now three feet too high requiring a gymnastic descent into a boat. The step down was bad enough onto a stable platform but into a rocking rowboat was a much more difficult descent with a potentially bruising and possibly wet fall.

So the posts had to be removed. They were steel, perforated on the long axis, the kind of steel posts used to string wire fencing. Each one was driven into the sandy mud lake shore, driven far enough that they couldn't just be pulled out by arm strength alone. I tried that. They were driven far enough down into the mud that pulling and pushing produced nothing. Removal needed more than just muscle power and will power.

Each set of two posts was bridged with a piece of two-by-six. Two rusty bolts held the two-by-sixes to each post. Those pieces of lumber connecting the steel posts turned out to be the answer.

First I had to think. This required some creativity. There was no way to pull up on the posts. There was no 'sky hook' from which to hang ropes or chains. My Dad had always kidded me about sky hooks, but in real life there weren't any.

Then it came to me. I went out to my Wrangler, unsnapped the hooks holding down the hood, released the latch, and raised the hood. There was the jack and jack handle. I got them out and walked around the cottage back to the beach.

My running shoes and socks came off, and I waded into the chilly waters of Stanley Lake. I dropped the jack onto the sand below the two-by-six between the first set of posts. The top of the jack was about three feet below the bottom edge of the two-by-six, so I had to find something to span the gap. Back up on shore, I looked around and finally had to go back up to the cottage. Behind I found some old pieces of lumber including lengths of four-by-fours and two-by-fours from eight inches to two feet.

Lugging seven of those pieces, I went back down to the beach, and within five minutes had rigged a post from the jack, resting on the lake bottom, to the two-by-six, supported by the steel posts. It was then that I realized I was being watched. Covertly. No one stood up on the bank staring at me. But several sets of eyes, from neighboring cottages, were casually scanning the scene. One neighbor sat in front of his bungalow pretending to fix a fishing line. The other sat on his porch with a radio talking to him.

I went on. The jack handle fit into the jack, and I started cranking. The jack rose a half inch, wood pushed against wood, the jack settled a little way into the sand, and I cranked more. Slowly, the left steel post rose, then the right. The movement was small. The evidence was an eddy of sand and mud around each post. I cranked again. More movement.

I savored the moment. No heroics here. No blasting the posts with dynamite. No digging for hours to get them loose. Just a simple mechanical trick. An automobile jack and some pieces of lumber pushing up with enough force to raise those steel posts. I cranked again. The left post jumped up several inches. It was loose. Another two inches of jack travel and the right post was also free.

Nonchalantly I pulled the piece of lumber away and slipped the jack out from under the two-by-six bridging the posts as they slowly fell into the water. All I had to do was drag the posts, still connected by the two-by-six, to the shoreline and a little ways up the embankment.

The second set of posts followed in short order. In half an hour I removed the posts and without a bit of strain on my back or arms. The jack and handle were back in the Jeep. I hacksawed the bolts off of the posts and dropped those heavy pieces of two-by-six, carried the posts to the back end of the cottage yard, and retreated to the cottage.

No one ever talked to me about my success that day. No male would do that. No one congratulated me. But within two days, both neighbors came over and introduced themselves. I passed an initiation ritual.

9

Gerald lived in a small house, more than a cottage, two doors in the direction opposite from Max. I met Gerald one morning when I was taking garbage out to the trash can behind the cottage.

"Good morning, my man!"

I turned. "Good morning."

Gerald was without question the best dressed and most impeccable of the residents of Stanley Lake. He was also one of the most unique. I guess you would really consider him an eccentric.

"And how fares the young man?"

I looked around. Then I looked bewildered. He meant me.

"I'm fine. And you?"

"In fine fettle, thank you. Heretofore, I have been sickly. Untowardly. However, I have since recuperated."

"Sorry to hear that."

"And yourself? Have you been well?"

"Oh sure."

"Excellent! The blessings of good health are to be praised and appreciated. One should sing songs to good health. Sing paeans of praise!"

I was finding out – and confirmed it through the months at the lake – that this is the way Gerald talked. All the time. Any time.

"Well, I guess I haven't done that."

"Ah! So much the pity. Consider the plight of the unwell, the sickly, the terminally ill, the feeble, the unhealthy, all of the poor souls who are less than perfectly well. They cannot sing paeans of praise for they have nothing to celebrate!"

The conversation continued in this way for another twenty minutes. I was happy, ready to sing paeans of praise when we went our separate ways. Whenever I met Gerald, whether on the road or at a social gathering, that is the way he talked. He drove me nuts. Other people had learned to tolerate him.

10

Walking out of the kitchen door to the backyard of the cottage one day, I noticed that the door sill and weather stripping were dirty. Years of sand, dirt, muck, and grease were caked on the wood and metal. Of course, an occasional brooming cleared some of it, but a brown-gray residue laid there unfazed by a plastic broom.

I stopped and looked, turned back into the kitchen, and walked over to the cabinet under the sink where we kept the cleaning supplies. I gathered up two kinds of cleaner, a cloth, some scrubber pads and went to work on the sill and metal weather stripping.

Working slowly on one part of the sill, I cleared the gunk away from a stretch of three inches and was rewarded with the gleam of blond oak. I mean I was rewarded! It looked good. So I scrubbed and swiped at another three inches. And another and another. Close to the ends of the sill, it took more effort to get down to the wood. There was a thicker accumulation of gunk because brooms couldn't get in there. And there was less wear from boots and shoes and sandals.

Then I started on the chrome weather stripping. The metal shone brilliantly where I cleaned, and I worked my way from the center of the strip first to one side and then the other. It went faster. At last I sat back to admire my work.

Checking the clock in the kitchen, I realized that I had spent almost two hours scraping, washing, and polishing! Total concentration. Now I knew what people said about the Zen of work, the Zen of anything. Absolute absorption in the task equalled timelessness. Could I do it again? Or did it happen by chance, at least in my life? We would have to see.

Sayings of Fred
It's not the size of the task but the soul you put into it.

11

Having taken out the old dock, I had to build and install a new one. This one would be lower for easier access to the boats. The lake level had dropped.

Stanley Lake is spring fed, the water flowing into the basin from several underground sources. The lake itself is a natural bowl formed millions of years ago by a glacier. The ice scoured out the bowl, and there were hundreds of these small bowl lakes all over southwestern Michigan. When the glacier receded, a chuck of ice was left in the basic. It eventually melted, and the bowl filled with water.

But what dictated the depth of Stanley Lake? Actually, a natural earthen dam at the eastern end of the lake. The water flowed out of the lake through a small outlet, and over the past decade or so, the dam dirt on that end of the lake eroded a few feet. So the water level dropped as much.

So I had to put posts in the sandy-muddy bottom on the lake in front of the cottage and then build a platform to rest on the posts. Four-by-four material for the posts was laying behind the cottage. All I had to do was saw it to length -- by hand. So I measured the three sets of posts, one nearest the shore, one halfway out on the new dock, and the last set the farthest out at a water depth of four and a half feet.

The posts would rest on the bottom, four feet apart. That way I could build a four-foot wide platform by cutting eight foot two-by-fours in half. Those two-by-fours and the planking for the platform I bought at the lumber company in Hastings, Michigan.

So I set to work. Cutting boards to length, test fitting them, assembling the first section of platform on the ground in the front of the cottage, and then nailing it all together. The work absorbed me. This was a different kind of thinking and planning than in my former desk job.

I spent the last half of the morning and all afternoon building. By late afternoon, I was done. The posts sat on the lake bottom, the two sections of platform, each eight feet long, rested on the posts. I pulled the big yellow boat and the Sunfish up and tied them up on posts.

A test entry into the big yellow boat confirmed the design. I was done! And I was very satisfied, with myself and with the project. That evening, after dinner, I went down to the shore and just sat there and looked at the new dock. The next day I painted the deck sections.

12

In the city and in a professional job, there is always urgency. When I had time on my hands in Chicago, I looked for something exciting, even demanding, to do. I had to keep up the pace.

Stanley Lake provided a totally different atmosphere. The pace, obviously, was much slower. The small tasks that made up the day could not be rushed. I learned, for example, that you can't build a fire in the wood burning stove by sticking a couple of logs in, stuffing paper next to them, slipping a couple pieces of kindling over the paper, lighting the paper with a match, and then walking away. A fire needs tending, particularly in starting it. You have to watch it and see if the kindling catches. As it does and burns well, you have to rearrange the logs and kindling and then add another log to take advantage of the first hot flames. All of that took time. I couldn't build a fire, make coffee, and cook oatmeal all at the same time. One thing at a time. One thing, taken slowly and carefully, at a time.

Creating a fire was another learning experience. Every fire is unique. Each log is slightly different. Perhaps a little thicker or longer. Sometimes thick at one end and narrow at the other. Kindling varies. And some wood is drier, catching the flames faster. While some fires are simply obstinate, created out of the driest wood and kindling, carefully arranged, yet failing to light on the first or second or even third try. An obstinate fire requires a persevering fire tender.

When there was spare time, and there was a lot of spare time in my summer at Stanley Lake, I filled it with watching and listening and felt no need to create activity, to run around, to have a radio playing. So one day in early June, with nothing else to do, I walked down to the shore in front of the cottage and sat down on the sloped dirt just to the right of the dock.

It was easy to sit there and just watch the waves or wavelets, more frequently wavelets on a lake that small, wash up against the dock posts and shore. A glance upward might catch a hawk circling over the trees across the lake. There was always something to see.

So I sat and watched water, turtles, breezes, birds, trees, and bugs. Sometimes I heard a distant human voice or someone starting a car. Time passed slowly and evenly and peacefully.

I looked out at the dock, a few feet of water under its center section, and saw a large black shape slide along. I leaned forward to look more carefully. The shape hesitated briefly and then undulated again. It was a fish. A very large fish! One bigger than I would have thought could exist in Stanley Lake. Maybe an apparition? No, clearly a large fish. I leaned farther forward and slid as quietly as I could toward the water. Motion was detected, and the fish slipped under the dock and out the left side, away from me. I could see its sides, and its length. A northern pike!

So there was at least one big northern in Stanley Lake, and I had the good fortune to see it cruising past my bit of beach. Later that summer I would run into that pike - again.

13

Max was in his boat drifting by the cottage. "Bluegills are on the beds!" he shouted up at me.

"What?"

"Damn bluegills are on the beds. They're biting. Better get a rod and come on down."

I did. Three fishing rods with cheap spin casting reels stood next to the door on the front porch. I took one and went down to the big yellow boat, pushed off, and rowed slowly out to Max.

"Here," he said as I pulled up alongside. He handed me a fistful of worms. "Just dump them in the bottom of the boat. They'll live long enough."

"Okay." I impaled a worm on the hook sideways, slipping the point of the hook through its midriff.

"No! No! Jesus, don't you know nothing' about fishing?"

"I sure don't," I said. No one had ever taken me fishing.

"Swing that hook over to me. Slow."

I did. Max grabbed the worm and got it back off the hook and then slipped it onto the hook headfirst, at least it looked headfirst to me. The result was a worm body along the full length of the hook from the point to the eyelet where the line was fixed. He adjusted the bobber on the line so the hook was about two feet below the little red and white ball.

"So what is this about the fish being on the beds?"

"Means they're mating. Totally focused on sex. And food. Just throw that hook in the water and you'll catch a fish."

I made a clumsy cast, good enough to get the hook and bobber and sinker five feet away from the boat. The hook sank slowly with the weight of the sinker until the bobber supported both hook and sinker. I did know enough to watch the bobber because a fish biting on the hook would cause the floating ball to bounce up and down.

I wasn't prepared for the bobber to disappear below the surface. The fish didn't just nibble, it grabbed and swallowed. I cranked the reel and pulled a bluegill out of the water, a seven inches of fish. Beautiful, bluish, greenish, and even narrow bands of yellow coloring.

Max looked over. "See how damn easy it is? Just got to catch them on the beds!"

I didn't know what to do with the fish.

"Well you're gonna have to take the damn fish off the hook if you want to catch any more!"

The hook was embedded deep in the throat of my catch, and I spent minutes trying to get it out.

"The fish is a goner. It's dead! Just pull the hook."

It came out, ripping flesh as it did.

"See that wire mesh basket in the back of the boat. That's where you put the fish. Then hang it over the side."

My lessons in fishing were coming one step at a time. Max was a good teacher. I got the basket, put the fish in it, and draped the basket and its short line over the side of the big yellow boat, the line tied to the center seat where I sat.

Another worm This time I managed to get in on more or less the right way. Another fish. In about half an hour I had a catch of dozen and a half little bluegills, my first experience at fishing and a very successful one!

14

Some men are blessed with fathers who fix cars and clean fish. I was blessed with a father who read books and loved to hike in forests. So I never learned how to adjust a carburetor or clean a fish.

So, after my first big catch, the eighteen bluegills, five or six inches long, clumped at the bottom of the wire mesh bag, I had to scrape off scales and get rid of the head and entrails. Max showed me the weathered table, nailed to the trunk of one of the oak trees, the fish cleaning place.

I grabbed one of my catch, wet and slimy, and laid it on the table without a clue about what to do next. Max stepped up and pinned the tail of the fish to the table surface with his thumb and deftly began scraping the scales from tail to head, against the grain, with a serrated knife. The scales are overlaid from head to tail, so scraping from tail to head lifts and loosens them. The glinting scales, with a soft sheen, spread out on the table around the dead fish.

Then, in another swift motion, Max chopped of the head. The final part of the process was to slit the body along the belly. Prying the two halves of the body apart, Max stuck his index finger inside and slipped it along from back to front. The organs of the fish spilled out onto the table, and Max was done. He held up the gutted, headless, scaleless body and said, "Go get a pan or a dish. We've got have someplace to put these little suckers."

I ran to the kitchen and brought back an old plastic dinner plate.

Max stood back from the table and handed me the knife. "Okay. It's all yours." So I picked up another of my victims and clamped it to the table with my thumb. My efforts at scaling were not as effective. But I got the job done. Whacking off the head was a little harder, and I missed on my first try, getting just half the head. With another slice, I got it all.

Slitting open the belly was no problem. I had moment of squeamishness about sticking a finger inside to slip out the guts. But I did it. The came sloshing and sliding out in a neat small pile. My first cleaned fish

As with all manual skills, practice helped. After five fish I had a pile of heads and guts and scales on the small table, and I was getting faster and better. Max nudged me aside and scraped the table bare, dropping the unwanted fish remains in a bucket alongside the table. I started in again. Twenty minutes later I had eighteen fish ready to sauté.

15

Of course, never having caught or cleaned fish before, I also didn't have a clue on how to cook them. Max, surrogate father, showed me. A box of corn meal stood in the cupboard next to the sink. I shook some of it onto a large plastic dinner plate. Then spread it out. After rinsing the small bodies under a faucet, Max dipped each one in the corn meal.

While he did that, I was heating oil in a fry pan. Medium heat. A small amount of oil. Those were my instructions. Max finished breading as

I got the pan ready for our feast. We laid each fish in the oil and watched the bubbles around the corn meal. I was ready to sit back and let the fish cook. Max didn't let me.

"They're only a quarter inch thick! Flip the sonsabitches over!"

I did. The corn meal was a light brown. When I got the last fish flipped, Max told me to get the first one out of the pan. That's how long it took to get the white flesh tender.

We sat down, nine fish in front of each of us along with a fork and knife. The trick was to lay the blade of the knife along the spine of the fish and slide the meat away from the vertebrae and ribs with the fork. Doing this gently but quickly produced a small piece of fish, maybe three inches by one inch, filleted, and tanned with corn meal on one side.

I tongued the morsel tentatively. It was mild, almost sweet, flavored by the corn meal. I was hooked, as hooked on the flavor as the fish had been on worms. In a few minutes we were done. There wasn't much meat there. But the taste lingered, and I knew why Max and the others on the lake waited patiently to catch thirty fish or more. That was the only way to get a meal! We had just enjoyed an appetizer.

Summer
16

Max drawled out his philosophy of life one afternoon while sucking on a can of beer: "Eating, drinking, sleeping, screwing, and fishing. That's what life is all about."

He put the can down on the stump of a tree next to his lounge chair and looked at me. "That's what people like you don't understand. You get into all that crap about working and doing something significant. Bullshit! You work to make money so you can eat, drink, sleep, screw, and fish. Nothin' else."

I shook my head. "Max, that's pointless. It doesn't get you anywhere."

"Where's to get?"

"A feeling of achievement. Knowing you've done something worthwhile."

"Naw. That's okay for guys like you. Maybe you can do something important. I don't know. But I know I can't. And don't want to. I want to get up in the morning and fix eggs and bacon and potatoes. Then I want to get in the boat and go fishing. Sit in the sun and pull in fish. I can sit in that boat and drink a beer and chase those damn little fish all over the lake.

After I'm done with that, I eat lunch and take a nap. Then I go fishin' again. Doesn't matter if I catch anything or not. Have another beer. Come in and take a shower. Put on some jeans that don't smell too bad and drive over to Mattie's place. A bunch of us sit around and drink draft beer and shoot the shit. Guys and women. Sometime that night I can go off with one of the women and get laid. Then I go home and sleep. Get up the next morning and do it all over again."

"Don't you get bored?"

Max stared out across the lake, talking slowly. "Hell no! The fishin's always different. The days are different. In the winter I ice fish. I can change my brand of beer. Different folks show up at Mattie's every night. There's a couple or three women I can make out with. What's to be bored about?"

He paused and again looked over at me.

"It's people like you who need some kind of extra stimulation," Max went on. "You can't enjoy a beer and fishin' for more than a day or two. You can't shot the shit talk at Mattie's for more than a night or two. Then you got to have something else to do. Something else to talk about. We talk about jack shit. Nothin' important. Just cozy up in the bar and shoot the shit. Nobody cares what anybody else says. People have arguments and don't care who wins. Nobody gets mad. If someone gets mad, they don't stay mad."

Here was my Zorba! Right in the middle of middle America. Max spelled out his version of life more simply and better than I ever could mine. He knew who he was. He knew what his life was all about. Me? I was searching. And maybe my life would never be that simple.

17

One morning I started out on my occasional jog along the undulating dirt road around the rim of the lake. A quarter mile down the road, I saw a figure walking toward me. A female. We approached. She waved. I slowed.

The woman was in her fifties, walking down the middle of the road in a housecoat loosely wrapped around her and quite clearly with nothing on underneath.

"Morning!" she said.

"Hi."

"New to the lake?"

"Yeah I'm staying in that dark green cottage down at the end. Fred brought me here."

"Good man, that Fred!" She spoke with emphasis and gestured enthusiastically. The robe slipped open.

To me, a young man, it was not a pleasant sight. She had a flabby abdomen and sagging breasts. And even in youth there really is something more appealing about a half-hidden female body. She didn't care.

"I'm Marty." She reached forward to shake my hand.

I hesitated.

"Afraid of shaking hands with a naked old bitch?"

"Uh..no...not afraid. Just..well, I guess…"

"That's okay. Everyone around here knows me. They've all seen me front and back. There's a reason I don't wear those underthings."

I waited, not sure this was a conversation I wanted to continue.

"See, if you know the history of clothing, underwear was created to keep people from soiling their good outer clothes. In them olden days, there was not a lot of ways for people to clean their clothes. Didn't have laundries. Didn't have dry cleaners. So you had to make damn sure you keep your skirts and pants and shirts and dresses and that stuff clean. So they developed underwear to pick up the dirty stuff from the body. Well, nowadays we can clean all that outwear stuff real easily, so there's no reason to wear underwear. And I don't."

With that, Marty wrapped herself up again. "And there's nothing wrong with the human body. Mine's past prime, but so are most women over the age forty. What the hell! I'm not trying to attract you young fella!"

I smiled. "Okay." I reached out to shake her hand. The robe opened again, and I didn't know whether to look or look away. So I did both.

Off and on through the summer, I met Marty again on the road, usually in the mornings. She came to some of the weekend gatherings, dressed in a skirt and blouse, wearing topsiders or sneakers without socks. And always, clearly and obviously, without underwear.

18

Fred took me up north in Michigan for three days. We drove the back roads, looking at small farms, rustic houses set back among trees, and a few survivalist enclaves along the way. Barker stood on the front seat of the truck with us, turning his head from side to side scanning the scenery. I've always been fascinated with the interest dogs take in the outside world when riding in a truck or car.

We meandered, making up the itinerary as we went along. At an intersection, we looked around and decided which way looked most inviting. No map on this random journey.

No deep philosophical discussions either. A lot of silence. There was a lot to see and nothing to see. No great vistas or magical glens popped into view. Instead, there were miles of forest and miles of land which had been clearcut and was now covered in brush. Some were farmed in forty acre patches.

The trip was a respite from the days at Stanley Lake, and yet when we got back, I was happy to see the cottage again. We had a relationship, an intimate relationship, that cottage and me.

I unlocked the back door and walked in. I needed to relieve the pressure on my bladder from the last three hours of driving and walked into the bathroom, looked down at the toilet, and stepped back. A chipmunk floated in the water, drowned. Fred came in.

"Another thirsty little critter," he said as he looked down on the floating carcass. "See, the stupid things get thirsty, probably from eating some of our potato chips, and go get a drink from the toilet. Trouble is, they fall in and can't get out."

Of course, I had to remove the body. I did it with fireplace tongs and a plastic shopping bag. We buried the chipmunk under one of the oak trees and didn't mark its grave.

19

Max invited me to come meet George the Writer. That is the way he was known at the lake. George the Writer.

George occupied one of the few two-story houses at the lake.

One of the peculiarities of houses built at this and other lakes is that the usual "front door" faces the lake. That's because people want to have their living rooms and big windows toward the water and beach for the view. Consequently, everyone enters these houses and cottages through the "back door."

In the case of George's house, this back door, set seven steps above ground level, lead into a hallway. To the right, several down the hall, was a door into the kitchen and an eating area. To the left were the stairs to the upstairs.

Max barged in. "Hey, George, you home!"

"Well Jesus Christ yes! What the hell are you doing here?" The voice, high and whiny, came from upstairs.

"Got someone for you to meet. Guy might want to become a writer."

"Dumb shit." George appeared on the stairs, backing down, holding on to rails on both sides of the stairwell.

Max turned to me. "George used to be sailor. He always backs down stairs like that. Just like on the ships he used to sail."

George descended, turned, and looked me over. "You serious?"

"About what?"

"Being a writer?"

"I guess so. Right now I'm just trying to figure out what to do with the rest of it."

"Jesus Christ, don't take up writing! Most goddamed frustrating thing you could ever thing of to do!"

"George, show him your manuscript," Max gestured to George and then me.

"Oh, showing off the eccentric old writer, huh Max?"

"Come on George, just show him what you are doing."

I expected to be handed a manuscript, maybe in a box or bound in some kind of folder. George led us to the front room. There were built-in bookcases on two walls. One of the bookcases was filled with books, hardcover and soft, old and new, large and small.

The other bookcase was three-fourths full of binders. "There's the manuscript!" George pointed proudly. "I've been writing ten pages a day for most days of the year and for the last seven years. There's 41 volumes here! I think I'm up to about four million words!"

"How many books are these?" I pointed to the binders.

"One book, man! One book. It just keeps getting longer and longer. I can't finish it. There are thousands of characters. By the time I figure out one plot, some other characters bring up another plot. So I keep writing."

I was dumbfounded. Struck dumb. How do you respond to someone who has written the equivalent of two hundred books and thinks it is all one book!

"Do you ever edit?" I asked.

"No, no, no. Editing is for fools. I like to write. I'll get an editor when I am done with this thing. I think I can finish it in another two or three years."

Max glanced over at me. He was clearly proud of this prodigious talent living right at Stanley Lake. I didn't know how to respond. So I did the polite and stupid thing: I lied. "Gee George, this is fantastic. I hope you find a publisher."

"When I am finished, publishers will be beating down my door to get this into print! It is the greatest piece of fiction since War and Peace."

I didn't want to say anything negative. But it was evident that George was having one hell of a good time writing this monstrous magnum opus. There was no other explanation for the incredible output of words and daily, weekly, monthly, annual dedication to pounding on a keyboard. Having a good time writing was good enough for George – and me.

Sayings of Fred
Enjoy the process because most of the time the product isn't worth shit.

20

Sitting on the end of the dock, I dangled my bare feet in the warm water, absently looking out at the water, scanning the shoreline with a blank mind. Through the weeks here at Stanley Lake I was used to seeing the occasional ripples fan out when one of our fishy residents surfaced to snatch at a bug. In fact, that was one of the cues that fishing was favorable during these early weeks of June.

I closed my eyes for a moment, to rest them, and leaned back on my elbows. Then I heard it, for the first time, the small splash. Soon there was another. Using our eyes so much, we ignore the sounds of the world around us, and now I was listening to fish jumping, just a few inches, above the water to pluck an insect out of the air for lunch.

You see, fish are actually noisy, if you are willing to be quiet enough to listen.

Sayings of Fred
The world is made up of very small sounds.

21

Fred and Barker reappeared on a Tuesday. I didn't know where he had gone. He didn't volunteer any information. And I didn't ask because I knew, now, that it didn't matter. It was just idle curiosity on my part. I was where I was supposed to be this summer, and it didn't matter where Fred had been.

He showed up just before noon on a partly cloudy, warm, and humid Michigan day. The air was heavy. A light haze, a heat and moisture haze, shrouded the trees on the western horizon.

Fred greeted me and then walked around the cottage and then outside. Barker, once again, plunged into Stanley Lake in hope of swatting a fish bear style. Fred motioned me to come sit next to him in one of the three folding aluminum chaise lounges in front of the cottage. We seemed to be ordained to conduct our dialogues on these rickety supports with their weathered straps and tarnished aluminum tubing frames.

"Let's talk about death and heroism." He never approached a subject obliquely. Always right to the point.

"Okay."

"I'm going to start with some lessons I got from Ernest Becker's *The Denial of Death*. I didn't want to have you read this stuff here this summer. You have other things to learn and do. By the way, how is the fishing?"

"Pretty good, actually." I told him about my time with Max and the lessons on fishing.

"Good. Max is a good teacher on the lake." He paused and looked out over the water which was just slightly rippled, probably from a few swimming turtles and the remains of the wake of a rowboat. He paused to collect and organize his thoughts.

"This is going to be a monologue. I hope not a lecture, but a monologue. You don't have to respond. Just sit back and try to listen. I am going to compress a lot of Becker's writing into a few words and a short time. Then if you want to read it sometime, go ahead.

"As humans, we have a special problem. Becker thought that we were different from other animals in this respect. I'm not going to speculate on whether or not we are different from the great apes or dolphins or whatever. It doesn't matter. We have a special problem.

"Here's the problem. We develop language. We can symbolize things. That means we can create a virtual reality with words and pictures and other symbols. See we didn't need to have the high tech computer people show us how to create a virtual reality. We all were doing it in our heads for years.

"The problem starts when we create a self as we develop language and symbols. Little kids learn that there is an 'I' and it is different from Mom and Dad and other people. I am separate. Now this leads to this first problem which is an aloneness. When 'I' become real, when 'I' realize that I am separate from others, then all of a sudden I am alone in the world. No one else can ever experience my experiences. No one can ever really understand my meanings, my life.

"That's scary. Then something even scarier happens. If 'I' exist, then 'I,' someday could possibly not exist. In fact, it is inevitable. I am going to die. So I am alone, as in separate, in this world, and someday I am going to not exist.

"Well Becker says that if you really believe this and accept it, you go crazy. No one can live with the idea that you are really separate and alone and that you are going to die. So we spend most of our lives denying that we are alone and that we are going to die.

"That's why we are so fascinated with communication. We want to believe that we really can be understood by someone else. Oh, I don't mean that the other person can understand that I want a glass of milk or that I am about to make a left turn in my car. That stuff is easy. No, I mean that the other person can understand my hurt and bewilderment and ecstasy and hopes and dreams. So we talk and write and create poems and paint pictures and do everything we can to make believe that we are being understood.

"Now here is my take on something that Becker doesn't explore. The people who study communication will tell you that when you talk the other person doesn't really understand what you are saying. The other person is talking to himself or herself about what you are saying and interpreting it in his or her own terms. Meaning doesn't get carried from one brain to another like water in a bucket. Meaning is created in one brain from the symbols being sent out by another one. The meaning created may or may not have much to do with the meaning being symbolized.

"Okay. Then we also spend our lives denying that we are going to really die. We create all kinds of immortality. We build buildings and name them after ourselves. We write books and expect they will be read forever in the future. We make babies and expect them to carry some part of us into the future in their genes. We also hope they carry part of our spirit or soul with them.

"A lot of people can't or don't want to create some kind of immortality. So they just use anesthetics to numb their brains. Like alcohol. Or pot or heroin. Or they get addicted to sex because during orgasm you are, for a moment, immortal. Or they seek ecstatic union with the universe in dancing or drumming or something like that.

"And there is one great way to anesthetize yourself that gets approval from almost everyone. That is by working. Working hard. Working intensely. Working long hours. If you do that, you don't dream at night. You don't have time to think during the day. You are always preoccupied by plans and goals and problems. You are always problem solving and planning and devising. And you can make a lot of money doing that and achieve status and be admired by a lot of people."

This was quite a load to inject into my mind! I was following Fred, and it made sense. I could see how, in my own life, I was doing both. I was trying to figure out some way to have some of me go on living after I died. And I was also pretty good at numbing myself. At least I was in the past.

"Now here's something that's really important. I am going to move on to the ideas of Victor Frankl. He was a psychiatrist..."

"I know," I interrupted. "I read his book when I was in college. One of my professors wanted us to read it. Frankl was one of the Jewish survivors of the German concentration camps in World War II."

"Right. And one of the points he made in his book is very, very important. In looking back at the concentration camp experience, he realized that the people who survived were mostly people who had cared for others. They shared even a meager amount of bread with someone else. They comforted others even when they were tired, hungry, and hurting themselves. In the face of death, these people, the survivors were focusing on other people.

"Frankl and Becker both talked about heroism. Frankl's idea was that real heroism exists when you do something or you relate to someone in the full knowledge that someday you are going to die.

"Let me tell you something from my own experience. I have known a couple of people who were in their late eighties and they were still reading books and studying and learning. I kept asking myself: why? Isn't that futile? How can they ever use the information? Why don't they just sit back, soak up the sun, go to bed early, and eat whatever they want to?

"Well they were heroic because even though they knew that they were going to die, probably in the next few years, they still enjoyed learning. And there are other elderly people facing death who want to meet people and create new friends. A young person would ask: why? Why bother creating a new relationship when it only has a few years to go? The answer is that it is heroic. It is engaging in the basis of living a good life while fully knowing that death is right around the corner. Frankl learned that in the concentration camp. I learned it from some of my older friends.

"Real heroism is everywhere around us. There are only a few of those real heroes, but they are everywhere. They don't get medals. No one puts on a show to recognize them. Who are they? *The real heroes are the people who not only cope with but grow and emerge in a world that is constantly changing.* They don't cling to dogmas or rituals. They don't live out a story determined by their parents and teachers and mentors. They don't sit around and daydream. They also don't run around frantically trying to stay busy and appear important. For all those reasons, those real heroes are hard to spot. But they are there."

With that, Fred got up and went into the cottage, leaving me to ponder and wonder. Barker stayed with me. The lesson, I guess, is that even at my age, I should be living life fully. It's a cliché. But if I sit and actually think about my own death, sometime in the future, and then think about what I'm doing today and tomorrow, it makes sense. I am alone in this world. I will die someday. I will never be fully understood. I will never be immortal. People will know parts of me. Parts of me will live on. And that is the best I can hope for, Barker laid his head between the two front paws after yawning. He could care less.

Sayings of Fred
You will understand a lot about human behavior if you realize that most people are striving to become immortal or else doing everything they can to ignore the inevitability of dying.

22

The locals call them blow snakes. They live on toads that are abundant around the cottages of Stanley Lake. Scientists call them hog nosed snakes. Some people call them puff adders.

And they are hilarious -- once you see their weird display.

Approach a blow snake and it raises up into a strike position, looking like a small version of a python or some other venomous snake. The only problem is that the blow snake has neither fangs nor venom. It is harmless. But the pretense is good enough to scare away most people and many other smaller creatures.

The silliness of the blow snake happens if the harasser, me in this case, takes a stick and pokes at it. The snake rolls over and plays dead! The ultimate passive-aggressive creature in the wilderness!

23

Max had me drive him to Mattie's, the roadhouse. In the rural Midwest, at least in Michigan, there are bars spaced along state highways, often between two small towns. These are the places where locals gather to drink and talk. Most of the time the conversations are peaceful and fights rarely break out, usually when an "outsider" comes in and creates a problem.

So we drove in my Wrangler to Mattie's, and Max insisted I come in and meet "the gang." I did. Five were seated in big maple chairs, some with arms, some without, at a large round table off to one side of the room. "Max" called the gathered gang. He waved and bowed. And then he introduced me to the members of the gang.

Shelley, dressed in jeans and denim shirt, was suntanned and had a carefully "done" hairdo. She was, I found out later, a beautician and hair stylist.

Another female, fortyish and with short hair, was introduced as Pat. She didn't smile. In later encounters, she didn't smile. Smiling was not part of Pat's repertoire. Her arms were stout, muscular, but still feminine. She never had much to say, and said it in short exclamations or sentences.

Mike was seated to Pat's right. He made up for Pat's reticence. Mike laughed, smiled, rocked in his chair, and, with his red hair, was the stereotypical Irish jokester. Which he was. Most of his jokes were dirty, a lot of them involving priests, nuns, and altar boys. He also made a big joke of being next to Pat at every gathering so that they could be "Pat and Mike." In addition to his red hair, Mike's distinguishing feature was a trio of large warts or growths, pink, one on his right cheek, two on the left. Mike dressed in worn khaki slacks and a V-neck sweater with no T-shirt underneath.

With every joke or witticism, Mike poked Pat with his left elbow, and she returned the blow without showing either humor or anger.

Butch was a big guy, two hundred fifty pounds or more on six feet of frame, with a beard turning to gray and long hair tied back in a ponytail, the fringes of that hair tinged with gray. At that first meeting, Butch grabbed my hand, and I expected to be crushed. But he gave a solid masculine grip which I appreciated. He shook my hand and arm vigorously. Butch leaned back in his chair most of the time, holding a mug of beer in one hand and then the other, sipping occasionally. He leaned toward the table only to pour more beer from the pitcher into his mug. Butch dressed in biker garb even though he drove a pickup. I never saw him on a motorcycle and don't think he owned one. He just liked to dress that way.

Ernie was the direct physical opposite of Butch: thin, short, hair cut almost to the scalp. He leaned forward, elbows on the table, a glass of beer resting between his hands, and usually looking down at the initials, words, and signs scraped into the tabletop.

And so they sat, occupants of the round table at Mattie's, talking about the weather, fishing, who was getting divorced, who was living together, and who, getting divorced, was already living with someone else. There were mild arguments about the best bait for catching bass, the relative merits of the two kinds of draft beers offered at Mattie's, how to grow sweet corn, and the perpetual country folks disputes between Ford and Chevy owners. With an occasional Dodge Ram throw-in.

I sat, listened, and observed. I didn't have anything to say about what they talking about. I sipped on a beer, sat back, and enjoyed the talk about central issues in the lives of these people. Easier than another lesson from Fred on this day!

Around ten o'clock, Max, sitting next to Pat, put his hand on her shoulder, leaned toward her, and whispered something. She nodded. They stood up simultaneously, scraping their chairs across the rough wooden floor. Max smiled and gave me a thumbs up. Everyone seemed to know what that meant. Max and Pat slid out the door. The conversation at the table went on.

I got up to leave a few minutes later. I gave a short wave, the group responded with a variety of waves, shakes, and nods, and walked to the door. Shelly followed.

"You're cute!" Shelly winked at me in the parking lot. "Come on and sit in my truck for a while." She grabbed my hand, and we walked over to the bright red Ford 250 at the edge of the gravel parking area.

The doors were unlocked. I got in the passenger side; Shelly on the driver's side. "So you're from Chicago, huh?"

"Yes. A year or so ago. I've been out west since then."

"Whereabouts?"

"Moab, Utah. And Flagstaff, Arizona."

"Pretty country?"

"I can't say it's pretty. Rugged. Beautiful. Wild sometimes."

"Not like here, huh?"

"No. I guess Stanley Lake is pretty."

"Yeah, there's some pretty sights around here." Her hand caught mine and held it lightly. She stroked the back of my hand and leaned over. At the same time, she put my left hand on her right thigh. And her right hand, freed of my hand, migrated to my left thigh. There was no question about where this was leading.

Shelly was a nice looking thirty-something, a little older than me. Her hair was blond, not natural, but not bleached to straw either. Her face was pleasant. Not beautiful, not pretty, but pleasant. She used minimum of makeup and was well tanned. Her eyes, a deep green, were set just the right distance apart, and a smile danced on her lips most of the time.

"Come on," Shelly winked. I kissed her. The glands were taking over. I was getting an invitation. Too obvious and too good to resist.

We necked for a while and slid closer on the bench seat of the pickup. My right hand reached over and touched her left breast, at which she twitched slightly and I thought I had screwed up, moving too fast. Wrong! She quickly unbuttoned her denim shirt and offered me her brassiered breasts. The heat was rising in both of us.

"Wait," I said, coming up for air.

"What's wrong?"

"Nothing. But let's do this right."

"What do you mean?"

"It's a warm night out. I've got some old sleeping bags in the Jeep. Let's do this outdoors."

"Is this some kind of kinky thing?"

"No. It's some kind of good thing."

"Well, okay." She wrapped her blouse over two nicely formed conical breasts, still brassiered, and we walked to the Jeep.

"Is there someplace we can do this without being seen?"

"I think so. In fact, right behind Mattie's here. There's a field behind some trees and bushes."

Grabbing the sleeping bags, I followed Shelly around behind the bar, past the garbage cans and big trash dumpster. We had a bright half moon, and Shelly found a break in the bushes, not really a trail, but a way to get through without being grabbed by branches. In twenty yards we emerged into a small clearing.

"How's this?"

"Great!" I spread the sleeping bags out, one on top of the other. Then I put my arms around Shelly and kissed her gently on the lips, a soft wet kiss.

"Wow! Where did you learn to kiss like that?"

"I had a good teacher."

I walked behind her and began a gently massage of her back, through the loose shirt. I pulled the shirt out from her jeans and continued the massage on her bare back and then undid the brassiere. Shelly arched her back and moved under my hands. "Oh my, you are good! Most guys just want to get to it."

She shed her shirt and brassiere as I circled around in front. We kissed and touched. She flipped open my western-style belt buckle and unbuttoned the top button of my jeans, quickly unzipped the fly, and reached for my penis.

Instead of rushing to the final act, we kissed and massaged and touched. The tempo varied. Sometimes we were passionate and rushed. Then we slowed down again, backing off slightly, laughing softly.

When Shelly finally dropped to the sleeping bags, I knew she was ready. We had sex. We had good sex. We didn't make love. Venus' teaching came back to me as we lay there, naked and relaxed, until mosquitoes discovered our warm sweaty sweet bodies.

Shelly rolled over and looked me right in the eyes, her face no more than a foot from mine. "I don't know who you are, mister, but you sure know how to make love. Wish you would teach some of the guys around here!"

24

Max was smarter than he let on. He did read, mostly fishing magazines.

There are, I now know, many different kinds of intelligence. Thank God! Some people have a kind of mechanical smarts. Others can learn about and understand how to grow things. Max was fishing-smart.

One day in early June he let me in on a bit of information that every good lake fisherman knows.

"Okay," said Max, "we been setting our bobbers to drop the hook about three to four feet below the water level. Today we're going to have to set them lower."

"Why?"

"Well let's just test this out. We'll start at three feet and if we catch anything we'll stay with that. If we don't, then we'll drop the hook a foot and try again. Keep do'in that until some little fishy bites on our worms."

We did exactly what he said and sure enough the first bites began with the hooks at five to six feet instead of three or four.

"Why, Max?" I asked again.

"Simple. You got to put your hook where the fish are feeding. They may be dumb, but they're not so stupid that they'll come looking for a hook and a worm. We gotta go where they are."

Max paused as the bobber on his line bounced slightly. With a deft two-inch snap of the rod, he set the hook into a bluegill and brought it to the surface. In the process of dislodging the hook from the side of the bluegill's mouth, Max went on. "The food for these little critters is mostly in warm water, but it's at the bottom of the warm water. Now you prob'ly think the water is all the same temperature, but it's not. The lake is warming up. There's a layer of warm water on top and cold water below. So we need to find how far down the warm water layer is. If we're too high, the hook is above the fish. If we're too low, then the hook is in the cold water and below where the fish are. Oh by the way, the place where the warm water ends is called the thermocline. That's all the science I know."

Max broke into his crooked smile. "Don't be no smartass now."

I grinned back and saw the bobber on my line bounce. A small flip of my rod handle and I had my first bluegill of the day.

As spring turned to summer, the thermocline descended until it was fifteen to twenty feet below the surface of the water and finally at the bottom of the lake. Now the bluegills could be anywhere. They are not bottom feeders. In fact I would find out sometime later that summer just the opposite as I caught fish above the water.

25

Somehow we got on to the topic of dying one night at Mattie's. What happens when you die? Where do you go? Seven of us sat around the big round table, each with a bottle of beer, no glasses. There were the usual offerings: reincarnation and heaven and hell the two most popular. No one at the table was a died-in-the-wool Christian with a strong opinion about heaven and hell. There were some conjectures on what hell might be like. Two voices were raised in defense of reincarnation, particularly reincarnation from or to the form of an animal. Mary Alice knew, for certain, absolutely and without question that she had been a squirrel in her previous existence.

Max and I sat quietly, I was still an outsider, allowed to sit in but not allowed to enter. If I did, eyes might roll to the ceiling or sneaky smiles creep onto faces. I was a Big-City Idiot who was being tolerated.

I did remember a conversation with Fred, however. He has just finished reading a book. In it, here is the description of an experience of Abraham Maslow, the humanistic psychologist, was described. Maslow had had a serious heart attack. In fact, he would die just a short time after that first heart attack. But in the interim, he talked about his existence as 'life after death.' Fred made a point of that. But we don't have to die physically or experience the near-death phenomenon. No. We can die in small and different ways during our lives. Nothing dramatic. Each time, however, we can remember that we are living 'life after death.'

Finally, Max spoke up. "Who the hell cares? Don't know anything about heaven or hell or any previous existences. I'm here. The beer is good. The table is steady. And I got an itch!" With that, he reached over and put an arm around Mary Alice. We knew what that meant.

I got up to leave. Said my goodbyes and walked to the door. Pat followed me. All the way to my Wrangler.

"Say, mister city slicker, I been talking to Shelly. Do me a favor, huh? Just give me a kiss?"

"Why?"

"'Cause you have now got a reputation around here. Shelly says you're the best kisser she ever had."

"I'm flattered. But I can't just going around giving kisses."

"Oh, come on. No hurt in it."

"Okay."

She moved a foot closer and leaned toward me. I leaned, and we kissed. I tried my best soft kiss, lips molded to hers.

"Wow! That's different." Pat stepped back. "Willing to come over to my place?"

And that invitation was obvious. I did have a reputation. Not the bad kind that promiscuous girls used to get in high school. A reputation as a lover. Thanks to Venus.

"No, really Pat. Can't do that. I appreciate the invitation, but I have to get back to the cottage."

"Okay." She pouted slightly. "You sure?"

"I'm sure."

That was the first of several encounters and invitations. From Pat and others. Two weeks later, Pat and I had sex, this time just off a slender trail jutting from a two-lane dirt road five miles from the cottage. I let my male libido take over. I needed to have sex. Heterosex, not masturbation. Would it be possible to make love again? Was that possible only with Venus? It obviously took a belief, something deep, from both people. One person couldn't make love if the other didn't know or understand.

So I became a teacher, for the first time in my life, of a woman. Shelly and I had sex fairly regularly. There was more to her than the bleached-blond hair. By August we were making love.

26

Supposedly the point of fishing is to catch fish. That was my error. It's true for some people, but not all. I discovered three levels of fishing at Stanley Lake.

In fishing on a small lake out of a big, comfortable rowboat there is a simple satisfaction in just sitting in the boat and throwing a line in the water. Of course, that is just too stupid for actual activity. The next best thing is to put a worm on the hook, cast into the water, thinking maybe the bait will sink to the right depth, and then sit back and wait. Nothing happens. But that is okay. The sun shines intermittently as the big white clouds drift by. It's cooler on the lake than on shore or in the cottage.

After some time and no bites, the fisherman -- me -- reels in the line and lifts the hook out of the water. The worm is nice and clean. This is the level of washing worms.

Cast the worm into the water again and wait of ten or fifteen minutes. Another retrieval. At this point, the worm has begins to disintegrate. It's soft and spongy. In another cast it will flip off of the hook. So I take it off myself and try again.

Washing worms passes the time, and people on shore or in other boats think that something legitimate is going on in my boat. That is good enough for me.

In the next level of fishing, the fisherman casts the hook and worm into the water and again waits. This time, the bobber bounces slightly after a few minutes. Reeling in the line shows a hook with no worm! So try again. Same result. This is the process of feeding fishing.

It happens because small fish can munch on the worm in small bites completely avoiding the tip of the hook. The positive aspect of feeding fish is that the small ones will grow into big ones faster because of the feeding.

The final level is catching fish. Here the fish actually bite on the worm, impale themselves of the end of the hook, and can be brought into the boat, later to be eaten. After a month and a half at Stanley Lake, I found that I enjoyed all three levels of fishing: washing worms, feeding fish, and catching fish. It didn't matter to me.

Sayings of Fred
If your only goal is to catch fish, you will spend most of your life disappointed.

27

The group was assembled at Mattie's big round table on a warm evening. I had been accepted into the group even though it was understood that I was a temporary member. At least I wasn't put into the class of summer residents, the obnoxious people from Kalamazoo, Battle Creek and Grand Rapids who showed up in late May, spent weekends at the local lakes, disrupted the routine of the year-round residents, and then left again in September. No, I was in a special class. The occasional visitor from another part of the country, like a guest from a distant planet.

The discussion centered around a county proposal to pave some of the back roads in the area. Sentiment ran strongly against the idea. People liked the idea of having washboardy and rutty roads that kept casual stragglers from finding the cabins and lakes. In fact, the residents at Stanley Lake many, many years before took down the one sign at the beginning of their road which identified Stanley Lake Road. In its place, they put up, without county permission and also without county money, another sign: Dead End.

As the conversation moved languidly, as slow as the day had gone, I poked my index finger into my empty beer bottle. I twisted my finger around, twisted the bottle around my finger, and then tried to pull my finger out. It was stuck.

Embarrassed, I just sat there with the bottle on my finger, pretending to play with it. Pat was the first one to notice. He looked but didn't say anything. Then Shelly piped up: "What's with your finger in that bottle?"

"Guess I've got to confess." I actually blushed slightly. "I think I've got it stuck in here." I demonstrated by trying to pull the finger out. No luck.

Of course, the whole group laughed. No one pointed out how stupid I was, but I know they were thinking it.

"Well how in the hell you going to get it out?" Max laughed.

"I don't know."

Pat reached over and pulled on the bottle. My knuckle joint dislocated slightly and I winced. "Ouch! I don't think that is going to work."

"Ever had trouble getting anything else out of a hole?"

Uproarious laughter. I had to laugh myself. The situation was ridiculous, and I knew it.

There followed an hour of brainstorming. Someone suggested going outside an breaking the bottle. That got shot down because it could be hazardous to my health to try to break the neck of the bottle, right where my finger was stuck. They tried pouring some beer on the finger and around it into the bottle. My finger-cork blocked that. We twisted the bottle. We poured warm water and then hot over the glass hoping it would expand and free my finger. Nothing worked.

It was getting late, and I was in no immediate danger nor was my finger, so the group dispersed and I went back to the cottage. I slept fitfully that night, mainly because every time I turned over in bed the bottle whacked either the wall or the bed frame. So I woke up early, a little dazed, and still toting the beer bottle on my right index finger.

I did manage to fix myself a breakfast in spite of the handicap and performed a real comedy act trying to eat with my right hand – my left being useless - with the bottle in the way of the opposed thumb. Shortly after finishing the cereal, I heard a car approach and doors slam.

Pat, Mike, and Shelly walked up to the screen door and, shading their eyes, looked inside. "Hey man, we've got the answer!"

I let them in. "So what is it?"

165

"Well we checked with Mike's brother-in-law who's an EMT." With that Mike produced a small syringe filled with some kind of clear fluid. "We're going to lubricate that sucker!"

He grabbed my hand and looked at it closely. Guiding the needle of the syringe against the glass, avoiding my skin thankfully, Mike got the point of the needle an inch into the neck of the bottle and started to squeeze the syringe. Sure enough, material inside oozed, every so slightly, out of the body of the syringe and onto my skin. I could feel it.

"What's in there?" I asked.

"Oh it's just some of Shelly's spermicidal jelly!" With that Mike had to pull the syringe away and all three of them bent double with laughter.

Well whatever would work was okay with me. I rotated the bottle to spread the jelly around and tried to get the thing off. Still no luck.

"Wait! Wait!" cried Shelly. "That was only phase one. Now we got to phase two."

"What's that?"

"Raise your arms over your head and walk around for a couple of minutes."

I started to walk around the cottage.

"No. No. Walk outside."

So we trooped outside, and I walked toward the lake. Just then Max appeared.

"Now if that isn't goddamndest thing I've ever seen! A guy walking around with three of his friends and his right hand up in the air with a beer bottle on one finger. What in the hell are you doing?"

"Just following orders, Max."

I walked for another couple of minutes, and then Mike grabbed my arm. He pulled my hand down and the bottle slipped off! The spermicidal jelly and a slight shrinking of my finger from holding it up got me out of that fix.

I'll never stick my finger in any kind of bottle, ever again.

28

July 28th -- the date blasted into my memory -- was hot and muggy. The air misty. You couldn't see more than a mile, and the sky was light yellow instead of its intended blue. I spent the day in lethargic activity, trying to get going and not succeeding. Washing two dishes, a fork and spoon from breakfast was a major effort.

By mid afternoon large cumulus clouds began to build over the western sky. They loomed over Stanley Lake and finally, right around six in the evening, slid on over. An ominous darkness descended on the cottage. A storm was coming. A waiting, threatening stillness enveloped the lake.

I turned on a few lights but sat in the front room, absently but expectantly, watching the sky and lake. Then the first rumble of distant thunder sounded. Another and another. The weather gods were playing their huge drums in the evening twilight, and soon I saw the yellow-blue flares of lightning in the clouds, dancing from one sodden mass to another.

This storm was in no hurry. It roared and flared to the west and north of Stanley Lake, taking its time, building, raising clouds to thirty thousand feet and higher, sucking moisture from Lake Michigan, forty miles away, and rolling eastward at a pace in keeping with its huge size.

Then came the first clap of thunder, nearby, with a clearer and whiter flash of lightning, a ground strike. Still the cloud-to-cloud lightning persisted and the rumbles rolled around the evening sky. Another CRACK!, closer this time, preceded by a bolt from Zeus. No playing around for this storm.

I waited. A small breeze waved the branches of the oak trees and wavelets crept across the lake. Within minutes the breeze became a howling gale and the wavelets grew into waves, as big as a forty-acre lake could muster. Entire limbs of the oak trees whipped back and forth. Small twigs began to rip off and blow sideways across the yards. The storm slashed onto the lake, the trees, and surrounding cottages and homes. The lights went out, nothing new in this rural setting. Lightning probably hit a power pole nearby. Darkness gripped the area tightly. I could see only when the nature-created flashbulbs of lightning flamed, briefly and fiercely.

I thought I ought to feel afraid. Instead I was intrigued. The oak tree limbs were whipped by the angry wind. I could hear them lashing the roof of the cottage and each other above the din of the wind and thunder. Natural furies maintained their pace for hours, and I just sat engulfed by the noise and flashes.

Then, with a suddenness that was eerie, the whole thing was over. No more lightning and thunder. The wind subsided to a mild bluster. I walked out the front door and stood there on the wet sand. The clouds had broken and cleared out and a half moon silvered the trees and lake and sand and me.

A cold front blew through in those few hours, collapsing the dank humidity of the day and hurling it up, down, and sideways as rain. Now, with the colder air slipping into the place, the storm marched eastward and Stanley Lake returned to quiet.

I slept soundly that night. The air was clear. The cottage cool. I pulled the sheet and wool blankets over my shoulders and didn't stir until the first light of morning. When I looked out of the front of the cottage that morning, I saw the swimming float was missing. Turning my eyes to the right I could see it beached at the east end of the lake.

After breakfast, I launched the big yellow boat and rowed down to the float, lassoed it, and, with much heaving on the oars, dragged it back to the cottage. The bobbing created by the storm's waves frayed the anchor rope through. With the float resting on the shore, I waded out and then swam through a few weeds to where I thought I had anchored the float. There, a foot under water, floated the end of the yellow polypropylene rope. Returning with the boat, I pulled the rope and anchor out of the muck and moved them to shore. Rooting around in the storage shed, I found more rope and had the float anchored again within the hour.

And that was my major accomplishment of that day.

29

Max drank beer. After an hour at the big round table he went to the bathroom a couple of times an hour after the first three bottles. We sat at the dark brown, beat up, carved-on, but solid table, him drinking his beer and me just sipping on mine. Max drank three to every one of mine.

Having drunk several glasses of water before coming to Mattie's that night, I developed a quick urge to empty my bladder -- just about the same time that Max felt the call. We went to the men's room together.

There was only one urinal.

"Old farts go first!" Max said as we went in and let the door slam shut behind us.

Then I noticed something for the first time. Max was only about five feet three inches tall. Short. The urinal was slightly above waist high to him.

"You know why some urinals are high and some low?" he asked.

"No idea." Between Fred and Max I got into the darndest conversations.

"Well, I'll tell you," Max went on. "There's no building code on urinals. So it's the plumber. A tall plumber puts the urinal up high where he can piss in it without splattering the floor. A short plumber puts it down low so he can get his pecker over it. Damndest thing! George Appel put in this urinal twenty five years ago, and George was about six foot four. Look at the damn thing!"

He pointed. It was high. So Max unzipped and got his equipment out. It was about six inches below the rim of the urinal.

"Watch this!"

Max stood back and held his penis at an upward angle. He let fly. The urine arced up and into the urinal.

"Sonofabtich I'm good!" He chortled and the result was a wavering flow of yellow fluid some of which missed the urinal.

The stream ended.

"Why don't you just use the toilet, Max?"

"Hell, that's no fun." He zipped.

I stepped up to the urinal and performed my mission in the usual style trying to ignore the wetness on the floor.

30

Nature requires the human adapt to its rules. Usual routines and rituals sometimes do not work.

One evening, two hours before sundown, I walked down to the dock. Another hatch was occurring. Insects hovered an inch above the surface of Stanley Lake. The bluegills and perch were leaping out of the water to snatch the bugs all across watery acres in front of me.

Time to do some fishing! I took the stairs two at a time going back up to the cottage, grabbed the fishing tackle box and one of the poles and headed back down to the big yellow boat. The line swung off a post of the dock, and I was launched into what looked like a fisherman's dream. Fish were feeding, leaping, hungrily snatching at the insects.

The standard small hook, used for fishing with worms, came off as I snipped the leader with my knife. In place of the hook I tied one of the few flies in the tackle box. I was no fly fisherman and had never, in fact, fished in Colorado or Utah. But I knew that these fish were snapping at insects, and I needed something that looked like an insect. So the fly.

I set the hook close to the bobber because the fish clearly were close to the surface. I cast and waited. Nothing! Bluegills and sunfish leaped all around the boat and me and the line in the water. Not a bite! I cast again. Still nothing. This was crazy! These fish were in a frenzy, and I couldn't get one to even look at the small fly tied to the end of the leader.

Then it hit me. There were so many bugs above the water that no self respecting fish was going to attack a fly on the water or below it. I had to hold the fly above the water. Which I did. Within a minute, I had a nice size bluegill on the hook. Taking it off and putting it in the wire basket, I tried again. Another catch. And another and another.

I was 'fishing' above water! I was 'fishing' with a fly suspended an inch above the calm water and actually catching fish! Soon I had a stringer of nice bluegills and one perch. I learned, again, that we need to adjust our methods and our thinking to what is happening in the real world of nature.

Sayings of Fred
The more you are able to adapt, the less you need to control.

31

Fred returned on Monday. Barker, of course, arrived with him and initiated his 'fishing' activities immediately.

Fred suggested going camping at one of the state campgrounds along Lake Michigan. I was ready for a change from cottage life. It took me a little over half an hour to get ready. We pulled out and headed north and west, arriving at Orchard Beach State Park four hours later, having stopped for lunch at one of those small town restaurants which serve the finest hearty, not exquisite, cuisine. Every time we made a stop like that, Fred started a conversation with someone shortly after our arrival, and the conversation evolved so that friendship followed. Fred had the names and addresses of hundreds of people, good and ordinary people, all across the Midwest and desert Southwest.

The park was deserted on this Monday, the weekend campers having left the afternoon before. We drove into the park and picked a campsite at its southern end. The tents went up easily just behind a small dune, maybe three or four feet high at most, with short bushes spaced far apart. From the campsite we could hear the waves slapping the beach sand. This was a new sensory experience to me, although I had camped alongside streams before with the sound of the rushing water.

Having settled in, we hiked, barefoot, along the beach for a mile or more until we came to a small island out in the lake, and then we waded out to the island, the deepest water coming to my crotch which was somewhat above Fred's waist. Barker, trustworthy companion, waded out as far as he could and then swam, effortlessly, alongside us until the depth diminished and he could put his paws on the sand below.

A grove of trees grew on the island, and we wandered out to its western edge where all of Lake Michigan spread to the horizon, Manitowoc, Wisconsin being somewhere on the other side. We sat. We watched and listened to the waves, small ones, washing ashore.

I was becoming more and more tuned into the sights, sounds, and smells of this natural world. I could turn off my monkey brain, the chattering internal conversations, more and more easily.

That evening, after a dinner of canned tomato soup and grilled cheese sandwiches made over my one burner camp stove, we built a small fire on the sand about fifteen feet from the water's edge. Just before sunset, the great Lake Michigan was calm. There were no waves. There was no sound other than the gentle crackling of the fire.

A sunset over a big lake is an orange wonder. The moist haze over the lake, the water evaporating from the lake producing that haze, refracts the rays of the sun, and it becomes a big orange ball near the horizon. In mid-summer, when we were there, sunset takes a long time, and then there is an afterglow, long past the time the sun disappears, until darkness envelopes the campground. I threw an occasional twig on the fire, just enough to keep it going.

We sat in the dark. Stars dotted the skies through overhead haze. Out toward the horizon looking through thicker haze, they faded, although in the intermediate sector, between overhead and the horizon, the stars twinkled most vigorously. Barker lapped up some lake water and retired to a prime spot near the fire.

I turned to Fred. "The weather is going to change tomorrow."

He sat silently for a while. "How do you know?"

"I don't know how I know."

"Sit there and don't think. Just let it come to you."

171

So I sat. And sat. Then it did come. "I heard the water change. The waves are a little bigger now. I can hear them. I think that is the beginning of something."

"We'll see," said Fred.

I more or less forgot my prediction and the exchange, mesmerized by the sounds of the fire and waves and the warm night air.

The next morning I poked my head out of the tent. It was cloudy. Two foot waves were stomping on the beach. The weather had changed. By listening, tuning in, being aware, somehow or another I got the message the night before.

We broke camp later that day when the rains began. No sense in sitting in tents on the beach when we had a dry cottage back at Stanley Lake.

Sayings of Fred
Intuition is just listening to subtle signals.

32

The conversation at Mattie's sometimes produced stories, oldtimer's stories. Max and Pat were good at telling them. This was the one time when Pat was animated at the table, although she still did not smile.

Max's favorite, told at every third or fourth meeting of the group, was about the winter that Stanley Lake froze over but the ice was not thick. It snowed for several days, covering the ice with a pure white blanket. A deer, seeing something across the lake, decided to walk across. It fell through the ice. Every time it put its forelegs on the ice, the sheet crumbled beneath them. Max and three of the other year around residents of the lake saw the deer trying to get back up on the ice.

They knew it was impossible for even one person to walk out to the deer, much less two or three. So they stood at the edge of the lake, talking, trying to figure out what to do. Finally the three decided to drag the big yellow boat, my favorite vehicle, down from its winter perch and slide it across the ice. The big yellow boat was flat-bottomed for all practical purposes. They got the boat onto the ice, and two of them, one being Max, got in and poled their way out to the deer. They managed to lasso the animal and drag it, on its side, onto the ice, and then pole the boat and deer back to shore. There the deer stood up and ran off with a piece of anchor rope around its neck! A year later Max swore he saw a deer with a length of yellow polypropylene rope around its neck.

There was also the story of the old lady at McGregor Lake who burned up in her shack when it caught fire. It was full of newspapers and magazines. The shack burned and smoldered for three days according to the story, probably exaggerated through the years.

And there was the crazy guy who ran up and down the centerline of state route M 89 stark naked until a sheriff's deputy got there. They had to lasso the guy.

There were always the stories of the big snowstorms and mild disputes over which ones were the biggest. The memories went all the way back to 1937 and included the big storm of 1950.

33

Nine large oak trees surrounded the cottage, growing up to sixty feet or more. Similar trees rimmed three quarters of the shoreline. One, in particular, in front of the cottage, only a few feet and leaning out from shore, provided an inspiration as I looked out from the screened porch.

For all my years I had seen pictures of rope swings, suspended from the large high branches of brawny trees, and the trajectory of the swing begins on land and loops out over water. People in these scenes in television commercials and motion pictures grab the rope and swoop out over the water, release their grips, and splash, laughing and flailing, into the water. I wanted a swing like that.

That Tuesday was quiet at the lake. The neighbors were gone. I was alone on the southwest corner. No one was out in a boat or walking along the road. I would make that swing!

Easier decided than done. The first and biggest problem was to loop the rope over a branch that was about twenty feet above the ground. The second and minor problem was to find the right rope, solved within an hour by driving to the hardware store and buying fifty feet of half-inch nylon rope.

The obvious way to get the rope over the branch without climbing was to throw a lighter rope or twine up and over. That supposedly easy maneuver turned out to be very, very difficult. I tied an anchor for one of the boats to some clothesline we had in the garage. Throwing the anchor, which probably weighed only a few pounds, turned out to be an athletic feat. If I got it high enough, the anchor fell back to the ground at my feet without going over the branch. If I threw it outward toward the branch, I couldn't get it high enough. Of course there were other trees and branches so there was no clear shot at the target branch. I spent forty five minutes involved in that futile exercise.

Climbing a ladder would also work, but we had no ladder taller than ten feet and that was a rickety old step ladder. No option.

So I sat and pondered the problem like a chimpanzees given a stick and some string to try to get a banana out of reach, but I didn't scratch my head chimp style.

I looked for creative solutions. Soon I had it! I got the stepladder and leaned it against the eaves of the cottage roof and climbed up on the roof. Now I was twelve feet closer to the limb and at a better angle. The only thing I had to worry about was falling off of the roof. My first try failed, but I maintained my perch.

One minor difficulty came from this new tactic. I had to climb down from the roof to get the anchor and rope. Which I did. Four tries later I had the clothes line over the limb. I tied the end of that line to the nylon rope and pulled it over the limb. A simple slip knot made a loop in the end of the nylon rope, and I pulled the free end until the loop closed around the branch. All I had to do was cut the nylon rope and I had my swing.

I tied a piece of four-by-four, about a foot long, to the rope and swung it out over the water as a test. It looked like it might work. Into the cottage for a change into swim trunks and I was back at the tree in a few minutes. Here a bit of intelligence and caution overtook me. I walked into the lake in front of the tree, limb, and swing to make sure that the water was deep enough. It was.

As a last preparation I sawed off a twelve-inch length of old rake handle and tied it to the rope about five feet above the ground. That was my handgrip.

I walked back a few feet holding the length of rake handle as it swung upward over my head in an arc. With a running jump, I swept out over the bank, over the shallow water at the nadir of the pendulum swing, and then upward as my momentum slowed. And I let go, flying out into the deeper water, dropping into it butt first. I didn't touch bottom. My swing was a success.

I played with the swing for more than an hour that afternoon. And on several more afternoons that summer.

34

So I had become a fisherman. I could catch bluegills about as regularly as Max. I learned the art of floating around on the lake, adjusting the depth of the hook-and-worm until the little creatures bit. And I could clean them.

But I had more to learn. Max and I finished our morning expedition simultaneously. He walked a over with a stringer of twelve fish, plus or minus a few. I had ten resting, sloppily, in the bottom of the wire basket which had been slung over the side of the big yellow boat for the last hour.

"You still cleaning and cooking those little suckers the way I showed you?"

"You bet."

"Well let's move on to a higher level here."

"Like what?"

"Here's how you filet a bluegill."

If you have never caught or even seen a bluegill from a small lake in Michigan, you cannot imagine how ludicrous it seemed to try to filet them. They are three to four inches longs, head to tail, for most of the year. There are a few bigger ones early in the spring. But by the time I had caught my ten, they were three to four inches long, two to three inches wide, and about three-quarters of an inch wide.

Max produced a thin curved knife from his tackle box. "Put one of those critters up there on the cleaning table." I did.

Max sliced off the head, gutted the fish in his usual efficient way. Grabbing the scaling tool, he scraped the scales from the body and rinsed it quickly in the clean but stale water in a bucket next to the table.

"Okay," he said, "Watch this."

The thin curved knife slipped into the flesh of the bluegill just behind where the head had once been attached and moved toward the tail. It carved out a filet, roughly circular, an inch and a half in diameter. Max flipped the fish over and repeated the operation.

"See? Simple as can be."

As always, simple to the practiced and skilled. My attempts at filleting were not quite as good. By the tenth fish, I did get two decent hunks of meat with no bones. Twenty filets from ten fish lay in a small pile on the cleaning table. I hadn't realized how little nutrition actually came off of the bluegills. But certainly the eating was easier, and with some corn meal breading on the outside, the filets created a decent serving of hors d'oeuvres.

A bluegill dinner required a supplement of rice and vegetables. A lot of them.

35

Fred told me that sailing on water, soaring on the air, and skiing on snow were all similar: each depended on natural forces and so they were great teachers. I found that out in sailing the Sunfish sailboat on Stanley Lake.

Fred gave me some instructions in how to sail, claiming that it is best learned by practice. He was right. The theory is fairly simple. If the wind is directly behind the boat, let the sail out as far as possible. That is sailing before the wind or downwind. The boat goes faster sailing at an angle to the wind with the sail set out at an angle to the hull. A few trials and errors and the sailor gets a sense of the right angle for the existing wind and the direction he wants to sail.

The trick is sailing into the wind. You can't do that directly. Tacking means sailing at an angle to the wind in one direction and then turning the boat sharply and heading in the opposite direction. The result is a zigzag path across the water but generally upwind.

A Sunfish on a small lake is the best way to learn. If worse comes to worse, the boat can be paddled back to the cottage or the sailor can get out in shallow water and drag it back.

Within a week I was a decent sailor. I goofed on occasion and made a bad turn or forgot to change the angle of the sail to the hull. But I could sail out in any direction and make it back to the dock in front of the cottage. A few times I rammed the shore and once smacked the dock.

The abrupt braking emphasized the physical element in sailing a small boat. The sailor is tightly linked to the boat and the water. As the boat heeled under the force of the wind, I leaned outward. When the wind lessened or stopped, I had to move my body back in toward the centerline. And all of this happened while holding the line that controlled the angle of the sail and while steering with the tiller. The result is a gymnastic set of leg, torso, and arm movements going on continuously while sailing.

What Fred didn't tell me was that sailing was a simple and efficient way to get into the here-and-now. It requires constant attention because the wind shifts across the water, particularly when there are clouds casting shadows on the water. Gusts and calm times alternate. You can see a breeze coming across the lake by a swatch of ripples move towards you.

Soon all of this becomes intuitive. No thought required. In fact, thinking gets in the way as it does with most athletic and physical activities. I could feel the breeze on the sail and the movement of the boat. I could predict when it would happen and what would happen -- again without thinking.

After a few minutes on the water, I melded with the boat. I sensed its motions. I felt the wind intuitively. I sensed its moods and changes. So here it was again. Sitting in the desert on a solo, I merged with the earth, the sand and rocks and cacti. Being with Venus, I could put away plans and goals and just exist in the moment. Now, sailing the Sunfish on Stanley Lake, produced the same effect. I was learning something.

Hours of sailing ended up in a luxurious fatigue, an experiential smorgasbord of physical exertion, exposure to the sun and wind, and a complete cessation of thinking.

There was muscular fatigue, parched skin, and an empty mind.

36

A luxuriant growth of weeds spread across the beach in front of the cottage. Sunny days and warm water grew a crop of slimy leaves that tangled my legs and dragged me down as I swam to the float, thirty feet away from shore. Of course, they wouldn't really drag me down, but two times my feet did get wrapped in the weeds. I could stand, about chest deep, in the water so I couldn't drown. But the feel of the leaves was really slimy -- creepy in the lingo of my youth.

How to get rid of the weeds? I approached Jack, my next-door neighbor to the south.

"Jack, is there some kind of chemical we can use to get rid of those darn weeds?"

"There sure is, but it's illegal. Poisons fish and turtles as long as it lays around. And that can be for a week or so."

"Well how do you keep the weeds down in front of your place?"

"Here. I'll show you." Jack walked to the cottage and pointed down the slope. There, laying in dense ground cover, was an old rusted set of bedsprings. "See that?"

"Yes."

"Well what you do is drag that down to the beach and then you drag it back and forth across the weeds. That'll uproot most of them. At least is shears them off down at the level of the sand."

So I slid-scrambled down the slope to the bedsprings and, sure enough, there was a length of dirty half-inch rope tied to two corners of the springs Yanking and struggling, I got the springs down to the water's edge and then into the sand.

Dragging that contraption was hard work. I pulled. I sweated. Back and forth across the twenty feet of beach front. Sure enough, the weeds pulled out or got cut off. They floated to the surface. I grabbed a leaf rake, up next to the cottage, and water-raked the leaves and stems to the shore, then heaving them up the slope.

I needed a break after half an hour and got several long drinks of water. Then back to my labors. By noon I had a sandy beach again, at least out to waist high. Beyond that, I couldn't drag the bedsprings.

After lunch, I carried one of the cheap folding chaise lounges down to the water. The day was hot and humid, so I sat in the water on the chaise, my butt in the water, my body in the spot of shade of the overhanging oak tree.

Asking a simple question of a neighbor gave me an answer. I didn't have to solve all problems by myself.

Sayings of Fred
Smart people have to ask dumb questions in order to learn.

37

The big yellow boat drifted along the northern shore of the lake, opposite the cottage, along a section of lake shore with no cottages. Just big oak trees and an occasional maple. My line was in the water, the bobber suspending the hook fifteen feet down. This a deeper section of the lake.

The fishing had been bad for a week or so. Bigger bluegills were gone, most of them on Max's hook, a few on mine. There was lots of good fish food in the water, and no fish needed a dessert of worm at this time of year.

I really didn't care if anything bit or not. The day was pleasant, a temperature in the mid 70s, a few clouds scooting by overhead, the sun bright but not overly warm.

Then the bobber dropped out of sight. Plunged into the depths of Stanley Lake. Usually this was a sign of a snag. The hook would get caught in something on the bottom of the lake. Snags are a pain. Half the time you pull and break the line. The other half of the time you drag up some large object or a load of sea weed.

I pulled, and whatever was on the other end of the line slowly came up toward the boat. Cranking the reel slowly and raising the tip of the arced rod, I lifted the load. Surely it must be a tire or something just as big! It weighed at ton.

Pull on the rod, watch it bend, lower it slightly, crank the reel. Repeat the process, a few feet of line at a time. Then I saw the bobber which meant there was another fifteen feet of line to go. I pulled, lowered the rod tip, and cranked until the bobber was at the tip of the reel. Something was still down there dragging the line.

I pulled the tip of the rod into the boat and slipped the bobber off. I had to dislodge whatever it was hanging on the hook. The lifting and cranking went a little easier now. Line slipped through the eyelets on the rod and onto the reel.

I had be close to having this load of seaweed or tire near the boat. I pulled on the rod again and leaned over the side of the big yellow boat. There, three feet below the surface, was the big northern pike! I had hooked the monster fish of Stanley Lake. I was shocked and got nervous immediately.

No need to. The pike took one look at me, shook his head, broke line, and descended once again to his home in the deep. Now I understood the proverbial "one that got away." A good story. No trophy.

38

On a Tuesday morning I drove the Wrangler into Hastings to buy groceries for the week. The route from Stanley Lake to the state highway wound on a zigzag of dirt roads, one-and-a-half lanes wide, through heavy woods. An occasional clear cut scarred the landscape on one side or the other, but those areas were just twenty acres. Among the woods were small farms and some rural home sites, mostly older houses with pickup trucks parked in front.

I drove slowly because of the narrow roads and sandy ruts and made a left turn onto the road that would finally get to the state highway. As I turned and drove another thirty yards, a large black bird, straddling the humped center of the roadway unfurled its wings and walked, then loped, beating slowly, until it took to the air with a wingspread that seemed almost as wide as the road itself. The great beast stroked the air gaining speed and altitude slowly, rising above the trees and turning to the right disappeared over the branches and leaves.

A turkey vulture roused from its feeding as the noisy Jeep approached. Stopping the Wrangler, I could see, just ahead, the carcass of an animal, probably a raccoon or woodchuck. I sat there for minutes, marveling at the events available to the casual itinerant on the back roads of Michigan.

39

Fred and I had a slow comfortable conversation one evening sitting in the front room of the cottage, away from the mosquitoes swarming around outside. The talk drifted from one topic to another.

At one point, Fred said something that stayed with me for a long time: "The thing about this place," he said looking at me, "is that the people here are living on the margins of society. This is out of the mainstream. And these folks want to be out of the urban, money-chasing mainstream."

He paused to look out at a solitary boat, putt-putting along with a trail of whitish blue smoke behind from the two cycle engine.

"Lots of creatures live on the margins. Deer prefer to live in a wooded area but with open meadows close by. On the margin between forest and meadow. Max has probably told you about fish feeding at the margin between warm and cold water in the lake. Turtles, obviously, live on the margin between water and land. Same for frogs."

Again a brief silence.

"And people have settled in places that are the margins between water and land. Or between sky and land, like on ridges. Look at where people build houses nowadays. Particularly vacation houses. Or resorts. They build them on or near mountains, on sea coasts, along rivers and inlets.

"If you look at sacred places, they often are on geographic margins. At the entrance to caves. At the foot of a mountain. On top of a mesa.

"So the people here at Stanley Lake are living on a geographic margin and on a social margin. They want to live their lives their own ways. And this is the place to do it."

Sayings of Fred
Some of the most interesting people in the world live
on the margins of society.

40

The big yellow rowboat provided a sensuous relaxing ride on Stanley Lake when there were gentle breezes. The three seats were far enough apart that I could put my butt between the rearmost two and dangle my legs over that middle seat and into the space between the front and middle seats. This was no way to fish but a great way to enjoy a moderately warm day on the lake.

I rowed to a place where I could anchor in shallows, stowed the oars, and then assumed my supine position. There were mini-swells on Stanley Lake and the boat bobbed up and down, a few inches from peak to valley. Breezes shift constantly in the summer. The direction changes ninety even a hundred and twenty degrees in ten minutes. The rowboat swung on its anchor rope, moving slowly to the east, north, or northeast and then back, perhaps to the south, southwest, and back.

Laying in the boat, looking up at the sky with its small early afternoon cumulus clouds, I was tranquilized by the bobbing and swinging. I merged with the random rhythm of the boat and the water and the breeze.

I breathed in the here-and-now during those minutes on Stanley Lake.

41

I swear I heard God laugh one night at Stanley Lake. No, I hadn't been drinking or smoking anything funny. I wasn't hallucinating from fasting. I was just sitting in front of the cottage just after sundown, no one around, when I heard a laugh, much too deep and resonant to have come from any human vocal cords.

Later, inside, I wrote this:
I thought I heard God laugh,

and I would like to hear it again:
at some small human foible, a delicate giggle;
at a cosmic joke, a universe-rattling rumble;
at my attempts at spirituality, a gentle smiling encouraging
chuckle;
at a huge obscenity perpetrated by a holy man trying to be God,
a rapturous howl;
at a holy joke, a snicker;
and at a prank, one of God's own pranks, played on you and me,
a guffaw.
Wouldn't it be fun to hear God laugh?
I think we need to listen.

Sayings of Fred
If God didn't have a sense of humor, how could we?

42

I was madder than hell. Somebody just around the curve of the shoreline had a radio blaring out across the lake. They laughed and screamed so loud that I could make out individual voices. Everybody on the lake knew these people who came up two or three times a year. Otherwise, their cabin sat empty.

When they arrived, they took over the lake. Their noise echoed back and forth across the lake. And there was nothing we could do. A few years ago, two residents approached the party of six who laughed the emissaries out of the cottage and off their property with the standard American refrain: It's a free country. Free even to impose on other people.

The following year, one year-round resident put her speakers out on her lawn and played classical music to counter the rock. That only motivated the six to increase the volume of their sound system.

So everyone sat back and put up with the noise that went on from late morning until well after sunset. It made me mad. I listened to small sounds and didn't want to hear this racket. And it made me even madder that there was no way to deal with those people. They listened to no suggestions or opinions from anyone outside their group.

I did come to one realization though. It was people with low self esteem, the ones who had no other basis for their self worth, who liked to impose their will on other through noise. In Germany, criminals are known as the "weak ones." Here the weak ones made noise with their stereos, outboard motors, motorcycles, and muffler-less cars.

Fall
43

Labor Day passed. The lake was busy and noisy that weekend. Some radios played loud enough to be heard along the shore. Boat motors chirped and barked from morning until late evening. People laughed. Maybe some cried silently in their small houses, but we couldn't hear them.

There are small wonders everywhere in the world. We hopped into Fred's pickup on the Wednesday after Labor Day and drove over to the Yankee Springs Recreation Area. We drove an intricate set of right and left turns to a straight road. About a mile down that road stood a sign, low and not very visible: The Pinery. Fred turned onto the dirt road where the sign pointed.

We bounced along through the usual stands of shrubs and small trees until we emerged into a stand of tall pines. Each tree reached at least forty feet in the air, and the canopy of their branches covered the entire area allowing only small patches of sunlight to fall on the ground. No vegetation grew on that totally shaded ground. No growing thing stood a chance of living much less prospering in the hallowed darkness.

It was a natural cathedral. The trees provided the vaulting. We got out and stood in the midst of this green ceilinged edifice. Three other vehicles were parked in the few acres of pines, but there were no sounds. People spoke softly, their voices muffled by awe.

There was no need to speak. It was a time to simply stand and look.

Sayings of Fred
Look for the small wonders of the world where you live.

44

As much as we try to predict events and control our world, the unexpected pops up, sometimes with a great good surprise. That happened a week later. I heard a vehicle drive up, and when I looked out through the screen door on the back of the cottage, there stood Venus!

"Hi!" As though I had expected her. As though this was the most normal, expected thing in the world.

"Hi!" Once again I felt inadequate -- but happy.

She walked up to the door, holding her backpack by one shoulder strap, and came in without need for invitation. The backpack dropped to the floor, and Venus kissed me.

All these weeks of masturbation. Of fantasizing. Of remembering and wanting her and using my good right hand as a substitute. Now she was here.

"Thought I'd stop by and see how you were doing up here in the wilds of Michigan!" Once again that infectious, honest smile as she grasped my shoulders and looked me right in the eye.

"I'm doing okay. In fact, I'm doing very well!" And I smiled back.

"Good. Fred told me you were here. I'm on my way to a friend's cabin in upstate New York. Thought maybe I could camp out here for a day or two!"

Of course she could! She could camp out here for the rest of my life!

We walked into the bedroom and created a nest for Venus. Sleeping bag piled on one of the beds, her favorite pillow, and an old wool blanket at the foot of the bed. Her 'security blanket.'

Then we sat in two big steel chairs in front of the cottage on a mild but humid evening. We talked. And we talked. Most of it trivial. Some important. It didn't matter.

The sky gradually darkened. That night, maybe because of the cold of the last few days, no mosquitoes attacked. The evening cooled but not uncomfortably, and we continued to sit in our hiking shorts and T-shirts, occasionally reaching out to touch fingers, to establish that brief physical contact.

We spent three languid days sitting in the sun once it reached up enough to warm us. We hiked. We took the big yellow boat out on Stanley Lake and drifted around. We drove into Hastings and had lunch in a small diner that served good food and allowed customer to linger over coffee or sodas.

Of course we also made love. Just once.

The Venus had to move on. She packed quickly and pecked me on the cheek. "Hang in there!" With that she was in her truck, backed out, and drove off down the rutted dirt road.

I felt let down. No, depressed. I wanted more, but there would be no more. Venus had to continue her work, whatever it was and wherever took her. I had to continue my journey.

45

The next morning I woke up in darkness. Looking at the electric clock, it told me that there should be light. There wasn't. I struggled out of the sleeping back and into sweat pants and shirt. Out in the main room I looked out and saw dimness. Not darkness but dimness.

It was drizzling. Up to this time the days had been sunny with some woolly lamb-like cloud occasionally slipping across the sky. Today it was cloudy and with a steady drizzle. Water ran off of the oak leaves and the cabin eaves. Everything was wet. My Jeep glistened with water on the hood and fenders.

Looking out front I could see the clouds almost touching Stanley Lake. Visibility had to be down to a quarter mile. The wetness was something between fog and drizzle, light enough that the lake water showed no signs of impact from droplets. Inside there was a pervasive dampness, and the cottage began to smell of cooking, oil heat, old furniture, and human occupancy.

I fixed breakfast without any energy. Everything took longer. Nothing seemed to be working quite right. I was depressed. Doubly depressed by the departure of Venus and the all encompassing wetness.

I tried reading by the light of a floor lamp next to the old couch in the living, dining, kitchen area. It was a struggle. I tried napping and that didn't work either. By eleven o'clock I pulled on a poncho, walked to the Jeep, and drove in to Hastings. The diner was full. The wet drove people indoors. No one smiled. Conversations were muted. I got a table in a corner and hunkered down. Unfortunately lunch lasted on forty five minutes even though I ate slowly and chewed each morsel twenty times are they taught us way back in elementary school.

I drove around aimlessly. Even stopped by Mattie's road house. Only two customers sat at the bar, both well known drunks. Eventually I had to go back to the cottage where I tried to busy myself doing some cleaning, organizing, and straightening. There is only so much of that to do in a cottage that consists of a bedroom bathroom, enclosed porch, and the dining, living, kitchen room in the center.

Existence went on that way for the rest of the day and the next two. The drizzle continued spasmodically. Where it wasn't actually coming down the west hung around and kept dripping from trees, structures, and vehicles.

46

On the fourth day the clouds lifted a little bit and nothing fell from the sky. But the wetness and dampness remained. Midmorning I heard a vehicle pull up. It was Fred in his truck. I look out the rear window in the kitchen. Fred just sat in the truck. He didn't move but was obviously awake and alive. Finally he climbed out and walked, very slowly up to the cottage.

I opened the door. "Hi, Fred!" I was so happy to see him. Anything to break the monotony of the past days. He just looked at me. No response.

Fred walked in and shed the wool shirt he was wearing. He seemed much older. "What's going on?" I was concerned. This was not the Fred I had know for part of two years.

"Well, I've got bad news. I'm afraid." He shook his head.

I waited. Nothing.

Then he looked up at me. "Venus is dead. She was killed in a head-on collision in New York. Some drunk crossed the centerline and nailed her truck. Not a chance in hell she could survive. Died on the spot."

Venus dead? No way. Human beings died. People died. Goddesses don't die. Angels don't die. Spiritual teachers don't die. Fred would never die. How could this happen?

I just stood there. Fred had no comforting words. I didn't have any for him. I fixed a pot of coffee, and we sat at the small table and drank our coffee. Not a word was spoken.

But my thoughts were coming a mile a minute. I wanted to be with Venus. I had wanted to marry her. At least be with her for the rest of my life. Then I knew, by myself, that that never could have happened. She belonged to all kinds of people. Many people. Not just me. So how could I marry her? Or hang around her? No way.

Then I felt the bottom drop out. I mean that literally. My guts sank. My lungs dropped to where my stomach used to be. My back collapsed. I was hunched over.

That's when the drizzle started again.

Later Fred told me that he had gotten the word from some mutual friends. Venus body was being shipped back to California where she had relatives. There were no belongings to take care of. The house in Flagstaff would be sold. Her truck had been totaled. She just disappeared.

Fred spent the night and took off early in the morning. The clouds and mist cleared. Stanley Lake was blue again.

47

The early September sun arced across the sky to the south. It doesn't work as well as a heater that low. Cooler weather encourages nap taking. So I laid down every afternoon, a little after lunch, on one of the two single beds and closed my eyes. Sleeping wasn't necessary, just some relaxation and a chance to let the mind wander.

Laying there, I heard a running rattling sound on the roof. At first, I thought it was a squirrel running from one end of the cottage to the other. They did that, jumping from one oak tree, using the cottage roof as a bridge, and then leaping onto another oak at the far end.

Then it happened again. But the sound ran from roughly the ridge of the roof to the edge. I drifted empty-minded and heard the rattling again. And again.

Curiosity got the better of this big male cat. I had to see if I could find out what was making the noise. So I walked out the back door and around to the side of the cottage. As I walked along an acorn bounced down the asphalt shingles of the roof and bopped me on the head!

So I discovered the source of the noise. Newton discovered gravity by getting hit on the head by an apple. I discovered the rattling noise by getting beaned by an acorn.

48

The next day warmed significantly. One of those beautiful eighty degree autumn days with a hint of humidity but none of the overwhelming wetness of summer. That evening, just after sunset, I launched the big yellow boat for one last time on Stanley Lake.

A few dips of the oars in the water and I was moving slowly toward the center of the lake. The water was still warm even as the air cooled.

I slid down with my butt on the bottom of the boat, head resting on one seat, and legs dangling over another. I looked up at the sky, now a deep blue with the stars popping into view a few hundred at a time.

Suddenly I was gripped with a terrible feeling of loneliness and anxiety. Fred's lesson of many months ago hit me in the gut. I was not looking at the present. The light reaching my eyes took centuries to get here. We had no idea what the universe was doing now, today. We could never know. The data took so long to get to us that we could only report on what had happened centuries and millennia ago.

Life seemed futile and insignificant. Why study anything? Why worry about the nature of the solar system? Why be concerned about anything beyond my guts and my glands. I wanted to be Max. And I knew I couldn't. That made me feel even worse.

49

There is a beginning of the end in every phase of life. Most of the time, we are unaware of it. This time I knew what was happening. The days were getting short. I woke up to darkness in the morning. The first real light slid through the oak leaves and branches around seven-thirty. The evenings were cool; the nights almost cold. It was time to begin closing up the cottage and heading back.

Taking out the dock was the first of a series of small steps that added up to the end of the summer, the end of my visit to Stanley Lake. The water was still warm in mid-September, although cooler than in July and August. Certainly, it was warmer than when I had launched the big yellow boat and put the new dock in.

The big yellow boat wallowed in the small waves. I untied it from the dock posts and pushed it toward shore. Clambering over the deck of the dock, I slipped into the water on the other side and pushed the Sunfish up on shore.

So I waded out to the last section of dock and lifted it off of the supports. It floated easily, and I pushed it toward shore. The wood drifted steadily and then bumped into sand in a few inches of water. The second, middle, section of dock followed. And then the innermost, the one resting on the shore. It didn't take much to lift the dock sections up onto the slope above the shore and slide them up, one at a time, well above the shore line.

There they would stay until next spring when someone else could face freezing feet to reconstruct the port.

The supports, the ones cut, screwed together, and positioned in May, lifted out of the muck with little effort and also floated to shore. They were no heavier than the deck sections. I dragged the supports next to the deck sections.

My next job was to pull the Sunfish up the slope, and that required muscle. I tugged and pulled on a line knotted to the stainless fitting on the bow and finally got it as high as I could. Walking back down to the shore, I swung the stern up to get it even farther away from the water, water which would turn to ice sometime in November or December.

I left the big yellow boat resting against the shore, its bow line wrapped around one of the small oaks on the slope. Maybe I could get in one or two more voyages before it was time to leave. That wouldn't happen.

That night a cold wind swooped down on Stanley Lake. The harbinger wind. Autumn was here.

50

Two days later, I sat on the lowest step of the stairs leading to the lake below the cottage. The sun shone brightly, an autumnal afternoon sun, already fairly low on the horizon, dropping noticeably each day as we approached the equinox.

The oaks had started to drop their leaves, although they retained most of them through the winter and well into spring. I saw a leaf floating, points up, looking like a small ancient boat, past me from left to right. Then another came by. A third drifted past, this one upside down, points down, rounded stem side up. Then another little boat. A steady succession of leaves came by.

I followed the latest one with my eyes and saw it move slowly around the edge of the lake, past the homes and cottages, and, amazingly, all the way around to the other side of the lake. It was so small that I lost sight of it. But in looking now to my left, I could this parading flotilla of oak leaves coming back around toward me. There was a continuous circle of leaves, moving counter clockwise around and around.

There was no wind, not even a breeze. Absolute calm lay on the waters. An enigmatic current carried the leaves circling in quiet dignity, from my perch to my right, around the curving shoreline, and back to my left and across from where I sat.

I was moved to write these words:

Small leaf ships sailing proudly
in front of me
making neither ripple nor wave
propelled by a mysterious force
-- not wind --
circling the shore
coming again by my station
not wavering or caring
a flotilla of brown oak leaves
in double column
going on and on
until the first strong breeze
then dispersed
and finally run aground.

51

It was a sweat shirt day. A sweat shirt with a long-sleeved T-shirt underneath. The temperature in the shade was only fifty degrees, and the sun provided no additional warmth. Cool was turning to cold, already in September. The hot steamy days were long gone.

I sat in the front room of the cottage with all its glass panels and read most of the day. There was nothing else to do. All the maintenance and cleaning were done. The dock was out of the water. The Sunfish stranded on shore. And on the prior day, I worked the big yellow boat up onto the shore. So there would be no more rowing, no more sitting in the big yellow boat feeling the small swells of Stanley Lake.

The sun sank behind cumulus clouds early that evening. I switched on every light in the cottage, the overheads and two table lamps, but a melancholy invaded the cottage and wrapped itself around me.

I poked my head out of the back door. The night air was cold. Cold and damp. There weren't many lights on down the road nor, as I walked to the front of the cottage, along the curving shoreline. I felt lonely and depressed. Where was Fred? I needed someone to talk to. I didn't need to go to Mattie's and sit around listening to the casual chatter. I needed real talk. Something of substance. I needed to talk about what mattered to me or even just listen to what mattered to someone else.

So I switched off the lights and crawled into bed early where I lay sleepless, listening to the silence of the night.

52

Fred arrived on a Friday, the fourth week in September. He settled in quickly, throwing his sleeping bag on one of the two beds in the bedroom, and we went outside to sit in the sun. The air temperature was in the low 70s, the humidity low, and only the slightest breeze blowing. Barker, perhaps demoralized by his fishing attempts, didn't go down to the shore. He parked himself in front of the cottage, in a spot of sunshine.

"Well," began Fred, "it's about time for us to give up the cottage. Pretty soon it'll be too cold to enjoy the lake. The color change will be beautiful around here. Although the oak just turn brown. There are some maples across the lake. They will do their usual thing. Red. Gold. Copper. All the usual colors."

"It's been a good summer," I said.

"Yes. I imagine it has."

We sat silently, the oak leaves barely fluttering in the breeze, only small ripple crossing the lake.

"What happened to you here?" Fred never came at any topic sideways. Straight on, direct, face it.

"Well," I smiled, "I learned that I could pull out the posts of an old dock and build a new one. And I learned how to catch fish and clean them. Even got fairly good at filleting bluegill."

Fred laughed his deep raucous laugh. "That's all good stuff. Was there more?"

"Yeah." On a more serious note, I continued. "I found out that there were lots of little sounds and noises out here. Things you could never hear in a busy, noise environment."

"Like what?"

"Like the sound fish jumping out of the water and splashing back in. The sound of acorns rolling down the roof of the cottage."

"That's good. Most people never get a chance to hear anything but their own voices, the voices of other people, and the noises of cars, planes, trains, printers, copy machines, telephones, furnace blowers, and all the other stuff where we live. Subtle sounds are drowned out."

"I learned some other things. I found out that it is important sometimes to just watch and wait. You can't force things. If the fish are hungry they will bite. If they aren't, they won't. I found out that just throwing a hook in the water and washing off the worms can be satisfying. In fact, Fred, there were days when I didn't want the fish to bite. It would have interrupted my good time on the water."

This time Fred chuckled. "I know what you mean. Sitting in a boat swaying and rocking! What a good time."

Then I blurted out: "I also know that I don't want to go back to Chicago. I don't want to get caught up in that job thing again. There has to be something else." I choked. The sudden emotion welled up from gut to throat, and I couldn't talk anymore.

We sat for a long time. No need to talk. Just sit and feel the air cool ever so slightly.

"You know what, Fred?" I paused. "I just realized this. I learned to feel my emotions here. I have run the gamut. I have felt really happy and really depressed. I got really mad a couple of times when things didn't go the way I wanted them to. I felt a lot of satisfaction on a couple of the jobs I did around the cottage. Strange, but one of the best was a solid good feeling when I spent three hours cleaning the door sill at the back door. And I had a couple times when I felt completely mellow."

Fred looked over at me. I went on. "Another thing that just popped into my head: I felt I was ready to die, I mean I could have died without regret, when I had those mellow feelings. Depression makes you think about maybe dying and ending it all. But in those really mellow times, I just could have sat back and let it all end right there.!"

"That's probably not so strange," Fred said. "Maybe what you experienced as mellowness is what Nirvana is all about. Maybe it is the best definition of what we would like Heaven to be. We can't live in that mellow state all our lives, but we can enjoy the times when it happens."

Saying of Fred
Learning is just an attitude toward experience.

53

We continued the conversation that evening after dinner.

"Let's talk about anesthesia," began Fred.

"You mean, like in operating rooms?" I was puzzled once again.

"No, let's talk about the anesthetics of everyday life. You ended your list of learnings this afternoon talking about emotions. See it took months in a quiet place like this, away from all the usual stress and commotion, for you to actually feel those feelings."

"That's true. I was pretty numb for most of my life."

"Okay, how did you get numb? How did you maintain it? What was the Novocain of the soul that you used?"

"Well, obviously one was work. When I worked, I didn't have time to feel much of anything. Of I would get frustrated sometimes if things didn't go right. Or I might feel good if I finished a job, and it turned out okay. But other than that, I really didn't feel much of anything."

"How about away from work?"

"One thing: if I worked hard enough and long enough, then I would be so tired in the evenings that I would just vege out. Sit there in a stupor watchin TV. Usually some sports thing on ESPN."

"Okay, so work served as an anesthetic during the work week. How about the weekends?"

"The main thing was to stay busy. Have something to do. I didn't want to be bored. I'd play tennis. I'd find someone to go to a move. I'd go out to dinner with Andrea. Maybe we've had sex."

"Interesting. You know what everyone asks on Friday afternoons at work? 'What are you going to do this weekend?' And you know what they ask on Monday morning: 'What did you do this weekend?' See, the important things is to do something."

"That's right. And I guess we did that to avoid having to deal with ourselves. If we just sat around, those damn emotions might come roaring up. Then we'd have to deal with them."

"Exactly. Now you used fairly innocuous kinds of anesthetics. Ones that aren't dangerous. In fact, they are socially acceptable. Even considered healthy. Work hard. Play hard. There are other ways to dull feelings. One is alcohol. You've seen it. I've seen it. Max here at the lake uses alcohol that way. Right?"

"Oh, yes! I went with him a couple of times. You're right. He sips beer here in the afternoon while he's fishing or just talking. Then he goes over to Mattie's and drinks with his buddies. And the women."

A pause. The breeze freshened for a few minutes, creating wavelets in the lake.

I went on. "Oh yes, and Max uses sex too. I see it now. There's the chase and the conquest. That keeps him occupied."

"And the buildup to the sex act and then the brief moment of ecstasy is another kind of anesthetic," Fred pointed out.

"I hadn't thought about that. I guess you're right. The only feeling we men have in that situation occurs right between our legs. The old brain goes blank."

Fred looked over at me. "You see there are lots of ways to not-feel. We have invented a whole bunch of them. Pot is another one. Hard drugs even more. Nicotine is a good one. Smoking cigarettes levels out the emotions. You never feel extremely happy, but you never feel really low either.

"But there are less obvious and more acceptable forms of numbing yourself like competing in a golf tournament or a chess tournament. Like getting deeply involved in the plot of a good murder mystery or sci fi novel. Or going to a movie or watching a drama on TV. Hundreds of ways to escape having to feel our feelings."

"But why?"

"Because," Fred looked down at the ground using a small stick to stir the dusty soil, "for most of us emotions are dangerous. They are how we got into trouble as kids. We got mad at our parents and were told we shouldn't. We fell in love with a girl and found out she could care less. We got excited about a school project, and our friends made fun of us. We experienced awe at the sight of a sunset on the shore of Lake Michigan, but everyone else was chattering about their social events and wouldn't listen. So anger and love and excitement and awe all became unacceptable. We needed to find some way to avoid those unacceptable feelings. Our culture provided everything we needed to deaden our souls."

"Hmm. That's too bad." And we fell silent again. The sun was no longer reflected in the lake. It peeked between the oaks on the far shore and slipped away.

54

The owners and renters of cottages on Michigan Lakes perform a ritual sometime in mid- to late September, maybe even into mid-October if the weather has stayed warm: the closing of the cottage. It is much more than just locking the door and leaving. The ritual takes a full day, sometimes a weekend.

It took me three days because I didn't want to leave. But the oak leaves had turned brown, although they wouldn't drop until later in the winter during wind and snowstorms or even next spring. The maples across the lake had changed to red and now were mostly bare.

The first step in the rite of closing, for me, was to bring in the furniture from the front deck, placing and stacking it in the glassed-in front room. Each piece was dusted with an old broom, getting rid of leaves and twigs and dust, and then lifted or dragged through the screen door and deposited in a corner or along the back wall.

Then I spent the better part of a day raking leaves into neat piles, loading them into the rusty wheelbarrow, and creating a berm along the fence at the back of the cottage lot, beyond the dirt driveway and parking area. That is where there were piles of rotting leaves from autumns past, testimony to this annual shutting down ceremony.

Melancholy is an old word, used by writers of past generations. Today we talk about depression, but melancholy is different. It is not as deep or painful as depression. Melancholy is a gentle sadness. I felt it those fall days at Stanley Lake.

The next day I couldn't procrastinate any longer. The remaining tasks wouldn't take long. The end was near. A flame flickered in the oil heater which had kept me warm for the last three weeks. I turned the metal handle on the oil valve. The flame didn't go out immediately since there was still some oil in the burner.

I flipped off the switch for the water pump and went out to the well pit remembering my soaking introduction to the pump and pit a few months before. The iron cover swung away easily, and I lowered myself into the pit. The pressure gauge came out easily. Water oozed out of the opening. I knew the pipes in the cottage were draining.

Returning to the cottage, I opened all of the faucets and listened to the dying gurgles of the water disappearing back into the well pit and ground. The toilet flushed with the water remaining in the tank and, of course, the stool did not refill. A small puddle remained at the bottom.

Going out to the storage shed, I got the plastic can of antifreeze, walked back to the cottage, and poured the green-blue liquid into the kitchen and bathroom sinks, to protect the drain traps from freezing in the winter cold, and then more into the toilet bowl.

I opened the door to the oil heater. No more fuel. No more flame. The cottage would hibernate for the winter.

Now I hurried. No sense in prolonging this agony, this melancholy agony. Walking quickly from room to room, I check that all the windows were down and latched. The front screen door hook was firmly in its mating eye, and the front door was locked and deadbolted. Out the back door I went locking it from outside.

Only one more action. Two front windows had hinged shutters. I rotated them across the glass and latched them tight in seconds.

My backpack and duffel bag were already in the Wrangler. I got in, started the engine, and drove away. I prefer memorial services or closed caskets. It serves no purpose for me to view a body. It serves no purpose for me to even have a casket with a body in it. We are better served by the memories of the deceased than by pretending that the body is somehow still the person. I was mourning the death summer and remembering the events and experiences of the Stanley Lake cottage. It was time to go back to the desert.

55

Well not quite that easy. As I backed the Wrangler away from the cottage, Max strolled up the road from his place. He raised his shotgun and fired a blast into the air. The "boom" reverberated over the lake. Several hundred oak leaves were ripped into tatters where the shot whipped upward into the trees.

"Thought I'd give you a send off," he smiled his crooked smile, showing the misshapen and missing teeth. "Good luck!" He lifted his can of beer in salute.

"Thanks, Max."

I shifted into low and started down the road. Shifted up into second as the Wrangler rounded the curve. There was George the Writer standing in the middle of the road. Waving at me. I slowed and stopped.

George the Writer walked up to the Jeep.

"What's going on?" I asked.

"Well we've been watching you getting ready to go. And we thought we ought to have a few of us wish you well."

"Thanks." I was ready to shift again, release the clutch, and take off.

George the Writer reached up and put his hand on the sill of the driver's side window. He looked at me directly, the first time he had done that. "Would you consider staying here?" "Why?"

"Well, I believe I will need an editor. I thought you might take on the job."

I smiled. "George the Writer, I appreciate the invitation, but I am not an editor. I wouldn't know where to begin. And I have some other stuff I need to do."

"Well, best of luck. And if you run out of things to do, I have a manuscript you can edit."

I waved. "Thanks." With that I began my journey down the dirt road back to civilization.

But one more person waited for me, just a few yards farther down the road. Marty stood in front of her place wearing, as usual, the minimal clothing needed to stay comfortable in the weather of the day. In this case, she had on an old coat and sweat socks. No shoes. Coat open down to show most of her cleavage.

"Get rid of your underwear," she shouted at me.

"Okay, Marty, I'll do just that!" I smiled. I laughed. What a great way to exit this place.

Sayings of Fred
Maybe underwear really isn't necessary.

56

The Wrangler makes a terrible racket at 65 miles an hour. The fiberglass hard shell is like a big drumhead, and the wind noise around the square corners of the windshield reverberates inside the vehicle.

I pushed down US-131 toward I-94 and then westward to Chicago. I was depressed. Not deeply. There was a small sadness in my belly which did not go away after a sigh. I breathed in for a long count and expelled for the same. Still the sadness would not go away.

I knew what it was. I would never be a Zorba or a Max. I was stuck with a brain that needed to learn and think and write. I could not sink into a routine, month after month, year after year, of fishing, eating, drinking, napping, and screwing. And that saddened me. I wanted to cast off the demons who forced me to search. I truly wanted to be able to sit back and enjoy the very small events in life. To go with the simple processes of living. And I couldn't.

So I was headed back to Chicago. Not to live. Not to work. To visit my friends and Andrea, and then resume this strange journey. I knew that this would be farewell to that world, forever. I had changed, was changing, would keep on changing.

Maybe Fred would have some answers, or at least some good questions. I knew better. Fred, at best, would have another set of experiences for me.

I didn't know how close I was to completing my journey with Fred. I would find out shortly.

HIATUS

I spent a few days in Chicago, even a greater stranger to my friends. Andrea once again listened empathically. She had found a partner, a lover and seemed happy.

Once again I ventured west, this time plummeting down state from Chicago to St. Louis and across Missouri, winding my way back to the southwest. My destination, this time, was Phoenix. The prospect of a warm comfortable winter appealed.

Finding a job was no problem. I had a skill, writing. I had experience in public relations and advertising. I worked efficiently. I was hired. Clients of the small agency were happy with my efforts. The owner-manager wanted me to commit to staying. I couldn't. I explained to him that I had something planned for the spring. As Phoenix warmed into the 80s in late April, I took off and drove to Moab one more time.

THIRD YEAR

SECTION V

Buena Vista

1

That Spring, early May, Fred sent me to Buena Vista, Colorado for the next and what turned out to be the final stop in my journey and where I was to contact Jake Barnes. For what purpose? As usual, I wasn't sure and Fred didn't tell me. All I knew was that Jake, a recluse, was a friend of Fred's and had a background in linguistics and communication.

"How do I contact Jake when I get there?" Reasonable?

"Just ask around."

"No address?"

"Nope. Jake moves around some. And where he lives is like the Indian Reservations. There aren't any street addresses. No numbers. Maybe not even a real name for the road where he's currently perched."

"So how do I find him?"

"Everyone in Buena Vista knows him. Well, almost everyone. Just ask."

2

I drove the Wrangler north out of Moab, three miles, to the scenic drive, Utah 128, and meandered along the curving byway up past Hittle

202

Landing, where I met Fred two years ago, and then continued northeast within sight of I-70 but turning right along the old road to the ghost town of Cisco and finally to the interstate where I joined a meager flow of traffic toward Colorado. It was late Spring, and most of the tourists were yet to come. A few RVs with senior couples, some semis, and an occasional pickup pierced the morning toward the clouds building over Colorado's western mesas.

The Wrangler, surprisingly comfortable on long highway drives, moved steadily, at sixty-five miles an hour, toward the Colorado line. Wind noise almost masked the country and western music from a Grand Junction station.

The Utah-Colorado line is unique. There is a distinct difference in the geology between the two states. You can see the two states as the state line signs announce the passage from one to the other. Utah stretches out, mostly flat, to the Bookcliffs northward and seemingly infinitely to the west. Colorado undulates with a hint of high mesas and mountains.

With an early lunch behind me, I drove through the Grand Junction area and wound my way along the Colorado River, the water mushing along on my left and in the opposite direction, high and roily from melting snow upstream. The highway followed the curves of the river, a more interesting and pleasant drive downward toward Grand Junction than the way I was going.

The small towns of western Colorado slipped by: Parachute, Rifle, and Glenwood Springs where I-70 shoots up Glenwood Canyon, the Colorado River now in even more of a rush as a result of steeper descent, one of the most beautiful interstate drives, although only twenty miles long in the United States. Exiting the canyon on its high end, we, the Wrangler and I, emerged into country with towering mesas on both sides but with peaks clearly showing to the south and directly ahead.

I stopped in Gypsum and bought a tightly wrapped sub sandwich at the local convenience store. Then onward and upward, truly on and up geographically, to Minturn to pick up US 24 southward over Tennessee Pass down into Leadville, grim high mountain town with the highest airport in the United States. Highway 24 then descended gradually, undulating slightly in places, until, coming over a rise, I looked down into the valley where Buena Vista nestled.

So I drove into the town, pronounced "bew-na vista" by the locals. A strange aspect of southwestern culture that some places with Spanish names are pronounced the way English speakers see the words while others retain their correct Spanish pronunciation. Pueblo, Colorado is uttered as "pew-ebb-low."

3

After spending the night in one of the mom-and-pop motels, I set out to look for Jake. I asked. And I found.

The woman in the coffee shop sold me a decaf mug and came around to draw a map - where I would find Jake. I thanked her. The windows of the coffee shop faced US 24 and, in the distance, Mount Princeton, rising and dominating to the west.

Having sipped coffee to the bottom of the mug, I took the napkin-map and drove west, along US 24 south and then turned onto the 162 Road westward up along the Chalk Cliffs. Jake's place was a small summer cabin, just off the 162 Road, in the lee of the Chalk Cliffs.

I drove up the rough dirt and gravel approach to the cabin and parked.

An extremely long and skinny man with unkempt hair, a beard, and a huge head sat on a bench in the shade of the small porch on the front of cabin.

"Are you Jake?"

"Yeah." Taciturn. Cold. Unfriendly.

"Fred told me to come over and get together with you."

"Okay." Jake held a long piece of wood in his hands smoothing the grain by rubbing a stone lengthwise. "Making an atlatl."

I had no idea what an atlatl was. I might find out but Jake wasn't going to tell me.

"Here's the deal." Jake never looked at me, just kept rubbing the stone on the wood. "I hike. You follow. Each time I will tell you something. No conversation. No discussion. No questions. I just tell whatever I want to. You listen. You follow. Then sometime you go back to Moab."

I nodded.

"You can bunk in the cabin," as Jake pointed with his head toward the door. I retrieved my sleeping bag, bag of clothes, and shaving kit and went inside. There was a wood burning stove, a sink, a propane cook stove, and two bedrooms, each with a bed made out of rough hewn logs. Jake's room was clearly his, a sleeping bag on the bed and a few essentials piled on an old pine dresser. Two shirts and one pair of pants on hangers suspended from a rod in an open closet. I took the other room, spread the sleeping bag out, put the shaving kit on a small shelf, and dropped the clothing bag in one corner.

"Nothing to do around here today." Jake didn't look up. "Might want to go back in to town and look around. We'll go for a hike in the morning."

I was dismissed.

4

We walked silently away from the cabin and up the dirt road, Jake in the lead. The trip took us a mile or so up the road and then off to a trail on the right. As we started up the trail, Jake began talking, almost as much to himself as me. But I could hear.

"Fred's big on this one thing about communication. He's probably gotten around to it with you. Here's the thing. When you talk, you objectify whatever it is you are talking about. An experience becomes a 'thing.' It's no longer an experience.

"If you talk about your feelings, they become 'things.' They are now outside of you. No longer inside. They are no longer feelings. The more you talk about a particular feeling, the more it becomes a 'thing.' Pretty soon it is just words. The feeling is gone.

"Primitive people are smart enough to know that you shouldn't talk too much. Particularly about important stuff. They experience it. They talk just enough to get their work done. To coordinate with each other. The rest of the time they stay pretty much quiet.

"But they do communicate. They do it with ceremony. Music. Dance. Chant. Whatever. That's why they seem distant and cold when we White people try to talk to them. We talk too much for their liking. Dance and music are experiences. They have common experiences. That's how they pull together.

"So we have these marvelous experiences. Great sex. Incredible sunrise over the mountains. Wonderful evening of music. Whatever. And what do we do? We talk about it! Crap. We talk all that stuff to death! We kill every damn thing that is good and wonderful and worthwhile by our insane need to yak about them.

"Same holds true for religion. The best way to kill God is to talk about God all the time. Pretty soon it is just a word. Mystics experience God.

And, by the way, they don't talk to God. They listen. They experience God. And they don't talk to each other about God. 'Hey I had a better conversation with God than you did.' Or 'you should have heard what God told me today.' Nope. They shut up and live with the experience.

"I wish we'd learn from the primitives. By the way, primitive has an antonym: sophisticated. The difference? Primitive means original, simple. Sophisticated? Something that moves away from the natural. Unnatural. It also means to corrupt or pervert. It also means to make complex. So I'd rather be primitive than sophisticated.

"I wish we'd learn from the mystics, too. They have a good way of dealing with the world. We just talk ourselves to death. We talk our ideas and feelings and relationships and every other damn thing to death!"

And that was the end of the lesson for the day. Jake stalked on. I followed. We hiked in silence; returned in silence; ate and went to sleep in silence.

Sayings of Fred
Talk about all your mundane and bad experiences;
remain silent about the precious ones.

5

Jake Barnes, I learned from some of residents of Buena Vista, lived alone, without a vehicle of any kind, by scrounging surplus food from stores, behind restaurants, and just begging. He didn't seem to have any kind of income at all. An occasional check arrived by mail which he immediately cashed and bought food and a few toiletries. The checks, according to rumor, came from a publishing house. So he may have had a book – or several – published in the past and still be getting royalties.

To get into town, Jake walked or bummed rides. He talked little. No one had ever gotten more than a few words out of him. He didn't smile. He wasn't friendly. But, on the other hand, he was no threat to anyone, and an advantage of rural Colorado was that Jake wasn't alone in his weirdness. There were lots of 'characters' in town and out in the woods.

However, Janie Meyers, local bookseller, had done some research after a customer commented on the fact that a former college professor had dropped out of academe and come to the Buena Vista area. Jane found that Jake Barnes had been a full professor of linguistics and communication at a major midwestern university. He had indeed published books, a total of seven. He resigned his position and left the university without a cloud of suspicion. There were no bad rumors about his behavior. He had been an exemplary scholar if not the best teacher.

Somewhere in his academic journey, Jake Barnes, in studying the experience of communication, not just the usual scholarly subjects, found himself becoming more and more skeptical, even cynical. Finally, he abandoned the university life and adopted a solitary, monkish style near Buena Vista. As near as anyone could figure out, he spent all his days taking walks around the cabin where he lived in the fall, winter, and spring. When the owners of the cabin reappeared in the summer, Jake hiked uphill and disappeared for three months. He was seen in and around some of the ghost towns west of Buena Vista.

How long he would continue this existence no one knew. And few people cared.

6

Gratuitously, Jake told me why he left the academic world, specifically teaching and doing research in communication.

"No one wants to learn about communication. At least not the real communication I was interested in. No. Everyone thinks they know how to communicate. Just try to put on a workshop on communication. No one will show up. They figure that they are communicating. No need to learn how to do that. It's like going to a seminar to find out how to put on your coat.

"Communication is profane. Not dirty. Just everyday, ordinary. So I quit. Why the hell get all involved and interested in something that no one really wants to know about."

We walked a mile or so.

"Oh you can teach courses in mass communication or graphic design or some other technological kind of communication. But how to establish an empathic and involved dialogue just doesn't fly."

7

"Here..." Jake handed me a rock, a six-inch one-pound hunk of Colorado. "What is this?"

"A rock."

"What's it feel like?"

I tried to describe the roughness and weight

"What's it look like?"

I said: "About a pound, gray and brown, mottled."

"Okay, that's a start. You could also describe its chemical composition… if you knew enough about geology."

A long pause which Jake got up and started walking. I followed carrying my rock.

"What's all this stuff around us?"

"Rocks."

"Yep. Rocks. All kinds of rocks. And there are other kinds of rocks in other places. So we can refer to everything that is more or less like that thing in your hand as rocks. Then we are abstracting.

"We could also point to rock in the ground or on the side that mountain over there or in a cliff. By abstracting we minimize the differences. We generalize.

"If you pay attention when you hear people talk, you'll start to realize that most of the time they are talking at very high levels of abstraction. There are a lot of levels of abstraction. First, at the sensuous level, there is the thing itself. Like your rock. Then there is the word to name the thing. And another word to include the word-thing in a bigger category. A lot of words to describe all the different versions of the same thing. That goes on and on. So when you talk about 'human beings,' you have gone way beyond any particular human being, or group of them, or culture, or nation.

"Now realize how dumb it is to talk about 'human nature.' How could you possibly know about human nature? That phrase implies that all humans, every last damn one of them, has some basic, elementary similarity. But when you take the very abstract idea of human nature and try to apply it to Jennie Smith down there in Buena Vista, turns out is doesn't work.

"So most of the time we are talking at levels that don't make much sense. Much sense if you want to deal with this particular situation, this person, today.

"That's why I spend my time out here hiking, looking at the mountains, putting one foot in front of the other. Not trying to communicate. Only when Fred sends someone do I try to say anything. And you'll notice that

I don't try to get into dialogue. Just monologue. I try to be true to my own findings in the field of communication."

"But isn't that futile? To just experience and not try to communicate?"

Jake looked at me sideways. I had broken the rule. I hadn't just listened.

"Only futile if you think experience without communication is meaningless." He stalked off obviously leaving me to turn back. Lesson learned. I guess.

8

Another day, another breakfast in silence, some motioning from Jake, and a stroll this time down the road. We turned to our right and jumped across the small creek, barely flowing at this time of year, and meandered into an aspen grove. No trail. Jake bushwhacked his way through the trees, and I didn't have the vaguest idea of where we were or where we were going.

"Here's how our highly prized communication works. Doesn't matter if it is talking or writing. We put words together. We may have some sort of intent. Something we want to get across. So we make a little speech. Or we write a note. Or a damn book.

"Then we give the message to someone and assume that what we intended is what the other person got. Well that's bullshit! They may get something. Usually not what we intended.

"See we talk to ourselves, in our heads, when we receive a message. We make up a message when we hear what the other person is saying. Or read whatever was written. We put our own meanings onto the words and phrases and metaphors. That's the message we 'get.'

"Sure it works on a very simple level. You can give directions and most of the time someone will get wherever you directed them. But, hey, if you are giving instructions to someone at a job, you better damn well see what they actually do! You may be surprised to see them doing something entirely different from what you had in mind. That's why supervisors are told to coach employees, not just give instructions or directions.

"But the more abstract, the more emotional, the more experiential the message you are trying to get across, the less likely it will get there. The best you can do is trigger some kind of meaning in the other person and hope it is something close to what you had in mind."

9

I won't try to describe any of the other hikes. Each time we went a different direction into a different setting. The only variation is that sometimes Jake didn't start talking until we were an hour or two out or sometimes on the way back, almost back at the cabin.

This time he waited until we were back on the road.

"There are two motives for people to talk or write a lot. Either ego or fear.

"Ego. 'See I know so much more than you and I need to educate you.' Or 'I know I am right on this issue and you are wrong, so I'm going to talk you into the right view. Talking and writing are the ultimate ego trips. Every message has behind it the idea that 'I am very important; what I think it important; what I know is important; what I believe is important.' So listen to me. 'The world rotates around me.' 'I am the center of the universe.' 'I am God.' 'Or I am God's appointed representative.' So listen to me.

"There was a brilliant mind many decades ago. Name of Moreno. Developed something called sociometry. After he got his doctorate and before he embarked on his professional career, he took a year or so and wrote a book. He wrote a book and titled it 'The Word.' In German, "Das Wort." You know, 'the word of God.' That took some guts. Most authors should use as a last resort.

"The other reason for talking is fear. If you talk a lot, you don't have to think or feel. You can just keep on yapping. And if you aren't doing the talking, you can sit and pretend to listen to someone yapping while you are trying to figure out what you are going to say. You don't even have to figure that out. Either way, you don't have to bother thinking. Or experiencing. Or feeling.

"The one time when we quit yakking and listening is when we are asleep. And that is when the demons come out. That is when we have the weird dreams. Nightmares. All about stuff we don't want to deal with. So we push it way back in our mind and it sits there until there is a quiet moment.

"Just listen all the talkers. Read the books. It's either someone proclaiming 'the word' or someone just trying to avoid feeling anything."

10

"Language is linear. One word comes after another. That's how we make sentences. That's syntax. It's got to be linear. That means one idea after another in some kind of sequence. That's rhetoric. Or story telling. Language is good for linear sequences. Like rituals. Like any chronological events.

"Language sucks for anything else. Lousy for spatial stuff. Worse for systems. Systems are multiple components put together in some complex way. That's why you need diagrams for systems. Can't describe a system in just words.

"That's why newspapers distort almost everything. What they are reporting is nonlinear. Systemic. But the poor sucker reporters have to write linearly. Example? Accidents. Accidents are always the result of multiple causes. Car accident? Poor driving skills combined with bad road conditions piled on top of a vehicle with lousy handling. Cause? Driver error? Weather? Bad car design? You have to pick one when you're reporting. Even when you're discussing the accident. One person emphasizes the driver's skills. Another looks at the wet road. Some smart engineering type focuses on the suspension system of the car. If the driver had better skills. If the road had been dry. If the suspension system and steering were designed better. If...if...if.

"You can't describe an ecological system in words. It's not linear. It's all the elements tied together. You have to diagram it. Show all the components. Show all the links."

11

"The idea behind every mystical discipline is to achieve awareness. Doesn't matter if it Christian, Jewish, Buddhist, Taoist, or Muslim. The goal is to get to a point where you are totally aware. In the 'now.' No extraneous thoughts. No train of thought. Just pure experience.

"Now you can't get there by talking. Talking takes you out of the 'now.' Same is true for listening to someone. The reason is that you end up talking to yourself about what the other person is saying. That's what we call listening.

"So you can't get there by talking to yourself either. That's called thinking. Some people call it 'monkey chatter.'

"To get to that level of total awareness, you have to stop talking, listening, talking to yourself. In other words, you have to stop all the stuff we call communication. Then you can achieve awareness. You become totally open to all the sensations. You become totally open to what is cooking inside of your psyche.

"If you want to avoid all those sensations and those meanderings of your psyche, you should talk a lot, listen some, and, if worse comes to worst, chatter to yourself. That's the value of communication."

12

On the next hike, the lesson – lecture – was brief.

"Some smart people some years ago figured out that most of the time we engage in mutual monologue. I talk. You talk. You don't respond to me. You just say what you were going to say. Then I say what I was going to say. So you have two people emoting

"In dialogue, you respond to the other person. You put aside everything that you want to say or need to say. You take in what the other person is saying. Try to understand it. And you respond.

"I tried teaching that a few times. We even got to the point of trying to learn how to engage in meditative dialogue. That's where you listen carefully, maybe even take notes, and then take a while to respond to the other person. I know in one case it took me three hours to respond because I needed to really meditate on what my partner had said. Can you imagine a world in which everyone really took the time to meditate on what a partner, a co-worker, a client was saying?"

13

"Do words have meanings? Sure. But probably not in the way you think. People go running to the dictionary to find out what a word means. Well here's how dictionaries are put together. The folks who create dictionaries make a record of how words are used. They collect sentences and phrases. Each of those is put on a card. Nowadays, I suppose they put them in a folder in a computer. Anyway, they collect all those examples. Then the write a meaning or several meanings from what they have collected.

"So a dictionary is nothing but a record of how words have been used in the past. It's not some kind of absolute authority on what a word means!

"When you talk, you always have to think about what the words you are spewing out mean to the listener. Doesn't matter what they mean to you or to the gal who put the dictionary together. It's only what the listener's meaning is.

"And you know where that meaning came from? Experience. Reading. Listening. All of those are unique to the individual. So every message has a unique meaning to the person receiving it."

14

"Let's face it. Words have emotional impact. They trigger feelings in people. Sometimes the feelings are so strong the person stops listening…or stops reading. And the same word can have exactly opposite effects.

"Here's an example. There are religious folk who belong to fundamentalist churches. They believe in some fundamental aspects of their religion. And remember that there are fundamentalist Muslims and fundamentalist Jews as well as fundamentalist Christians. Probably are fundamentalist Buddhists and Hindus and Taoists and so on. To those people, being labeled fundamentalist triggers good feelings. That is what they want to be.

"But there are a slew of other folks who get uptight when someone starts talking fundamentalist. They get a very visceral reaction, and it is not a good, positive visceral reaction. They get upset. Angry.

"And man are we good at using these kinds of words to label each other! Liberal versus conservative. Believer versus nonbeliever. Nationalist versus internationalist. And on and on!"

15

"You see, there's a great danger in naming. Naming anything. But particularly naming very awesome or precious or wonderful things. That's why, in many religions, there is no name for the deity. The best 'names' are 'the Great Unknown,' 'the Great Spirit,' 'That Which is Beyond Us,' or 'the More Than Human.'

"By naming you limit and when you limit, you defile. See, you can never describe all of anything. At best you are picking out a couple of features. Try describing a chair in complete detail. Any chair. You can go on for paragraph after paragraph. Its appearance. The construction details. How it is used. Where it came from. The materials of which it is made. On and on and on. All for a simple physical object.

"And then people think they can describe something very complex. The only thing they do is over simplify. They limit. They define and defile. Every beautiful, wonderful event, sight, or experience becomes a few sentences.

"So the best bet is to shut up, look and listen, and file away what you can into your own memory."

16

"There's an interesting phenomenon in language. Take any word that has some standard meaning. You know, like the word 'food.' If you repeat it over and over and over, it loses its meaning. It becomes just a set of sounds. 'F' followed by 'oo' and then ''d.'

"The same thing happens when you type a word over and over on a keyboard. The meaning disappears and it become just a string of letters. Of course, when you stop, the meaning comes back. It just disappears while you are repeating it over and over.

"That effect is semantic satiation. You satiate the brain.

"Now here's an observation. Not a discovery or a proven fact or something verified by science. Just an observation on my part.

"If you take an experience, say a sunset over a lake, and start talking about the experience to people afterward, the experience become less and less an experience. It turns into a report on the experience. Eventually, there is no more sensuous or experiential aspect to it.

"I think that by talking or writing, we objectify experiences and feelings and relationships. That has good and bad features. The bad feature is that we kill the experience itself or the feeling or the relationship. It becomes words.

"Now what's the good feature? Well you can also kill bad experiences. Take something bad that might happen to you, like a minor auto accident.

It shakes you up. But if you start telling people about it, over and over, to different people, of course, because you don't want to bore one or two friends with the same story. Just keep on repeating it. Eventually, the accident's emotional impact is reduced. It is no longer as bad an experience as when it happened.

"That's why I think people like to talk about their surgeries, you know the standard joke about old people, or about their injuries or accidents or whatever. Intuitively, they know that if they keep talking about it long enough, the pain and agony begin to go away.

"That even works in grieving. The worst thing to do in grieving is to keep it all inside. The best thing to do is to talk about the death or loss. Talk about the loneliness or whatever. Just talk and talk. That probably will speed up the grieving process.

"I don't know if you know this, but there are 'talking therapies' in counseling and psychotherapy. The best known is psychoanalysis. But a lot of counseling is based on having the patient talk about her or his feelings, experiences, background, whatever. I think that these talking therapies often are a kind of semantic and emotional satiation. If you talk about your mean old father or your abusive partner long enough, the feelings are objectified, externalized. They become just words. Then maybe you can move on.

"There is one other benefit of semantic satiation. Take a brief phrase and repeat it over and over. Take the Jesus prayer: *'Lord Jesus Christ, son of God, have mercy on me.'* In *The Way of the Pilgrim*, the Russian *strannik* repeats it over and over again. Many mystical disciplines use this technique. It may be the repetition of a single word or sound. Or some phrase. That constant repetition makes the meaning of the phrase or word go away. And the mystic arrives at a state of awareness. Why? Because the constant inner yakkety-yak can't happen in the midst of semantic satiation. So the mystic quits creating messages while repeating the manta. Repeating it either out loud or mentally. Either way, the semantic satiation occurs. With a good result."

17

"What I was saying the other day is very important. Here is why. I really strongly believe that you should not talk about the precious moments in your life. Don't yak-yak-yak about the fantastic time you had hiking in the Sangre de Cristo mountains. Reserve that for your inner intimate life. Keep it to yourself. Imagine it. Relive it. Visualize it again. But for Fred's sake, never, ever start talking about it.

"Unless you really want to destroy the experience. It's like taking a picture of the mountains here in Colorado. There is no way you can capture the size, dominance, ruggedness, and all of the mountains in photos. The photos aren't big enough. Same is true of the Grand Canyon. Any of these big places.

"Well you can have big experiences. Trying to describe them is like trying to take one photo of the Grand Canyon and then showing it to people. They will never appreciate your experiences. They are yours. Keep them."

18

"It's like we're programmed to talk. That the first inclination for most people. Let me talk!

"I meet someone, and they start out with 'Let me tell you about…'

"Or 'Did you hear about?'

"Just go to a restaurant or airport or any public place and everyone is talking. Are they saying much? Probably not. Just making noise. Watch the people on the other end of the talk. Are they listening? Probably not. Just waiting for their turn to talk."

"People even talk in movies. They talk where it is an annoyance to other people. That's how strong the impulse is to talk"

19

On one of our hikes, Jake turned around and said, "Borborygmus." Not another word!

I shook my head and knew better than to try to ask for an explanation. I went to the library in Buena Vista two days later. Borborymus is the sound made in the intestines as stuff moves through them.

20

"The great unanswered question about communication, in my mind, is why people are afraid of silence. We have to fill that void. Can't stand to have any silence.

"There was some research done on public school teachers, probably high school, and the researchers timed the space between the teacher asking a question and the teacher then answering her or his own question. You know what it was? Something like three seconds! Teachers can't stand silence!

"I have a guess about why we can't stand silence. I think silence puts us back on feeling our feelings, seeing the reality of the world around us, acknowledging the real relationship we have with the other person. And all of that scares us.

"Here's why I think it scares us. Talking – communicating – is life. It means we're alive. Silence is the absence of life. It is death. So we just keep on talking to keep the Grim Reaper at bay."

21

"We like to think that words really work. That communication really does work. You know, that meaning is transferred. That we can control ourselves and our environment by talking and writing.

"Ain't so! The world of words is no substitute for feelings and experiences and silent relating to another person. But boy do we believe!

"You know, if words were so powerful, we could talk ourselves to orgasm! Without touching a single part of the old anatomy!"

22

"The most important communication skill? No question or doubt. It's not giving a speech or debating or writing a poem or creating a fantastic graphics presentation.

"Nope! The most important communication skill is listening. Problem is, that requires shutting up. Not talking. At least not talking as much.

"To listen, you have to be attentive. You have to try to figure out what the other person is really trying to communicate. You have to watch the nonverbal stuff. You know, the facial expressions and tone of voice and body posture. You have to stop and ask questions. You have to be able to say 'I didn't understand that, is there some other way you can explain it?' Those are all ways to listen.

"As I said before, what we *call* listening is just being quiet and trying to figure out what to say when I have a chance. That's not listening. That's preparing to talk!"

23

"Another guy and I went into a church. We were 'hired' as consultants. Actually they paid our airfare, housing, and food. They wanted better communication among the members of their congregation. So we went in and facilitated communication. We encouraged people to talk. These were the leaders of the church. There were some members of committees. We spent a whole Saturday, morning, afternoon, and evening getting them to talk. About their values. Their ideals. Their goals and objectives.

"What happened? A royal mess. See they really did communicate. For the first time. Trouble is there were a lot of different values and ideals and goals. Some of them at odds with other ones. So what we ended up doing is having people see all the differences. They got see the real conflicts in values and ideals. That had never happened before.

"They weren't real happy. In fact, we had to quit the communication facilitation. It wasn't working. Everyone started out thinking that by communicating everyone would pull together and get along. Just the opposite happened.

"The congregation got along because they didn't communicate. They all just assumed that they believed the same stuff. Joe over there just assumed that Marjorie over here believed the same as he did. That Saturday he found out that Marjorie believed in some things that he thought were blasphemous.

"That's when I quit facilitating communication for groups. For organizations. Let 'em charge on doing what they're doing and don't rock the boat."

Sayings of Fred
Sometimes you're better off with your assumptions
than with real knowledge of what someone else thinks.

24

"I spent some time in a university teaching people about language and communication. I learned a lot in those few years. What did I learn? Simple.
"Silence."
And there was silence. Jake never explained.

25

The area around Buena Vista, Colorado is some of the most spectacular in all of the Western United States. A wall of mountains rises to the west, huge fourteen thousand foot peaks running continuously from south to north as far as the spectator can see. To the east is a rim of lower mountains, more rounded, less spectacular, but creating a river valley, the Arkansas river flowing between the two boundaries. As a result, there is lush vegetation, by Colorado standards, in the valley and stark purple-black canted faces high up in the mountains.

Each day as Jake and I set out on those walks and hikes, I got to enjoy the vistas. The social environment was a cold as the wind on top of the peaks. The contrast struck me several times. I came back from each outing with a feeling of frustration over the lack of conversation. It was all one way. Each brief 'lecturette' from Jake followed by nothing. On the other hand, the views were incredible, and the act of walking activated my senses so that the sights and sounds and smells were amplified. Maybe that was also the result of the months of working with Fred and Venus and the time spent at Stanley Lake. I was sensually enhanced by the landscape and spiritually depleted during my time with Jake outside of Buena Vista.

26

So what did I learn from the weeks with Jake? It took a long while. I wanted to forget everything he said because it attacked what I most wanted to do and be. I had a message now. I had learned some things. I also had a lifetime, not yet a very long one, but nonetheless a lifetime to call on. I just knew I could 'get the message across' if I tried hard enough.

The lessons of Jake Barnes did eventually sink in.

If I wanted to be a writer and create messages, I would have to be aware that I would not be 'communicating' a single meaning in the minds of readers. I would be creating a small or large Rorschach test depending on the number of words in the piece. People would read into my words and sentences. They would create some kind of meaning from my writing, and it wouldn't necessarily be the meaning I had when I put the words on a computer screen. In fact, the odds are that they wouldn't.

The other trade-off in becoming a writer is that I would objectify my own experiences in the process of putting them into words for other people to read. So I would lose some immediacy, some of the sensuous and emotional value of the experiences. That meant I would have to decide carefully what to write about. Certain experiences would remain forever locked into my brain if I wanted to have them as my own. Others I could afford to expose, like film, and have them printed for others to see.

Both were lessons in humility. There was no way I could become the guru, teacher, bringer-of-light and simply transfer what I knew and believed to others. And even if I tried, I would lose something of myself in the process.

ENDING

1

I knew that our time together was coming to an end. I could feel Fred beginning to pull back even as we sat at the bank of the Colorado River where I had met him two years before. Of course, this was the right place to terminate. Of course it was.

Fred sat in his beat-up chaise lounge with the faded yellow vinyl strips alternating with the once-white now-off-white strips. He was focused on the red rock cliffs across the river. Faithful Barker parked himself in the shade under the chaise.

"There are some things I need to know," I started.

He turned to me. "So ask."

"Now, after all this time, I can look back and see your mentoring and teaching. Even though it was subtle. Even though it was occasional. There was a pattern. Are you part of an organization or a movement?"

"Yes and no," he said, turning to me. "There are thousands of us all over the world. All you have to do is make yourself available, and one of us turns up in your life."

"Does this movement have a name?"

"No. Not an official name. It's called wisdom. It's called spirituality. It's called a natural way of living. It's called a lot of things."

"But it's not New Age or Christian or mysticism?"

"No. It's called whatever you want it to be called. But what you call it doesn't matter. In fact, you are better off not calling it anything at all.

Didn't we go through all that business of naming and what it does? Let's apply that lesson here."

"Okay. Yeah. I see. But is there some kind of organization?"

"No. Absolutely not. If you have an organization then you need to have facilities. Someone has to manage things. You need money to pay salaries and to buy buildings and pay taxes. The next thing you know, you are devoting most of your time to maintaining the organization, and you lose sight of the purpose. In fact, you can't practice what you preach.

"In an organization, you have a hierarchy. Then people begin to vie for the upper spots and the top spot. The organization generates competition between people. That drains energy from the purpose. Soon you have people so involved in the organization that they forget what it is all about.

"So why have an organization?" Fred looked over at me. Barker glanced up at the same time.

Sayings of Fred
Organizations always outgrow their missions
because the organization becomes the mission.

Then he continued. "Here's something very few people realize or have even thought about. When Jesus lived, the standard way to minister and heal and teach was to stay in one place and develop a following of the people in the area. That's what all the teachers and healers did. But not Jesus. His ministry was itinerant. He moved from place to place. That was seen as very peculiar. Very strange. He broke the tradition. He colored outside the lines. But he taught me and others something. You don't need to have a place. Everywhere is okay. You can learn the important lessons wherever you happen to be.

"Buddha taught me the same thing. He didn't need a temple. He didn't need a fancy place, a big chair, a podium or stage. He sat beside a tree next to a river and taught. So we can do the same."

"Confucius walked around China with a group of students and followers. He got into conversations with them. He got into conversations with all kinds of people. Along the way he taught, and he learned."

"But don't you need some guidance? Some principles? Something?"

"Nope. There's no creed, no dogma, no 'book.' There are thousands of books and tales and fables and dramas. There's no need for one book. You can find lessons in a thousand places, ten thousand places. Each of those places, each book or play or story or poem will reach some people in some way. So having a lot of sources allows a lot of people to be reached."

Sayings of Fred
There's no need for one book, because you can learn from all books, all places, all people.

"In my case you had me read those books by Herman Hesse. They had an impact."

"Sure. For someone else they might not mean a thing. So that other person should read something else. It's the same set of lessons. It doesn't matter who the author is. It doesn't matter the format or medium. It's the lessons that count."

"But there is more than just reading or watching plays? Right?"

"Absolutely. The big lesson is to shut up and listen. If someone can't read, they are not cut off from the lessons. We can listen to people. There is a lot of wisdom available from our friends and neighbors and parents. From our siblings. But it takes some effort to shut up, quit talking, and listen. We have to listen with the 'third ear.' That's a phrase some psychiatrist came up with. It's good. Listen with the third ear. Stop interpreting and judging and evaluating what is being said. Take it in."

"What about traditional sources of wisdom? You know like teachers and ministers?"

"There are some people in every profession who are worth listening to. There are teachers, priests, ministers, coaches, doctors, and business managers who have good lessons to teach. If we listen. There are also a lot of those people who are just stuck in their professional ruts. There have nothing to give, no wisdom. They can give useful information, even knowledge. But no wisdom."

"Is there a way to figure out who has this wisdom you keep talking about?"

"Sure. Listen carefully to life stories. Read between the lines. Find the people who have survived failures. Good people grow and gain wisdom from failure. They go on. Other people just curl up and die after failure. I don't mean die literally, but they use anesthetics like alcohol or other drugs. Some people never take a chance. They can't fail and haven't failed because they don't try anything. Those are the people to avoid.

"Look for the ones who have had a major illness and survived and learned from it. Look for the ones who have helped a friend die. Look for anyone who has endured pain and suffering and gained from it."

Fred had spoken with such passion a few times before. He sat quietly, now looking at the red brown river flowing in front of us. I waited.

He began again, less vehemently. "You will become one of us. You will be a teacher. My only advice is to pass on what you have learned, not what you have been taught. Learning is within you and real. Teaching comes from the outside and may become learning, but it may also simply be something that sounds good."

Again there was a pause. "The most important learning for me was to shut up and listen to my body. You need to do the same. Isn't that what we spent so much time on?"

I nodded as he looked at me.

"There is a natural wisdom there. You body is telling you things all the time. When it needs exercise. When it needs sleep. When it needs food. When it needs the sun. Listen to those messages and then follow them. That's important. There are people who hear the messages but don't take the time to respond. They ignore the messages and just go on doing whatever they are doing.

"And listen to your soul. That is the other part of natural wisdom. Your soul is trying to speak to you all the time. Stop being so busy that you can't hear. Listen to those soul messages and follow them. Follow them. Don't ignore them.

"See that's the beauty of what you have experienced these past few years. You don't need a lot of wisdom from books or other people. Your body and soul are speaking to you all the time. Listen and respond."

Again silence.

He turned to look at me again. "It's natural wisdom that comes from within. You can confirm and learn from listening to others in person or through books. But you are also programmed by your inner nature to do the right things."

With that we sat silently until almost sunset.

Sayings of Fred
Pass on what you have learned, not what you have been taught.

2

Fred took me on one last field trip. We drove from Moab along the Colorado River canyon where I had first met Fred and continued to Grand Junction and on over to Glenwood Spring where we hung a right off of the interstate and through the downtown area. Our route continued up Colorado 82 to Snowmass some thirty miles from Glenwood. This is not the Village of Snowmass and ski area. Snowmass is a junction on Colorado 82 and not much more. Here we turned right again and drove several miles into a bowl to the Cistercian Abbey at Snowmass.

"What are we doing here?"

Fred: "We are going to the evening service at the monastery."

"Do they let us in?"

"Only on Thursday evenings."

The road up to the monastery was dirt, and we bounced along in my Wrangler until arriving at a small parking area. A few other cars were there. Two followed behind us at some distance.

The sun was dropping toward the mountains west of the monastery, across the open meadow. We slid out of my Jeep, and Fred led the way to the entrance to the monastery. We were met by a friendly but reserved monk who pointed us down a hallway. The sanctuary was to our left about a hundred feet or so down the corridor. It was small and rustic. People sat in pews and we took seats in one toward the rear of the sanctuary. There were no monks in sight.

Fred leaned over to me. "These men chose to be here. And they abide by the rules. Very little talking. No extraneous noise. The chose to live with men of similar beliefs and values. That is important. Where you live and with whom you live dictates who you are.

Sayings of Fred
You become more and more like who and what surrounds you, and you can choose who and what surrounds you.

A few stragglers wandered in, and then the monks appeared in single file taking their assigned positions at the front. I remember very little of the details that evening. I do remember an overall warm feeling: peace and tranquility.

The service itself was simple. There were no ornate trappings. No complex rituals. It was in keeping with the austerity of the building and the men.

We walked out a little over an hour later. Alpenglow spread across the western sky in that mountain setting. It lasts well beyond sunset to a special kind of twilight that occurs at that altitude. We drove away and to Glenwood Springs where we stopped for coffee and donuts.

"So what did we learn?" Fred looked at me as he slurped his coffee.

"I don't know!" I was instantly irritated. He kept asking me questions for which I had no answer. "I didn't learn anything. I sort of enjoyed the experience. What was I supposed to learn?"

"What do you know about the Cistercians?"

"They're monks. They live in a monastery."

"Ah but you see the Cistercians -- they're also called Trappists -- are a special kind of monk. For centuries they were forbidden to communicate with each other. All their communication was directed toward their God."

"Okay. That's interesting. But so what? I'm not Catholic. I'm not a monk, and I don't intend to become one. Among other things there is no way I could do without sex for the rest of my life."

"Well, I wanted you to experience the service this evening with these monks. I wanted you to see and hear and touch and smell the place where they work and worship. Because they are models of simplicity. Of a simple life. They don't own anything individually. They work at physical labor. They live in a plain place."

"And that teaches us?"

"That it doesn't take much to live well. All we need to do is get our values straight. To focus on the right parts of life."

"I guess that's right. You sure don't have much."

"No, I don't. Once upon a time, I did. But not anymore. I learned my lesson. The more house, the more rooms, the more time I had to spend cleaning and painting and papering. The more vehicles I owned, the more maintenance I had to have done. The more appliances and gadgets, the more I got frustrated when they didn't work right. So I minimized my living space, my vehicles, my appliances and gadgets."

"And it's working for you?"

"Sure it is. I am well. But there is something else we need to understand about the Trappists. They are mystics. They deal directly with God through meditation. Remember meditation? They call it centering prayer, but basically it's the same thing. Other people call is contemplative prayer."

"How could I forget meditation? You taught me well."

"Remember the lesson of the monks" said Fred, "Your possessions own you as much as you own them. For every thing you own, you have to be concerned about safeguarding it, maintaining it, repairing it, using it, and on and on. The more you own, the more you are tied down. The more expensive your possessions, the more you have to worry about having them stolen or damaged. You have to buy insurance and locks and security systems. The bigger your possessions are the more you have to provide space for them. You have to buy or rent that space. The more ingenious and wonderful the possessions, the more you have to be concerned about whether or not they" keep on working. You have to buy maintenance contracts."

"So the moral of the story is to own as little as possible?"

"Exactly."

"And that is the lesson for this day?"

"Well here's the additional lesson from the Trappists and all mystics. They have a lot in common. There are mystics in Judaism and among the Muslims. They are Kabbalists and the Sufi. Of course, the Zen Buddhists also practice meditation. It's interesting because they all have very similar ways of speaking and dealing with the world. In spite of the huge differences between their 'religions,' the practitioners are similar. In fact, the 'religions' are often at war with one another, but the mystics can communicate with each other because they share a common experience."

"Now that's interesting. They share the ability to connect with their God, their Spirit, or whatever. Maybe there is hope for the world yet."

"Ah don't get carried away! There is hope for the mystics. But they are only a fraction of one percent of the religious who are only a portion of the population of the world."

At least I was beginning to share the way of the mystic, and I knew now that I had a bond with others across the world.

Sayings of Fred
Your possessions own you as much as you own them.

3

Two days later, Fred sat, once again, in one of those old beat-up aluminum and vinyl strap chairs in his yard, possibly the very one he had perched on when we met two years before, and he motioned me over.

Barker stood up and meandered over to me as I sat down. For the first time, he looked up at me and then laid his chin on my foot, as if to say that I was now accepted into his doggy version of the new world that opened to me.

"There's one other thing I need to say about what has happened to you and who I am. One of the outcomes of your stay at Stanley Lake was the idea that there are a lot of people living on the fringes of society. Not a huge number, but certainly some.

"Well you need to realize that a priest, a shaman, a minister, and a teacher – the really good ones – live on the margins of their organization, their community, their society. If you are totally a part of an organization, you get all caught up in the games and politics. You try to get ahead. You want to earn more money. Get more recognition. Whatever. If you live completely inside the local community, you get all caught up in the issues and politics there. You will want more freedom for your kind of people. You will want rules or laws to control other people. All that stuff. And if you buy into your society - your culture - totally, you will have to ignore your soul and your body.

"The ideal priest or shaman has only one allegiance, and that is to the spirit that moves him or her. It is not to the organization or the community or the society at large. It is to the inner voice.

"And the same is true for a writer. Keep that in mind."

4

As Fred and I stood up and began folding our chaises, he looked up at the sky, a deepening blue as daylight faded.

"There are a few very fortunate people who live a unique life. That life is no guarantee of perpetual happiness or even contentment. No, it's a life guaranteed to provide depression, ecstasy, anger, and serenity. All of the human emotions. It's a full life. At the end, people who live that way have no regrets.

"That life exists when a person is doing soul work, living in a soul place, and relating to a soul mate. The work, the place, and the mate may change over time, but the conditions are there. It happens to very few. You're lucky if you get two out of the three for some brief time. You're even fortunate to have one occasionally because for most people none of that ever happens.

"I've been very fortunate to do what I am doing, to live here, and to have Valeria. Very fortunate."

I never met Valeria. His wife? Partner? Friend? I would never know.

5

As I packed up the Jeep and got ready to leave, Fred sat in one of those chaises under the tree, this time with a sweater and a small black knit cap on his head. I walked over to him.

"Thanks, Fred."

"You are more than welcome. And remember that what you have heard and read and experienced is timeless. It comes from discovery. Just takes a few people to create the conditions for discovery."

6

And so I became a writer. I am sitting at my keyboard in a three bedroom, one-and-three-quarter-bath house just outside of Williams, Arizona. I can see Bill Williams Mountain and, in the distance, some smoke is rising along the horizon where the Forest Service has lighted a prescribed burn to reduce the chances of severe wildfires in the future.

Much to my surprise I got a call from Andrea one day. She wanted to know if she could come out and visit. I agreed and picked her up at the Flagstaff airport two weeks later. She stayed in my house, and we traveled around northern Arizona visiting the Grand Canyon, the local national monuments, and Sedona. We ate out several times in the local diners in Williams. She planned to stay a week. At the end of the sixth day we sat down and talked. She wanted to move to Flagstaff. The last relationship in Chicago hadn't worked out. She was bored with her job. Bored and stressed as the same time.

We negotiated her move. She was welcome to live with me until she could find a place of her own. After she came the need to move on never came up. We melded our possessions and furniture. We melded our lives and souls. We got married.

I have been moderately successful, earning enough that, together with the income provided by Andrea we are able to enjoy life. We live simply. We cook most of our meals here at the house and eat outdoors as much as possible. My one luxury is a sunroom where I can sit in even the coldest, snowiest weather and look out on the world in comfort. On sunny cold days, I sit there in briefs, careful not to sunburn myself where I did some years ago.

I make most of my income from writing. I don't try to communicate. That part of the lessons finally sank in. My goals now are to evoke images, maybe stimulate some memories, create smiles, and induce moods. I tell stories.

Andrea works for the U. S. Forest Service, Kaibab National Forest. She enjoys her work because it allows her to be outdoors much of the time. We have sex and occasionally make love in the forests when the weather is warm. In the late fall and winter, we drive an hour or two south and make love in the desert.

I walk, jog, hike, cross country ski, and snowshoe as the weather permits. My pulse rate is in the low 60s and my blood pressure 120 over 65. I am well. In every sense of the word. My bowel movements are chocolate brown and float most of the time. My urine is clear at least once a day, usually for most of the day.

And there has been convergence. I did examine my past and have been able to use it without being a prisoner to it. I do have some goals and plans and look to the future. I believe I am in touch with the world around me, the people and the more-than-human beings also. Also my body. And I do look inward listen to my soul on occasion. But most importantly, I try very hard to live in the here-and-now blending the lessons of the past, the vision of my own future, the demands of my own culture and peoples, and yet also the messages of my soul.

7

I never saw Fred again after our last encounter. I don't know if he is alive or dead, although for some reason I cannot imagine him dying. I returned to Mill Creek Canyon just two months ago on one of my periodic retreats. I walked from the parking area up through a sandy open area and at its end I saw an older woman, in her late sixties or early seventies, hunched over with a stick in her hand. A younger woman, thirty or so, crouched beside her.

The older woman was drawing something in the sand. I passed within a few yards. There, in the sand, was a simple cross. The older woman was talking, pointing to the lines and sectors. There was the future and the past, the outer and inner worlds, once again, being explained to someone who would become a seeker.

I turned around and walked back to my Jeep. The cycle was beginning over again here at Mill Creek Canyon and perhaps other places on the continent and in the world. A quester, a mentor, several hundred lessons, and a transformation.

I felt a quiet satisfaction and prayed for the young woman that she might listen to her soul and find her vocation, her partner, her place in the world.

EPILOGUE

In every human life there is a tragic element. A tragic flaw. A final lesson, one of my own, was that it is important to discover that tragic flaw in yourself – no one else can define or identify it for you.

That flaw is inherent. It is not a problem to overcome, a deficiency to eradicate through education, counseling, or meditation. No, the flaw is part of you and your life. You have to learn to live with it.

My flaw? That I am trapped in a life of words. As much as I want to be a more sensuous and aware being, I am doomed to write, label, analyze, and describe, and in doing so I miss many of the wonders of the world around me. I can live with that.